New Life Clarity Publishing

205 West 300 South, Brigham City, Utah 84302
Http://newlifeclarity.com/

Printed in the United States of America
ISBN-978-0-578-59038-7
Library of Congress Control Number: 2019955420
Copyright@2019 B.D. Powell

WILLIAM MCFADDEN AND THE PUZZLE ORGAN

By

B.D. Powell

To my wife, for never giving up on me.

Always and forever

TABLE OF CONTENTS

Chapter 1
THE HOUSE RULES

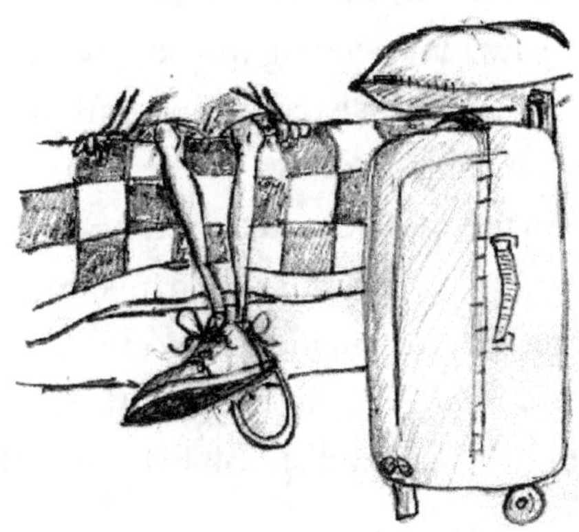

William folded the edges of the paper carefully. Each crease had to be perfect. "Whatever you do, don't move!" he warned.

"Is this safe?" Andy asked.

"What do you mean? Of course it's safe. I've never missed before. Besides, I paid you ten whole dollars. Put that apple on your head!" William commanded. He wasn't about to have Andy back out of their deal.

Andy balanced the apple above his forehead and waited for William to finish. "But what if you miss?" he asked nervously.

"If I miss, I'll give you a hundred dollars. But you have to swear to not move an inch," William demanded. Finishing the last fold, he held a perfectly constructed boomerang. He had always been great at origami, but this was something his father had shown him how to make.

"What happens if I flinch?" Andy murmured.

"You could lose an eye," William teased. He rolled his eyes thinking Andy was being a coward

"Is this really what we have to do when I come over to your house?"

"No. We could go outside, but that stranger keeps wandering around out there. I saw him peeking into my window."

"I saw him, too!" Andy insisted. "That dark hood is creepy. Didn't you call the police?" he shivered.

"No, I'm not a wimp. Besides, if anything happens, I'll put his eye out with my boomerang," William said, inspecting his work of perfection. "So, if you'd rather go outside, it's no big deal, but we might see the stranger in a dark hood. . ." He trailed off, fishing for an answer.

Andy looked at the door and shook his head. "I'll take my chances in here," he replied.

"Well, let's get on with it," William said. He waved his boomerang in the air, practicing his aim. He licked his lips with anticipation. After all, it wasn't often he was able to have fun with Mrs. Burbank around.

The apple wobbled back and forth atop Andy's head. "I think I have to go home," he whimpered.

"Don't be such a scaredy-cat. If you don't hold still, I might miss," William insisted. He walked away from Andy, counting his steps. "One, two, three . . . twenty-nine . . ."

"Okay, that's far enough," Andy cried out.

William turned and stared down Andy on the far side of the room like it was a showdown at high noon.

"Are you sure we should be doing this inside?" Andy asked, quivering.

William knew this trick. Rickey Thompson had wormed his way out of their deal and kept a crisp ten dollars in his pocket without ever seeing the edge of his boomerang. He wasn't going to fall for that again.

"You worry too much," William said. "My house is the biggest mansion in the neighborhood. There's more than enough space in my living room."

"You could still hit something."

"Like your eye?" William flippantly replied. He didn't want to wait anymore. The anticipation of trying his latest paper creation was killing him. He couldn't even wait for a countdown and launched his arm forward, letting the boomerang go. It sailed through the air toward Andy's head.

There was no time for Andy to flinch. A split second later, the boomerang struck the apple squarely in the middle, toppling it to the floor.

"Ahhh!" Andy screamed post-mortem.

"Yes!" William declared, holding one fist in the air triumphantly. "Perfect hit."

Andy bent down and picked up the apple. The boomerang was buried deep inside. It had nearly cut it in two. "I didn't believe a paper boomerang could do that! What if it had really hit me in the eye?" Andy quivered at the thought.

"You would have been a Cyclops," William chuckled. "Stop worrying. I told you I never miss." He pursed his lips and thought for a moment. "Well, I *almost* never miss."

"*Almost! Almost!* What do you mean *almost?!*"

"There was this one time. But let's not worry about it," William said, not wanting to explain why Justin, another neighborhood friend, had gone home with a very awkward haircut that day.

"Are you kidding me!? I would think that the chess club captain had to be more honest than that," Andy said in disbelief. "Doesn't being a part of that club make you have to be more trustworthy or something?"

It was true William was captain, but he was the head of lots of clubs. It wasn't because he was popular. Rather, he was just smarter than most. Math was a walk in the park and chemistry was as easy as an afternoon nap. It must have been a family trait since his father was the same. Regardless, he failed to see how it forced him to be honest about his bad boomerang experiences in the past. It was only once anyway.

A shriek thundered from a nearby hallway.

William shuddered, knowing exactly what it was. It meant there was going to be more screaming and a dissertation on the house rules. He just didn't know which rule had been broken.

"What was that?" cried Andy.

"That's Mrs. Burbank, my aunt," William sighed.

Loud, angry footsteps pounded against the floor. "WILLIAM!" shrilled a voice. The vibrations echoed off the wall and nearly knocked Andy backwards.

"It wasn't me! I told him not to throw it inside," Andy said. His face was white as a ghost hearing the thunderous wails from around the corner. The apple tumbled from his hand and hit the ground, splitting in two. "I have to go home," he gulped, racing out the front door before he finished his sentence.

"Yes, Aunt," William called out.

Mrs. Burbank stormed into the room, a surprisingly short, stout woman with a face redder than a tomato and a nose with flared nostrils. She stood over him authoritatively, wearing a striped dress that dragged across the ground. She thought the stripes were slimming, but they only accentuated her pear-like figure. In one hand, she was holding her trusty pen that did most of her dirty work. In the other, she was holding a list of rules. It was so long that, like her dress, it dragged on the floor behind her. This list was of particular length compared to others. William could see it stretch down the hallway, past five bathrooms, and up two flights of stairs. Most of her lists only made it half that length. William could always deduce how angry she was based on its length. It must have been something terrible to bring her all the way to the ground level of the mansion with a list so absurdly long.

"That's the last straw!" Mrs. Burbank cried.

William shrugged his shoulders and tried to think. He couldn't recall anything that he had done to provoke her.

"You know exactly what you did," Mrs. Burbank roared. "Don't play coy with me."

Of course, it was normally like this. He never knew what he'd done wrong until Mrs. Burbank told him.

"Aunty, I don't remember," William protested. Sometimes Mrs. Burbank let off clues by batting her eyes quickly or nodding her head in one direction. He tried to guess what he'd done by investigating her angry glares. Things were always better if he could figure it out before she told him.

"Well?" she replied with a blank stare devoid of hints.

William tried to think fast. The only thing that crossed his mind was how silly Mrs. Burbank looked when she was furious. He wasn't sure if it was the stripes bouncing up and down or her face that looked like a tea kettle about to explode.

Mrs. Burbank puffed loudly through her nostrils like her pipes were about to burst. "How many times do I have to say it? Call me Mrs. Burbank, not 'aunt,' 'aunty,' or any other related words! I refuse to be an aunt to an undisciplined animal like you!"

"Sorry, but there are too many rules," William replied. He didn't want to be bad or upset Mrs. Burbank. There was simply no other alternative. No one could keep rules straight from a list that could wrap around a mansion. Every list she had grew ten times daily. It never ended.

"You seem to have a special knack for breaking all the rules!" Mrs. Burbank boomed.

William tried not to look at Mrs. Burbank. He found it amusing that even though her stripes were supposed to be straight, they looked like a wobbled line going around her hips. He bit his lip to stop a grin. He knew it was rude, but the added sight of a ripe tomato face atop a roly-poly woman made it hard to refrain.

"You think this is funny? How could you use glue? Do we need a rule for this?!" Mrs. Burbank demanded.

William's eyes widened. He had altogether forgotten, caught up in his boomerang prospects. It hadn't been intentional, of course. He had mixed his father's glue recipe to perfection just before it spilled all over the toilet seat. It was the strongest batch that he had ever made. He had resolved to clean it up, but that was earlier. "I didn't mean to," he vainly protested.

Mrs. Burbank wasn't about to listen. She placed her trusty pen against the list.

William lowered his head. *Another rule? Really?* He tried not to worry about it too much.

Like a python toying with his prey, Mrs. Burbank paced around William. Her dress coiled around his shoes.

William wondered if Mrs. Burbank's anger could rub off her dress and turn it into a real-life cobra ready to attack him.

Furiously, the pen went to the end of the list and feverishly scratched a new rule. Mrs. Burbank vocalized the rule as she wrote. "No glue of any sorts! That includes all glue recipes!"

"I was trying to fix the thing in the bathroom, and the glue spilled. Honestly, I meant to clean it up. It was an accident. I just forgot." He stopped protesting, knowing Mrs. Burbank's unflinching rules meant nothing he said was going to change his inevitable punishment.

"I have cared for you for months while your father is missing. As repayment, I get a nasty red ring where the toilet seat had to be pried away. Honestly, I cannot put up with you any longer!"

What did she mean by that? She had been in the mansion for six months, that much was true. But William relied on himself. He did his own laundry, made his own meals, cleaned the mansion, finished the to-do lists, and mowed the lawn. He hardly saw how she could claim she 'cared for him.' "If you would let me look for my father, I could find him. You wouldn't have to watch me anymore," he protested.

"How many times have we been over this?" Mrs. Burbank trailed down the list of rules with her eyes. "Rule four-hundred and thirty-six says you are forbidden to look for him."

William had no idea that Mrs. Burbank had made it into a rule. "Why not? He's been missing for months, and no one is doing any-thing!" he argued. It made his blood boil talking about it.

"Do you recall the fire you started last time you went looking for him?" Mrs. Burbank reminded him. "Besides, you couldn't be more wrong! There are detectives, police, and people looking for him," she said vaguely. "One silly little boy isn't going to make a difference."

"I could find him," William insisted. "You wait, I'll do it." He folded his arms defiantly.

Mrs. Burbank threw her hands on her hips. "Don't be ridiculous! You're an impatient young boy. No wonder your father left."

"He didn't leave!" William snapped. He felt his face flush and wondered if he was redder than Mrs. Burbank.

"Important, wealthy men like your father don't just disappear into thin air," Mrs. Burbank challenged.

"Well, he didn't leave." William insisted again. He took a deep breath to calm himself down.

"You're just going to have to accept the truth, though I doubt it will ever sink in. I'm all you have, and it's going to take more than glue to scare me off."

William knew why Mrs. Burbank wouldn't leave. It was a sim-ple answer: money. His father had been bursting at the seams with it. Who wouldn't want to live in a gigantic, beautiful home? With William around, she didn't have to do a single chore. She had fired most of the house staff just because she needed to create work as punishment for breaking rules.

"Maybe you would have better luck teaching Charley," William muttered. He hadn't meant to be heard, but it was loud enough to reach Mrs. Burbank's ears.

"Funny you should mention him, because he is on his way," Mrs. Burbank said, turning around and arching her back while examining her list of rules. "Oh, how I despise him."

That was an odd thing to say. Mrs. Burbank didn't allow Charley over even though he was a close family friend. He was probably related as a distant cousin or something, but William couldn't be sure. It had never been important to know how they were connected. All he knew was when Charley was around, there was going to be a good time. That was until Mrs. Burbank came along. She thought he was a bad influence. Indeed, it would have been an unusual occurrence if she gave him an invitation.

"You asked him to come over?" William questioned. He was more than puzzled.

"Yes, he is taking you to stay with your Uncle Ben for a week. As soon as you finish your glue punishment, you're leaving!"

What did that mean? Who was Uncle Ben? William didn't know his family well, but he was certain his father had never mentioned a brother. "Uncle? I don't have an uncle."

Mrs. Burbank turned sharply and put her finger over his lips. "You most certainly do, and I will not hear any arguments! Your uncle has generously offered to give me time off, which I desperately need." She dramatically threw her arm onto her forehead. "I don't think I can take much more without collapsing." Her back bent into a dramatic pose, contorting the striped dress. "He'll call me every few days to check in, so don't do anything foolish. I'll come get you in a week or so." She smiled with anticipation.

William didn't mind having time away. In fact, he needed it more than Mrs. Burbank. But who in the world was Uncle Ben? It didn't matter, honestly. If there was a chance for him to get away, even for a few days, he was taking it. However, there was another matter to deal with first: Mrs. Burbank had mentioned punishment. "Let's get the punishment over with," William mumbled. He shrank backwards and cowered sheepishly, waiting for judgment. Mrs. Burbank's punishments were never pleasant.

"The glue incident cannot go unpunished. Also, I know you threw that boomerang inside. That breaks rules 36, 108, and 205." She paused to think, placing her hand to her chin. "Brush your teeth forty times . . ."

Brushing his teeth didn't sound that bad. He shrugged his shoulders, thinking he'd gotten off easily, but the rest was yet to come.

". . . with a toilet brush," Mrs. Burbank finished.

"What?!" He gulped hard, but it didn't get rid of the knot that formed in the back of his throat.

"The crime fits the punishment," she said firmly. Mrs. Burbank grabbed William by the ear and marched to the nearest bathroom. She placed a toilet brush on the counter. With one hand, she raised a half-used tube of toothpaste into the air and squished. A long stream of creamy white mint mixed with baking soda fell downward onto the bristles.

Mrs. Burbank stood commandingly behind William as he picked up the toilet brush. *At least it smells minty fresh.* Stroke by stroke, he counted to forty. His gums turned a bright red, throbbing with pain. When he was done, his lips barely closed over his mouth. His swollen cheeks were puffing outward awkwardly like he had been punched.

Mrs. Burbank looked satisfied. "Maybe you'll learn manners someday. Go and pack your things. You don't have long before Charley arrives."

William went up three flights of stairs to his room with drool falling from his mouth. He had gotten used to punishments like this. It was getting easier to get past them all the time, but this one would be much simpler. He had something to look forward to. He licked his tender gums with his tongue, trying to keep his spit from falling out. He couldn't wait to leave.

He grabbed a bag and carelessly threw in a pair of shorts, a shirt, and an extra pair of shoes. Lost in thought, he kept dropping stuff in. He would have preferred looking for his father, but Mrs. Burbank never would have allowed it. Secretly he wondered if his Uncle Ben might know something. If his father had a brother, it seemed logical that he might be able to help. Even a small clue could change everything.

Finished packing, he pushed the bag closed even though it was bursting at the seams. He sat on top to force the edges together and zipped it tightly. Ready to go, he flopped on his bed, dreaming about being free from Mrs. Burbank. The mansion didn't matter. None of it did. All he wanted was his father back. Well, it was almost all he wanted; It might have been fun to tear the list of rules up too. William licked his sore gums, trying to imagine they were getting better already.

The doorbell rang. It must have been Charley.

William grabbed his suitcase and walked down the hall. As soon as he passed his father's office, he stopped and turned around. Books and trinkets littered the room. All of them were important to his father, but none more than the wall.

William looked behind his father's desk. The wall was littered with pieces of paper, each with a special quote turned face down. Why his father had them was something he'd never understood. There were hundreds of them coalescing into a pattern that pin-wheeled outward peculiarly. When his father spoke about the wall, he would say, "It's all about the pattern. Do you see the puzzle? Do you see it, William?" His father loved puzzles, but William had never understood. William loved good quotes too, but to him that's all the wall was. There was no puzzle, no mystery that he could see, yet his father persisted in trying to convince him that it was there.

He closed his eyes and reached high on the wall. The first note his hand brushed, he unpinned. It didn't matter which one he picked;

he didn't need to turn it over to know which quote was written on the other side. His father had made him memorize the pattern, every single piece of paper. He would never forget it. It was one of the few tangible connections he still had with his dad.

"'Genius is one percent inspiration and ninety-nine percent perspiration.' Thomas Edison," he said. He turned the paper over to see the quote on the other side as predicted. He sat in his father's chair, holding the quote tightly. The edges wrinkled as he squeezed. He didn't think there was another person in the world who could understand how he missed his father. With his father constantly busy with work, they hadn't had all that much time together before. It made every minute with him important. Now even that was gone. His whole world felt like it had imploded.

William glanced at the pictures on top of his father's desk. There were only two that were ever there. The first he would never understand. It was hardly a picture at all, looking more like an amorphous blob of blue. His father would tell him that it represented the "eternal expanse of the mind," whatever that meant. But his father seemed to find meaning in its blue nebulous shape. In fact, there were a few times that he'd found his father staring at it. When he later asked, his father had said it took him back to a time before all this, but that answer was just as hazy as the picture.

William had seen the other picture many times before. He'd never paid much attention to it. His father stood holding a pointy hat next to two men, one on either side of him. On his left, a thin, straight-backed character was smiling and leaning up against his father's shoulder. Oddly, his one blue eye peered at the camera while his other, a stark green, darted awkwardly sideways. It was a bit disturbing to see the cross-eyed gaze and it sent chills up and down Williams spine every time he saw it. He quickly darted his eyes to the other side of the picture where there was a much shorter character. He was far too petite to lean on his father's shoulder, being barely tall enough to lean against his knee. He was sporting a bright green suit and bowler hat that made him look like a character out of a comic book.

William looked over the picture, again confused at the odd characters. Had his father taken the picture at a circus? Where else would these kinds of characters meet? Scrutinizing, he leaned in and studied the background. A contraption with a twisted mess of tubes sprawled out in all directions. William wanted a better look, but most of it was covered by the foreground. He had never seen anything like that at a circus. Whatever it was certainly seemed more interesting than the old hat in his father's hand. Regardless, everyone's attention in the picture was devoted to looking at the hat. It didn't look like a special hat. In fact, William thought it might have been one he had seen through an antique store window the other day. The hat was being triumphantly held as if it was a trophy, and everyone in the picture was wide eyed, gleaming with excitement as they stared. Along the bottom, no surprise, his father had written a quote: *"If we worked on the assumption that what is accepted as true really is true, then there would be little hope for advance." -Orville Wright.*

"William!" bellowed Mrs. Burbank's shrill voice from downstairs.

How her voice carried up so many flights was beyond William.

"Do I need to come up there? Don't make me write another rule!" roared Mrs. Burbank again.

His time was up. He put the picture in his bag for safekeeping and followed the list of rules downstairs until he stopped at Mrs. Burbank's feet.

Mrs. Burbank was tapping her foot impatiently. She was holding the end of the list and writing another rule. "You are no longer allowed more than five minutes to come downstairs," she said, irritated.

William was too excited about leaving. He didn't care what new rule was being added. He pretended to absorb the rule and nodded.

Behind Mrs. Burbank, there was Charley, leaning against the front door frame like he was posing for a magazine. His light brown hair spiked upward, rivaling Elvis's. He even had the sideburns to match. He always kept a whiff of cologne on him too, but his clothing left something to be desired. His tight t-shirt, with a heavy-metal electric guitar printed across the front, was too short and left his midriff exposed when he moved. When William ran up to him to give a high five, his belly button came into view. His hair wiggled as they slapped hands.

William reached for Charley's other hand and they did a secret handshake. Hands raced through the air, bumping at a blinding pace, but William's favorite part was the chest bump at the end.

"Good to see you," Charley said in his usual mellow voice.

"You too," William replied. "How's the latest girlfriend?" That was always a good question to get Charley talking. He had no shortage of hysterical oddities to tell.

"She was a babe," Charley said, grimacing. "But we broke up. She wanted me to eat fish. I only eat meat."

"Isn't fish meat?" William asked, anticipating a ridiculous answer.

"I suppose, but it's not a manly meat. Manly meats are limited to steak and pork. Chicken may be somewhere in the middle," Charley replied, convinced he was right.

Mrs. Burbank put the list down. Her face was laced with disapproval already. "NO, no, no. Absolutely no talking about girls. He's too young. I never should have called. Stop filling him with all sorts of ideas."

"Sorry," Charley said. He leaned toward William and whispered, "She's uptight today. Did she eat fish?"

"No, but she had steak last night."

"Yeah, that's an aggressive meat."

"I can hear you. Enough funny business. It's time for you to leave. I'll be expecting a call from your uncle," Mrs. Burbank said. She waved her hands in the air, brushing them out the door.

William grabbed his coat. He didn't want to wait another minute.

The wind outside was cold. It nipped his bare legs, brushing past his shorts. The snow crunched under his footsteps. He didn't care how cold it was. He wasn't going back to face Mrs. Burbank again so he could change into pants. He hated pants. If Charley could deal with it in a midriff t-shirt, he could handle it.

William brushed away the snow in front of him and made a path to Charley's 1983 GMC Ventura van. The side door was bent and the edge was open, letting snow fall inside. His arms gave three hard tugs before the door squeaked open enough to let him in. He threw his bag into the car and jumped inside. It took another three pulls to get the door closed again. Avoiding a pile of snow on the ground, he climbed up front, where the windows were duct-taped shut. Luckily, no snow was falling through, but the seat belt looked badly worn. He wondered if he would do better in the backseat. *If the wind blows hard enough, will the van fall apart?*

Charley turned the key and the engine roared. The stereo blared loudly, making the windows vibrate. It was 1990's rock music, Charley's favorite.

William was surprised that the van hadn't broken down yet. He half expected a wheel to fall off the minute it started. Warm air rushed at him through the vents. He was grateful the heater worked. The engine squealed and the tires drove over the snow-packed road. He leaned to look back at the mansion. It was going to be a good week. He could just tell. With any luck, his uncle would help him find his father.

Hunched beneath a snow-laden bush, on the side of the mansion, a quiet figure dressed in a dark cloak was watching, a hood pulled back just above the eye line. No one would have noticed him spying.

Through the branches, a van could be seen. Loud music blared from it as it drove down the road and was lost in falling snow.

"You will help me," the figure muttered as if William was standing next to him. "Or you'll never find your father."

Chapter 2

AN ODD WELCOME

Anew song came through the van speakers. It was nice to hear a new rhythm because the same songs repeating were starting to make the drive dull. Charley cranked up the volume, making the van throb to the beat. Leaning against his window, William watched the snow fall. He felt his skull vibrating with the glass. As his head bounced, he turned and caught glimpses of Charley, head banging in the driver's seat, one fist punching the air. When a famous guitar riff blared through the stereo, Charley clamped the steering wheel with his knees and strummed an air guitar. William smiled. It was good to be with Charley.

Turning off the main road, the van pushed through a snow drift. As the road narrowed off in the distance, it was hard to see any road at all. This was an area less traveled. Overgrown trees lined the sides. The van swerved to avoid the occasional low-hanging branch, but even the slightest move caused it to fishtail against the thick, fresh-laden snow.

Rickety noises came screeching from the struggling van as it tried to keep itself from sliding over the shoulder of the road.

William tried not to listen to the whining belts and popping engine. All it did was cause anxiety. *This van could strand us on an abandoned road.* Still, he was happier here than with Mrs. Burbank.

"Are you okay?" Charley yelled over his music.

"What?" William yelled back.

Charley turned the radio down just enough to be heard. "Mrs. Burbank seemed more uptight than usual," he said.

"You can say that again," William replied with a nod. "Her rules are out of control." Since Charley didn't come over much, he was sure Charley didn't know how bad it had gotten.

"She's just looking out for you."

"By torturing me? She had me drink a jar of pickle juice when I forgot to put the toilet seat down!"

"Ew! That's bad. Maybe things will be better with your uncle?" Charley banged his head harder when one of his favorite grunge bands came on.

William half expected Charley to turn up the radio again, but he didn't. He was grateful, because he needed someone to talk to. "That would be something if things got better with my uncle. My luck has been terrible lately. My dad vanished six months ago, Mrs. Burbank throws her rules at me constantly, and now I'm headed off to who knows where." He leaned his head against the window.

"Come on. Look on the bright side. Your dad was always good at staying positive. What would he say right now?" Charley asked, swerving to miss another tree branch.

That was an easy question. William gave a half-baked smile thinking about his father. "'When one door closes, another door opens; but we often look so long and so regretfully upon the closed door, that we do not see the one which has opened for us.' Alexander Graham Bell."

Charley's face scrunched together like he was confused. "What?"

"It's what my father would say. He had a quote for every occasion. It means we look too much at bad things in the past. It makes us forget the good things that might be in the future."

"That's good advice, dude. Your dad knew lots of stuff."

"You should see his quotes. He made me memorize everyone in perfect order," William said. He looked out the window, staring into the trees. "I wonder if he will ever come back," he sighed.

"I'm sure he will!" Charley insisted. He saw William's head dropping. "Just you wait, your uncle is going to have some answers for us."

William shrugged, hoping Charley was right. It had been six months without a hint of his father. Not a clue, not even a trace of him was left behind. It wasn't always easy to keep his hopes up anymore.

Charley slammed on the brakes. His head lurched forward. The tires skidded atop the icy road. William fell forward, his seat belt cinched across his shoulder. The van slid ten feet.

William pulled back from his seat belt. He raised his head to look out. His neck was already sore from whiplash. The van had stopped short of colliding with a gate. Inches from the hood, its black ominous bars towered over them. It was hard to see because most of it was covered in snow.

"I think we're here," Charley said. His white-knuckled hands gripped the steering wheel, but his voice was unusually calm.

"How do you know?"

"Look," Charley said. He unclenched his fingers and pointed out the windshield.

William followed Charley's outstretched finger. On the gate, in snowcapped iron letters, MCFADDEN was spelled out. Wildly colorful spray paint covered half of them. Others were badly scratched and dented like they had been vandalized.

"That's my family's name all right, but what's with the spray paint?" William questioned.

"I've seen gates like this before. They're mostly to keep out bears. Maybe a bear scratched it?" Charley suggested, shrugging his shoulders.

"A bear with spray paint?" William questioned. He knew Charley wasn't dumb. He just had his moments where he didn't think clearly. Like the time he thought dogs could talk after seeing a movie. He'd spent two hours trying to get a dog to speak before he realized that he had been watching voiceovers.

"It could happen. I've seen some weird stuff on the internet. Trained bears and everything," Charley said, nodding his head. "Trust me, it could happen."

William was in disbelief. There was no use arguing. Charley would defend his point of view to the end. Instead he glared out the window. Was someone supposed to greet them? He wasn't sure that he could get to the gate through the thick snow. He wished he had worn pants and brought a snow shovel.

Charley honked the horn. The sound echoed against the trees. "So now what?" he asked.

"I don't see anybody. We're in the middle of nowhere," William replied. They could go back, but he certainly wouldn't head home to Mrs. Burbank. Interrupting her week of rest would have been a death sentence.

A loud screech came from the gate's rusty hinges as it slowly opened. William looked at Charley with his eyes wide. He almost expected Charley to tell him that he was playing a joke, but Charley looked just as puzzled.

Charley backed up the van as a pile of snow rolled along the ground in front of the gate as it opened. There was a clear road ahead of them. "Do we go in?" he asked in a tense voice that was two octaves too high.

William didn't think they had an option. "If you want to explain to Mrs. Burbank why she doesn't get a week off, then by all means, turn around."

Charley pressed the gas, and the van rolled past the black gate.

William looked out the back window. The gate slammed closed with a crash.

"Are you sure your uncle invited you to come?" Charley asked, looking over his shoulder at the iron bars.

"That's what Mrs. Burbank told me," William mumbled. "But she can get pretty angry. Maybe she was trying to get rid of me?" It was a stretch to think that Mrs. Burbank would send him out into a heavily forested road behind a black gate, but he didn't have a better explanation for why they were there. He wasn't even sure that this Uncle Ben was real.

"Great," Charley said in a long, low tone. "So, we could be driving to a juvenile detention facility where she plans to lock you up and to teach you manners for all we know?"

"I doubt it," William said. Mrs. Burbank had never tried to get rid of him per se. She had tried to lock him outside overnight, dropped him off at the wrong house ten miles away, and left him on the subway, but these were just because she was angry. She was never trying to permanently get rid of him. Or was she?

"She's pretty serious about her discipline stuff," Charley pointed out. "I wouldn't put it past her to send you to some psychiatric facility. How do we know that your uncle even lives here anyway?"

"We don't, but why was my family's name on the gate?" William questioned, looking at the tightly shut iron bars. "Besides, I don't think we can go back anymore."

Charley shook his head. "Come on, old Bessy. You can do this. Steady now," he said to his van. His hands patted the steering wheel like it was a horse. Moments later, the van pushed down the snowy road.

The sun was setting in the distance. Their surroundings were becoming a dark blur in the night. It was hard to see the hills ahead through unplowed drifts that rested across every hilltop. The tires spun madly going up. Going down was an entirely different matter; bald tires careened out of control, swerving at the last minute to avoid danger.

The van made it to another hilltop and perched on the edge, about to slide down. "What is that up ahead?" Charley said. He was squinting his eyes at a ghostly figure. The headlights flashed across a man in the middle of the road as it careened downward across the icy ground.

William saw the ghostly figure blurred before his eyes. It wasn't until the van slipped back up the hill and came to a stop a few feet away that he got another glimpse. The figure was a scrawny man with an umbrella held over his head shielding his pale, dirty face from the snow falling. He was thin as a twig with prominent cheekbones. His face had a deep hollow for one eye socket while the other was covered with a pirate patch. Black flies the size of bumblebees swirled around his head under the protection of the umbrella. He was standing in front of a tunnel like he was guarding it. It was too dark to see inside. *Is this my uncle?*

Charley rolled down the window and turned off the music. "Excuse me!" he yelled.

The wiry man snapped his umbrella shut, sending flies buzzing in every direction. He strode quickly through the snow and stuck his head through the open window. Flies swarmed together again like a black rain cloud over his wild hair and dirty face that smelled like it hadn't been washed in years. The flies carried the reeking stench into the van. Charley recoiled into the passenger's seat and plugged his nose, grimacing. William swatted at the flies with both hands. His cheeks puffed out, holding his breath.

"Can I help you?" slurred the stranger. Drool ran through empty holes where teeth should have been. His eye twitched quickly.

"We're looking for my Uncle Ben," William replied, pinching his nose. Even plugging his nose wasn't filtering all the stench. It was so thick he could taste it now.

"What? Who are you?" growled the man.

William wasn't sure that he wanted to tell him. Whoever this was seemed a little off. Most people are at least aware of their personal hygiene. This man wasn't even aware that insects followed him. Who has black flies follow them anyway? "William," he reluctantly answered.

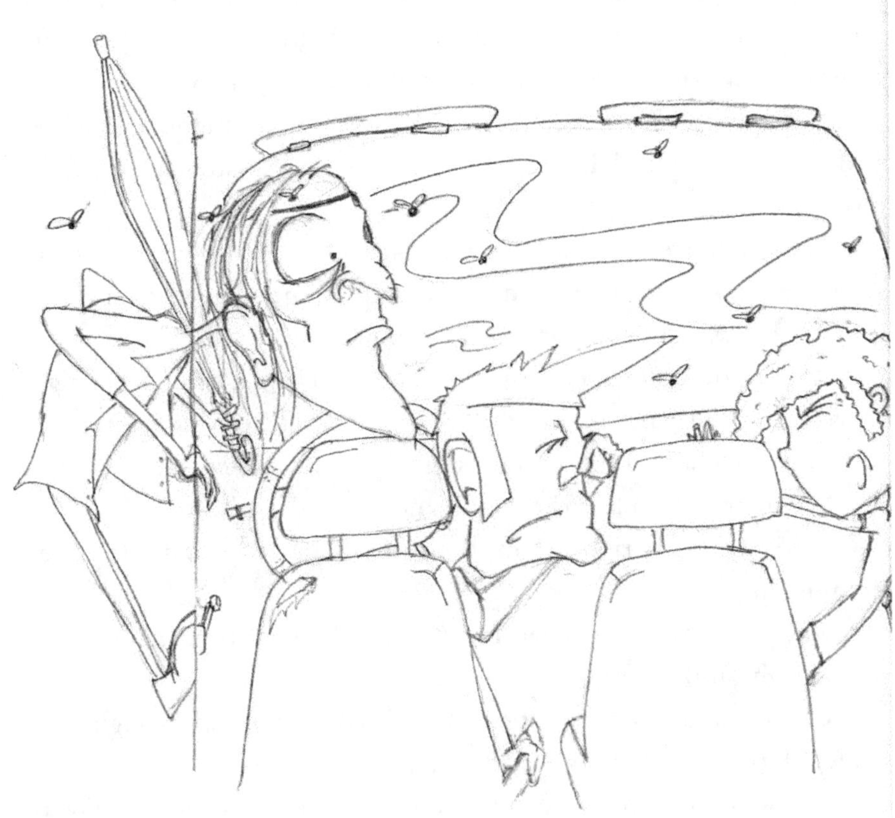

One eye stared at William, but it felt like two. The man's blank stare went straight through him. It made William glad the other eye was covered. William wasn't debating whether the man was insane or not. There was no doubt he had lost a few marbles. It made William wonder if there really was a detention facility nearby—and if this was one of their escaped victims.

Breaking his stare, the man looked perplexed then almost angry. His head shook back and forth. "No, no, no, no . . ." he mumbled repeatedly in disbelief. After a run of denial, he suddenly stopped. Like a dime flipping, his emotions turned. A sinister smile replaced his disgruntled appearance as he stared again. "Yes, yes, yes, yes . . ." he said, becoming louder with each word. "I'll help by giving directions," chuckled the man. "Whatever you do, don't change them."

"Okay, sure. Whatever you say. I have a great memory," Charley said in a hurry. He tightened his lips to keep the stench out of his mouth.

William puffed his cheeks out and nodded agreeably. He was nauseated. At this point, he would say anything to get the stranger out of the van. He was sure Charley would too.

"After you enter the tunnel, turn right. Then take another right. Once you're that far, take another right. Finally, take your last turn."

"Let me guess. Take another right?" Charley asked sarcastically.

The man shot him a dirty look and nodded his head.

"Got it. Right, right, right, then right," Charley said. He gave a thumbs-up.

The man pulled his head back, opened his umbrella, and strode out of sight into the tunnel.

Charley swatted at the flies and turned on the fan as high as he could. "Holy cow, that guy smelled like manure."

"How could anyone smell that bad?" William questioned. The directions were a little peculiar but not out of reason. He wondered if it was a good idea to trust the mangy stranger at all. "Wouldn't four rights drive us in a circle?" he asked.

Charley squinted his face like he was concentrating. He held up his fingers and counted to four rights. "Yeah, I guess that could bring you into a circle. Oh, maybe a square."

"So, we're driving into a dark tunnel and then in a circle?" William said. He watched Charley curl one side of his lip and scrunch his nose. He knew that face. It was Charley's dumb-face. He made it when he thought something was ridiculous.

"He said don't change the directions," Charley replied, scrunching his nose tighter.

Without another plan, Charley slipped the van forward on the snow, crushing the stranger's snowy footprints and entering the tunnel. It was surprisingly light inside, but only immediately around the car. A soft halo of light rested around the rickety van. It followed them as they drove, lighting a few feet around them.

Road signs covered the walls, pointing in all directions. Many of them weren't in English and some were from distant places. William recognized a few: the Taj Mahal, the Great Wall of China, Yellowstone, Salt Lake City. Each was accompanied by an arrow pointing off into the darkness. Other signs had only numbers on them. It wasn't any ordinary tunnel for sure. It made William wonder what would happen if they followed the signs. Would they end up in Japan or wherever the sign pointed? It seemed more logical to follow a sign than a bunch of right turns.

The tunnel came to an intersection, forcing the van to choose. The wheels squeaked around the corner to the right. No sooner had they turned right than another intersection came up.

"I hope that smelly guy knew what he was talking about," Charley said. There was a hint of anxiety in his voice. "Are you sure your family never had a facility for crazy people?"

William shook his head. He could admit that his family wasn't normal. Most families don't live in a place with 526 rooms, but that didn't mean they had a facility of some sort. William agreed that the place was odd, but when it came down to brass tacks, it was just a tunnel with a bunch of road signs. He had seen peculiar things before. This wouldn't even rank in the top ten on his list.

Charley turned right again. Just like before, they entered another turn immediately following. Now it really felt like they had just driven in a circle. William thought his suspicion was confirmed when he saw the end of the tunnel come into view. The bright light from the exit grew until the van emerged. Brilliant sunlight gleamed on the road ahead. It blinded William coming in through the windshield.

William blinked several times adjusting his eyes to the light. He furrowed his brow and peered out the window. His jaw dropped. Not a drop of snow was on the ground. It was a beautiful spring evening with birds chirping and flowers in bloom. "Where is all the snow?" he asked, shaking his head in disbelief. He was glad it was gone, but it just didn't seem possible. The events of the night jumped immediately to the top of his list of peculiar things. They weren't in Kansas anymore.

"Who cares? Love that sun! I could use a nice farmer's tan," Charley said. He didn't seem to care whether it was strange or not. He just seemed to be glad to be out of the tunnel. "Look over there," Charley said, pointing across a grassy field at the end of the road.

Not far off, William saw a large red brick building. It stretched in either direction with a central portion at the end of the road that had a large circular roof with an overhang supported by columns. Underneath appeared to be a front door. A wide set of stairs led underneath the overhang to the entrance.

"I guess my uncle lives in there?" William asked with a shrug. He had absolutely no idea where they were or what this building was. He thought it looked more like a national monument than a home.

"Isn't it like a McFadden to have the biggest house on the hill," Charley snickered.

The van was whining louder than normal after its struggle with the snow. Charley stepped on the gas to urge it along and the van gave a loud pop. Smoke billowed up from under the hood. "NO!" Charley yelled.

"Is the van okay?" William asked. He knew it wasn't.

"Last time it did this, I had to sell my guitar to fix it," Charley said.

He dropped his head to the steering wheel.

The van sputtered and rolled to a stop. Charley got out, mumbling to himself. Black smoke rolled into the sky when he opened the hood. Despite the soot, Charley put his face into the engine compartment.

William got out of the van too. The only thing he could see was the building at the end of the row. There was nothing else for miles.

"Aww." Charley coughed. He stumbled back from the van with his face covered in black soot. "It's a lost cause. She isn't going anywhere without some tender loving care and a few parts." He wiped his face with his shirt.

"Maybe my uncle can help?" William asked. If there really was an Uncle Ben, he thought.

"You mean the one that lives in the psych facility?" Charley spun his finger around his ear like it was crazy. "Besides, that place looks abandoned." He spat soot from his mouth.

"There's only one way to find out," William replied. He started walking down the road toward the building.

Charley looked at his van again and slumped his shoulders. "Why? Why?" He turned and followed William.

Near the front door, William didn't feel much better. Charley was right--it did look abandoned. There was spray paint covering parts of the building. Broken glass was strewn on the ground from shattered windows that had been boarded over. Yard statues had fallen to the ground. Flower beds were taken over by weeds that trickled onto the stairs.

William approached the door. A large metal knocker shaped like a puzzle piece hung before him, swaths of spray paint dashed across it. He lifted it with some difficulty and let go. It made a crashing bang as it struck. It was its last knock; the rusty hinge came loose and it fell to the ground.

Minutes passed.

"Okay, believe me now? It's abandoned," Charley said. He turned to go back to his precious van.

William turned to leave as a dust cloud rolled into the air. The door was opening.

Chapter 3

SECRETS IN THE HALLS

Villiam coughed and waved the dust away. When it settled, he was looking at a pair of neatly pressed suit pants. Either side was filled with legs like columns that stretched up the doorway and attached to a waist. The other end had feet that dwarfed a clown's. Long coat tails dangled behind them and nearly touched the floor. The door was surprisingly large, yet the man in the suit made it look like it was built for a midget.

William gapped his jaw open wide. *There's no such thing as giants? Right?* He looked at Charley, eyes wide.

"Wow, you're huge!" Charley commented loudly.

William punched Charley in the arm. This being his first encounter with a giant, he didn't want to be rude. Of course, this couldn't have been a giant because they aren't real; just as imaginary as a unicorn or leprechaun. It must just be an extraordinarily large person. He

29

leaned forward to identify the monstrously large character. A stomach and broad pair of shoulders came into view, but the face remained safely hidden behind the door's archway. Perhaps he could make out the shadowy outline of a chin. It was far past the top of the door. He couldn't be certain. "Excuse us. We're here to see my Uncle Ben," he stated apologetically.

The man leaned down, his waist bending in half to get his shoulders to his knees. A gruff face poked out from the door. Wrinkles adorned his forehead, which was filled with brown spots. The lines stretched downward and attached to a pair of bushy grey eyebrows. They were overgrown, like weeds out of control, covering most of his eyes. The hair didn't stop there. It was thick down to a bushy mustache that weaved together with a lush beard. Both had brown flecks that had yet to turn grey. They cascaded over the front of his mouth, keeping his lips hidden behind the foliage. For all the hair on his face, it was odd that he was bald on top. His face looked more like he belonged on a street motorcycle in black leather than in a neatly pressed suit.

"I'm Jay," he said in a low vibrating tone that made his mustache ruffle. "Come in." His face disappeared from under the doorframe as his waist straightened. His heels clicked together formally. Clownishly large feet turned properly, spinning around. Moments later, he was disappearing into the dark of a hall.

William thought it was an odd welcoming party. But then again, this entire trip had been odd. A giant butler was just one more thing to add to the list. He stepped out of the gleaming sunlight into the cold, dark hall. Jay was disappearing quickly. Charley mumbled something behind him, but he didn't bother to listen to what it was--probably some comment about not following giants or entering rundown houses. But he knew if he ran inside, Charley was certain to follow. He hurried to catch Jay.

A few steps into the hall, William picked up his pace and looked around. The hall was dimly lit. Light poured through shabby drapes that covered boarded windows. It was a sad sight. The vandalism didn't stop on the outside; ratty wallpaper and torn portraits lined the walls that extended through a network of halls branching off in every direction.

Not paying much attention to his feet, William began to stumble into a hole in the ground. He looked down just in the nick of time to jump over broken floorboards. How can my uncle live here? On his tiptoes, he moved between the good parts of the floor, like he was trying to skip between cracks in tiles. It slowed him down, but Jay didn't look like he was going to wait. He looked at Charley hopping over the splintered wood too. Charley was hanging his tongue out, deep in concentration, as he planned each jump carefully. He had managed to get ahead of William since his longer legs allowed him to skip a greater distance, but it was nothing compared to Jay's tree-trunk legs that gave him enormous steps. It took William and Charley a healthy skip-jog to keep up.

The hallways were endless, and even at a quick skipping pace, it seemed like they would never get anywhere. The amazement wasn't just because the hallways were long. No, William could see that each had at least one staircase that connected to two more hallways and two more staircases. Like a honeycomb blossoming into a nightmare maze, the crisscross of halls and stairs would be terrifying to get lost in. Without Jay guiding them, they would be up the creek without a paddle. William picked up his pace to stay close on Jay's heels. He considered that if he got too close, Jay might hit him with his foot. However, he would rather be kicked than lost.

Getting used to the constant skipping motion, William became comfortable in his rhythm. He tried to catch up to Charley several times, but each time he caught him, he managed to fall back again. He resolved that he could comfortably stay a few feet behind him, and he let his attention turn back to his surroundings. Really, the only thing of interest, other than the shabby condition of the place, were portraits on the wall. Disappointingly, many had torn edges and smeared faces, but William didn't think that he could expect much else given the condition of the hall. Afterall, if they didn't take care of the floor, why would they take care of portraits?

The pictures rushed past him like signs in a subway tunnel. Who were these people? There must have been thousands of them. There was a metal name plate below each that glinted as he ran by, but while hopping, he couldn't have read them if his life depended on it. Then something caught his eye.

A gold plate below a portrait gleamed at him like a spinner drawing in a fish. He wasn't sure why this one seemed different. He slowed his pace just enough to make out the words. To his surprise, he recognized them. He stopped out right, resolving that he could catch up. He needed to know what was written on that plate. *I can run fast. All I need is a few seconds anyway.*

Charley didn't notice William slip away. He was too focused on keeping up his pace, his tongue hanging out of his mouth with a small tip of drool now at the end.

William moved in close. The inscription, a blur before, came into focus: *It is possible to fly without motors, but not without knowledge and skill. - Wilbur Wright.* He knew this quote from his father's wall. *Who does this portrait belong too?* He searched for a name, but it was gone, scratched away. If that wasn't enough, the portrait had a torn edge that hung down over the face. It looked deliberately ruined. He lifted the torn edge. A pair of light-brown eyes and neatly combed hair looked oddly familiar. He pushed at the torn edge until it stuck to the wall and stayed in place. It allowed him to step back to take a better look.

He jumped in disbelief. His father's fair skin and sharp jaw line were unmistakable, like a red crayon mixed in a pile of green. He couldn't believe his eyes. A double take didn't change a thing. It was a portrait of his father. Younger, slimmer, but it was him. There was no mistaking it.

He turned to show Charley, completely forgetting that he had fallen behind. His quick stop had turned out to be more like a long detour. He frantically called out, "Jay! Charley!"

The sound echoed through the halls. It was answered with utter silence.

Chapter 4

THE PUZZLE ORGAN

William's footsteps creaked against the splitting floorboards as he ventured down a hallway. There was no point running; it would only get him more lost. He scuffed his foot against the ground, trying to leave a mark, hoping it would act like a trail of breadcrumbs. It wasn't working well. Each turn made him wonder how far down the rabbit hole he had gotten. He shivered at the thought of being stuck in a maze of halls and staircases. *I need something to occupy me.* He looked to the only company he had, the portraits. One by one he read them. Each had a name accompanied by an honorary achievement:

Sir Allen, for discovering the art of levitation.

Mr. Peabody Donight, for the invention of transparent clothing.

Ferddie Winkey, for inventing the earthquake machine.

Patricia Stokes, for the discovery of weather manipulation.

It was entertaining enough to keep himself from conjuring horrific images of being hopelessly lost in the network of halls.

One by one, the portraits passed. There was no way to read them all. He was starting to think they continued forever when they were abruptly replaced by doors. Like the portraits, each was labeled: *Nolen Burger, Emma Stonefield, Harold Pithington.* Some of the names he recognized from the portraits. *If my father has a portrait, does he have a door too?*

William reached down to try and open one but couldn't find a doorknob. He shook his head, puzzled. The hallway was dimly lit, but he could see well enough to know that none of the other doors next to him had doorknobs either. *Why would there be so many doors with no way to open them?*

He bent to one knee, looking for a lock, switch, or anything. What he found reminded him of his father. In place of a handle, a picture puzzle was in front of him. He hadn't noticed it before since it was flat against the door. It was just like the ones his father used to keep around the mansion. It was one reason William knew his father loved puzzles so much. His father would go on and on: "Try this puzzle, William." "I bet you can't do that one." It was a game between the two of them to see who could solve them faster. William's father usually won, but William had a real knack for solving them quickly too.

William moved the pieces of the picture puzzle that replaced the doorknob. A scratching noise echoed off the walls like fingers on a chalkboard as they shifted. One by one, the pieces came together to form a picture of a purple tiger with large walrus teeth. William had never seen a purple tiger before, and he was pretty sure that no tiger in the animal kingdom had teeth that large.

The second the puzzle was solved, there was a click. The door sprang open a crack. Getting back to his feet, he edged his fingers along the door to open it. It was dark inside. "Hello?" He closed his eyes and listened hard for a reply. "HELLO," he called out again into the silence.

Finally, there was a shuffling noise with thumping footsteps. William might have mistaken it for Mrs. Burbank until they got closer. Following each step was a scratching noise like claws dragging along the ground. His blood ran cold. "Is anyone there?" he whispered, hunkered behind the door. He suddenly wished he hadn't opened it. Peeking just over the edge of the door, his eyes spotted something. Through the darkness, two bright dots flashed in his direction like a reflection off a mirror. It reminded him of his neighbor's cat at night. There was no mistaking it: a pair of eyes were staring directly at him.

William stopped breathing. He slowly started to close the door, hoping he could walk away. As the door closed, a loud screech came from one of its rusty hinges, and the eyes in the dark raced toward him. A roar thundered from the blackness. He pushed the door with his might and turned his back to keep it closed, legs braced against the ground as a loud thump struck the door.

William's heart was racing. His lungs were hyperventilating. Whether it was adrenaline fueling his imagination or not, he couldn't tell, but he thought he saw a flash of purple and two large teeth before the door closed. There was no way he was opening the door to find out. His legs started moving, carrying him down the hallway. He didn't dare take time to look over his shoulder.

Twelve halls and seven flights of stairs later, he couldn't move another step. He sat against the ground and wiped sweat from his forehead. Shaken, he saw more doors surrounding him. He wasn't about to open another one. But, like a needle in a haystack, there it was: a door with his father's name on it. The label read, *Arthur McFadden: Principal of the McFadden Institute.* His eyebrows peaked with curiosity on what was inside, but he wasn't sure he dared open it. At least, not after the purple tiger encounter.

"Psst," he heard over his shoulder. He stopped and listened closely, wiping sweat off his brow. There was nothing but silence.

"Psst," came again. He turned around quickly, but he saw nothing but an empty hall. *Could it be my imagination?* He had already seen a possible giant, a dizzying array of halls and a purple tiger. Maybe this was all just a dream that he was going to wake up from in a minute. He closed his eyes and pinched himself just to be sure. All he felt was stinging on his arm where his fingers pinched together tightly.

"Psst."

"Is someone there?" he asked. He turned around several times to check if someone was present. There was nothing out of the ordinary. His voice quivered. He could hear soft giggling.

A powerful, familiar stench filled his nose and burned his nostrils. He pinched his nose to stop the smell as best he could.

"Lost your way?" asked the voice with a chuckle.

"Maybe," William called out. He didn't want to sound lost.

"Need help?"

William smelled the stench getting stronger. "Who are you?"

"I'm a friend. Your friend. More accurately, I was your father's friend."

"Where are you?" William asked.

"The real question is, where are *you?* I'm right here," the voice said from behind him.

William turned sharply. The man he had seen at the tunnel, outside this place in the snow, was standing in front of him, flies, eye patch and all. The stench hadn't improved since he last saw him. William had hoped that both he and Charley recoiling in their seats when the man stuck his head into the van would have tipped him off that he needed a bath. "My father's friend?" he asked in a nasal tone.

"Yes, I was. Until . . ." He hesitated and looked at the ground.

"Until what?" William asked. He shooed flies buzzing around his head.

The man looked confused. "What does it matter? We were good friends once. That's all that matters now. Yes, that is all that matters." His eye rolled in its socket.

"What's your name?" William asked. The man was standing closer to him than before. He was inching his way into William's personal space. William took a step back, trying to regain comfort.

"Mr. Millner," he replied. "You'll never get lost with me. No, never. I know this place like the back of my hand." He tilted his nose toward William.

"I could use some help," William said. He held his arm straight out, his elbow locked, keeping a barrier between them.

"I know. I saw what you were doing. You shouldn't open doors around here. It can be very dangerous," Mr. Millner said. He pushed his nose into William's outstretched hand.

William quickly pulled back his arm, afraid it might be permanently tainted. "You were spying on me?" He put his hand to his nose to make sure it wasn't too stinky. He recoiled. It smelled terrible. He shook his hand in the air, hoping it would air out. "What was that thing anyway?" he asked. "It could have killed me."

"I wasn't spying on you, and yes, it could have killed you. A bit of advice: don't go places you aren't supposed to."

William shook his head. "Why is that thing even inside this place?"

"It was locked up until you opened the door. It was safe," Mr. Millner giggled. "Since you're unharmed, it isn't that important anyway. What really matters is where you're supposed to go, and I know where that is. You'll never get lost with me. No, never. I always know. It's that way." Mr. Millner pointed.

William looked beyond Mr. Millner's finger down a darkened hallway. He was hoping that Mr. Millner's finger would have pointed at the door with his father's name on it. "Is there another purple tiger behind that door too?" he asked, pointing at his father's door.

"Of course not!" Mr. Millner shook his head. "Don't be ridiculous!" He folded his arms and turned like he was offended.

"Sorry, I didn't mean to make you angry," William apologized. "I saw my dad's name and thought. . ." He was quickly interrupted.

"I'm not mad. Not at you, at least." Mr. Millner's smiled. His wild emotions turned on a dime. Happy as a clown, he marched to the door. The picture puzzle whirled under his fingertips.

"Are you sure it's safe?" William asked. He was glad he wasn't the one opening it, just in case.

"It's perfectly safe," Mr. Millner replied as he pushed the edge of the door open. It jammed. Mr. Millner planted his feet and heaved, but the door didn't budge.

There were no roars that William could hear. No pounding footsteps. Maybe it was safe? He moved alongside Mr. Millner and pushed too.

The door inched open until they could see inside. It was a mess: papers scattered, a bed turned over, dresser drawers turned inside out, and a phone resting on the ground. The room was torn to pieces. Not one corner of it was left untouched. Why would someone do that? "It looks like someone was looking for something," William said.

"Yes, it does. Though your dad was never tidy anyway," Mr. Millner said, leaning over William's shoulder and looking into the room. "How did you know him?" William asked.

"We used to be really good friends. I'll prove it," Mr. Millner said. He reached for his pocket and pulled out a picture. "See?" He shoved the picture squarely into William's chest. William took the picture. Oddly, it was the same one he had taken off his father's desk.

Mr. Millner pointed to the tall man leaning on his father's shoulder. "That's me." He smiled, pointing at the different colored eyes. He pulled up his eye patch to show one green eye sunken in a deep socket, skewed awkwardly to one side. Then he pointed at the other one, as blue as the sea, like it was an unmistakable birthmark.

William couldn't argue. How many people had eyes like that? If it hadn't been for the eyes, however, there was no way to identify him. The photo barely resembled Mr. Millner's mangled state. "My, you've changed," he said as politely as possible.

"Those were the days. We were quite the trio," Mr. Millner said proudly.

"Who's this other man?" William asked, pointing to the small figure leaning against his father's knee.

"Oh, Uncle Ben. Well, he's not really an uncle. We just call him that." Mr. Millner snatched the picture and tucked it safely in his pocket. "Not many people are smarter than him." He paused and placed his hand to his chin like he was thinking. "Except for your father, of course. He was the best. With the three of us together, no puzzle stood a chance."

William shook his head. *So, Ben isn't my Uncle?* He didn't know what to think of this place. Things were becoming stranger by the minute. It was even odd that he was growing use to Mr. Millner's stench. He didn't think you could get used to a smell that tremendous, but he didn't need to plug his nose anymore. He looked about the room. "I wonder what they were looking for?" he asked. He was speaking more to himself than asking a direct question to Mr. Millner. Regardless, he got an answer.

"I couldn't say," Mr. Millner said. "Oh, but look at this." He bent down and picked up a small wooden box from the floor. "Your father always had handy charms lying around." He handed it to William.

"What's this?"

"It's one of your father's trinkets," Mr. Millner said. "I always used to love his inventions. I got to try some of his best ones. Open it!" He clapped his hands with excitement.

William opened the box, half expecting to see another puzzle.

Instead, he was surprised to see a watch. It had a button on the side with the letters *A.M.,* his father's initials. A thick brown wristband connected it at the base. It was nice looking, but it had no numbers on the face. "How does it tell time?" he asked. He turned it over to make sure he hadn't missed something.

Mr. Millner chuckled. "It's not that kind of watch. It's your father's Never-Lost Watch. I used to have one too. When I was young and a freshman here, your father gave me one. I don't get lost anymore though." Mr. Millner let his lips buzz and scoffed in the air like it was preposterous that he would ever become lost now. "You'll never get lost again." He leaned in close, interlocking his fingers as he waited eagerly for William to try it.

Freshman? What was Mr. Millner talking about? William felt pressured with Mr. Millner leaning over him. He put the watch on his wrist. It was comfortable, but he failed to see how it could keep him from getting lost. "Now what?"

"Why don't I show you why you came here?" Mr. Millner suggested, teeming with excitement as his tiptoes jumped up and down against the ground.

Why I came? "I came to meet my Uncle Ben."

Mr. Millner chuckled. "Oh, I'm afraid not. You came for the puzzle organ."

William tilted his head to one side. "What? "He had never heard of a puzzle organ. And he certainly hadn't come for it.

"I'll bet your Uncle Ben is at the puzzle organ right now. If you want to find him, let's go," Mr. Millner said with a snicker.

"Okay." William narrowed his eyes and shook his head. "Let's go, I guess." He was uncertain how he felt about it. However, he didn't want to stay and open more doors. That much he was certain of.

"Push the button and talk, silly," Mr. Millner said, pointing to the Never-Lost watch. His hand bounced up and down over the button with one finger outstretched. "You can take yourself."

William reluctantly pressed the button. *How can a watch keep you from getting lost?* He put his lips close to his wrist. "Take me to the puzzle organ," he whispered. His eyes widened as he saw the arrow on the watch spring to life and point down the hall.

"Now all we must do is follow," Mr. Millner said gleefully. He clapped his hands together and spun in a circle.

William followed the watch but was terribly confused about the whole situation. An explanation would be nice, but Mr. Millner didn't seem balanced in the head. He couldn't have been. He barely noticed the flies landing around his nose and buzzing into his open mouth. No sane person would have allowed that.

If William missed a turn, the watch patiently redirected him until he arrived at a large room. As soon as he entered, he could see several hallways opening to this same spot. He wouldn't have thought it unusual if one other hall ended here, but it was as if there were five or six hallways that opened up to this very spot. Even in his mansion back home, he couldn't think of a room with that many halls leading to it. It made it feel like a central point. There was obviously more than one way to get to this room. *Do all the hallways lead here?*

A few more steps into the room, he jumped a pothole in the floor and looked about. For the most part, it was circular with a pair of dusty couches directly in the center. They were made of a voluptuous velvet that was nearly rubbed away leaving the underlying fibers exposed. Both were obviously positioned in a deliberate fashion, facing one side of the oval room. It was this side that caught his attention. Rather than several halls entering, there was a large curtain with golden tassels. The tassels stood motionless but shimmered in the dim light just like a shiny golden coin would have. It was certainly an oddity. It reminded William of a theater with a small stage upfront, though there was no step up to get to the curtain. It simply hung from the top of the ceiling to the mangled floorboards below. Had he not known any better, he would have sat down and waited for the show to begin. What was even more peculiar was the arrow pointed directly at it.

William hesitated, but Mr. Millner marched forward and flung the curtain, disappearing behind it. William followed cautiously.

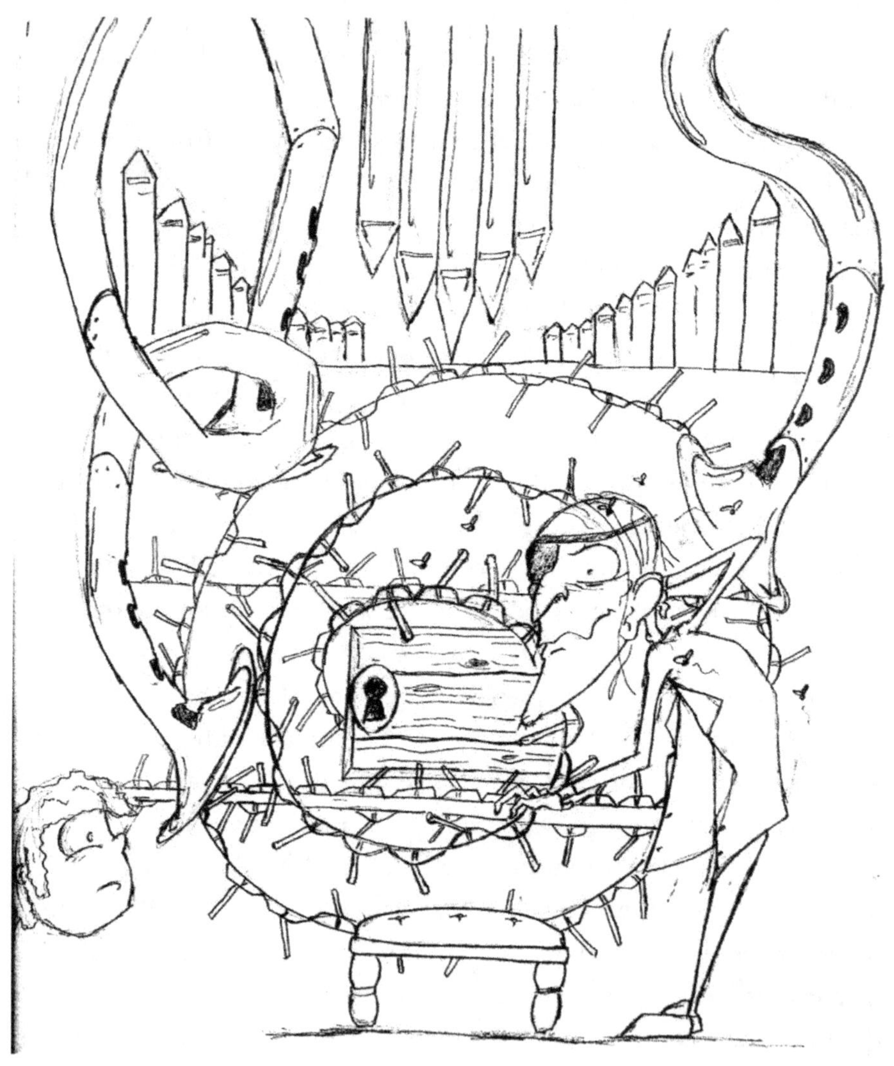

On the other side, Mr. Millner stood next to a peculiar object with a simple bench in front. He beckoned for William to come sit.

In front of William, handles scattered in all directions in a spiral fashion like they were on a rollercoaster twisting around. The short wooden handles looked like they only pulled in one direction. Some were up high and others down low. Even upside-down ones seemed to be permitted. It was hard to see any real organization, but it felt like they were meant to be in a pattern of sorts. If he had to guess their focal point, it looked like they were circling around a small, locked wooden cabinet. Enormous organ pipes twisted down from the ceiling on either side of him. Some of them were straight and pointed downward, as William would have expected a typical pipe organ would have looked. However, others, with an end more like a trombone, twisted through the air, cascading around the small bench where he was sitting. Pipes were on all sides of him.

"This is why you're here," said Mr. Millner with a sinister smile.

William was indeed puzzled. *Why does this look so familiar?* "Could I see that picture again?" he asked.

Mr. Millner took it from his pocket like he was cradling a baby and gently placed it in William's hand.

William wasn't interested in seeing Mr. Millner again. He was more interested in what was in the background. The twisted metal pipes matched exactly. The photo had been taken in this very spot. "What's this thing for?" he asked.

"Why, don't you know?" Mr. Millner's eyes widened and he put one hand over his mouth, flabbergasted. "The puzzle organ is a deadly puzzle."

It didn't look deadly. Confusing with all its handles, but certainly not dangerous. "So, it's a puzzle?"

"Of course. Didn't you know that already? And you're going to solve it!" Mr. Millner danced gleefully like only a madman could.

Solve it? *How do you solve a musical instrument?* "I'm not sure that I can," William said. He wondered if Mr. Millner had finally lost the last good parts that his mind had to offer.

"Of course you can. You just need some help. That's all, help."

"What happens if I solve the puzzle organ?" asked William. This was getting odder by the minute.

Mr. Millner pointed to the locked cupboard. "It opens!" He giggled.

"What's in it?"

Mr. Millner dropped his excitement and gazed at William. His facial wrinkles straightened as he opened his mouth wide. There was no giggling anymore. "The most precious thing in the world," he said. Teardrops gathered in his eyes. They pooled, ready to fall to the floor. He put his hands together like he was praying. "I need to get inside," he muttered. "I mean, we need to get inside. Your dad did it, but no one before him or after him. Lots of people have tried. Most of those ended up going deaf and giving up. Not your dad. We made a good team together," Mr. Millner said. He rubbed his fingers sensually over the locked cupboard.

"People went deaf trying to solve this?" William asked.

"Oh yes. Many people. But you are going to do it. Yes, you are."

William shook his head. "I don't think so." He had just about enough of this.

Mr. Millner's face laced with anger. "Yes, you are!" he demanded in a loud tone.

Taken back, William almost fell to the ground. He wondered what he had done to make him so angry. He tried not to look into Mr. Millner's eyes furiously beating down on him. The tension made him squirm uneasily.

William looked down at the puzzle organ. The curtain ruffled. His eyes couldn't have been off Mr. Millner for more than a moment, but when he turned around, Mr. Millner was gone. *Did he storm off in a rage?* "You there? Mr. Millner? Where did you go?" William called out. There was no answer. He turned around, looking in every direction. He was alone.

"So, I'm supposed to solve this thing? It doesn't look dangerous," he said to himself. Then again, he had to consider that he was in a place where even opening a door was dangerous. The handles, scattered about him, were tantalizing. There were so many. Over and over again, he tried to convince himself that organs weren't dangerous. Was there anything wrong with trying to pull one of the handles? He reached toward one, but chills running up and down his spine made him stop. It made him think of Andy, his friend that didn't even dare to have an apple taken off his head with a paper boomerang. "I'm no chicken," he muttered. He picked a handle at random and pulled firmly.

Almost immediately, a loud rumble roared down the pipes. The organ filled with a deafening bang that erupted. The blast sent him flying backwards like a ball from a cannon.

Chapter 5

UNCLE BEN

Soaring through the air, William spun into the curtain. It caught him like a net catching a fish. Tumbling downward, he unrolled and struck the floor with a thud. The air came bursting from his lungs. Dizzy, he rolled onto his back. His body was filled with pain. *What happened?* "Hello? Mr. Millner?" he called. His ears were ringing, and his voice echoed in his head from the blast. He tried to sit up but wobbled unsteadily back to the ground. He tried once again but couldn't keep his feet under him.

William saw a hand come out of nowhere. It pressed a pill against his lips, urging him to take it. He opened his mouth to protest, but the second he tried, the pill was flung past his teeth. It rolled on his tongue, heading toward his throat. It had a fuzzy texture, making it particular-

49

ly awful brushing against the sides of his mouth. It traveled past his uvula, scratching the back of his esophagus like he was swallowing a hairbrush. His tongue felt like he had licked a wet dog. He smacked his lips together and curled his tongue. The aftertaste was like moldy cheese. It only took a few seconds for the pill to work, though. His hearing cleared and his pain vanished.

Feeling better, William looked up to a small person standing over him in a lively green suit. He was no more than three feet tall. He had a pointy nose, a pointy chin, and a pointy beard. His hair was slicked back at the sides and teeming with grease. It nestled on the back of his head, where it came to a point that covered his neck. It looked like an arrow pointing down his back. He was the pointiest person William had ever seen. In fact, the only round thing on him was a green bowler hat atop his head. William couldn't help but conjure images of cabbage, marshmallow cereal, and four-leafed clovers. Whoever he was, he looked like a leprechaun. He wondered if it would be rude to jokingly ask where his pot of gold was.

"Can you hear me?" the man half screamed.

William nodded. "Loud and clear." He was a little disappointed at the absence of an Irish accent.

"Good. You're fortunate that I was here and always carry Mr. Spirin's Miracle Medicine. It cures almost anything if you take it in time. My first bit of advice: never leave home without it. The last person that did something as brazen as you ended up wearing hearing aids for the rest of her life. You should feel lucky you're not deaf."

William snapped his fingers next to his ears to test his hearing again. Moments ago, he'd felt like he had been shot from a cannon. Now he felt fantastic. What was in that medicine? He wanted more.

William reached to shake an outstretched hand. "Who are you?" he asked.

"I thought you would have deduced that by now," the short man replied, pointing his nose in the air and holding one hand against his suit jacket like he was posing for a picture. He waited for William to recognize him. When he realized that he wasn't as well-known as he thought, he leaned in close and shook his head. "I am the infamous Uncle Ben."

"*You're* Uncle Ben?" William replied. It came off a little rude. He didn't mean it that way. He must have been jostled more than he thought because at second glance, he recognized him albeit Uncle Ben was just shorter than he had expected. He got to his feet to more properly greet him.

Ben took the green bowler hat off. A large bald spot came into view. The whole of his head was nearly hairless except for the rim that sat below his hat. It was deceptive. "And you're William," he stated with a small bow.

"Yes," William replied awkwardly, bowing back.

"How I've wanted to meet you. A near spitting image of your father. You are skinnier than he was, however." He chuckled with his lips closed tightly. It made a curious smirk. "Your dad had a good head between his shoulders. I always admired that about him. He was my first teacher, you know. Taught me practically everything. Of course, I perfected things. The student became the master in a sense," Ben told him proudly.

"I saw a picture of the two of you with Mr. Millner," William said.

"Mr. Millner, you say. Why? Have you seen him?" Ben asked curiously. He narrowed his gaze, making William feel uncomfortable.

"Yes, but he left. I'm not sure what happened to him. He was here a minute ago."

Ben shivered uneasily. He paced a few times and then came to a standstill. "I hope he didn't fill you with any ideas. Anyway, you say he had a picture?"

"Yes. It had all three of you together."

Uncle Ben looked past William, reminiscing. His eyes became moist as he held one hand to his heart. "Those were the days. I miss your father. He was courageous, smart as a whip, and almost never wrong. Of course, I was the only one who caught his little mistakes. No one else matched his intelligence like I did. Fools, really. It was your father and me back then. Well, more like me and your father. Over the years, I have lost touch with him. Now it's only me out here, putting myself on the line. I wanted to visit him but keeping watch over the puzzle organ is time consuming these days."

"Do you know where he is?" William eagerly asked.

Ben hesitated to answer the question. He paced back and forth on the floor, keeping William held in suspense. "No, I don't."

William's small hopes dashed apart again. He had been hopeful this wasn't going to be just a trip Mrs. Burbank had sent him on to get away from him. Now that sliver of hope was gone, yet something about Ben didn't sit right, like he wasn't being entirely honest. It nagged at him.

"I heard he vanished," Ben said. He shook his head, disappointed.

"I always knew he would get into trouble someday. He had a knack for it. He was always second best. Unfortunately, I urgently need his help."

William was taken back. Was Ben looking for his father too? The idea of having help finding his father gave him a flicker of hope again. "Why are you looking for him?"

"Opening the puzzle. It's the only thing that your father ever beat me at. But I don't need to tell you that."

"What?" William asked, confused. "I'm sorry, I don't understand."

"Really?" Ben said, clearly baffled. "Do you mean to say you don't know anything about this place?"

William felt embarrassed shaking his head.

"And the puzzle organ?"

He shrugged his shoulders.

"I thought for certain that . . . how are you supposed to . . .? I'm sure your father told you something. This doesn't make sense at all."

William agreed. It didn't make sense. "Should I know something about the puzzle organ?" he asked hesitantly.

"Yes! Of course you should!" Ben said. He stamped the ground in frustration. "This must be very confusing to you, but we need your help."

"I would be happy to help," William said. The thrill of looking for his father echoed in his voice. He stumbled for something intelligent to say. "My dad used to quote Thomas Edison in times like this: 'Many of life's failures are people who did not realize how close they were to success when they gave up.'"

"Your father did love his quotes," Ben replied. "But they never helped that much."

"He had a whole wall of them in his office. And I—"

"I'm sure that's very interesting, but don't you know anything about the puzzle organ? Anything at all?" Ben's tone was turning desperate.

"Only that it threw me across the room. What is it?" William asked, looking back at the strange contraption.

"This might explain a thing or two," Uncle Ben replied. He flung a picture through the air at William.

William grabbed the photo. It was the same one as before, only this one had circles and formulas scribbled across the front. He held it up to compare it with the puzzle organ directly. There were subtle differences. Pipes were bent differently, handles had been moved into a new pattern, and extra knobs were added. But altogether, it was about the same. The only real difference he could see was a small cabinet. It was open in the picture.

Uncle Ben stood in front of the puzzle organ and let out a sigh. "That was the first time anyone had opened the puzzle organ for as long as can be remembered. It took the three of us to do it."

"What did you find?"

"Why, the key to knowing everything. Ideally, you would have known that by now." There was a tension in his voice. "You see the hat in the picture?" Ben pointed at the photo.

William remembered seeing something in his father's hand. Sure enough, it was clutched tightly in his father's grasp. It resembled an old, pointy wizard hat with patches, but he didn't see anything special about it.

"It's a thinking cap," Ben stated, pointing repeatedly at the photo.

"A what?" William asked. He looked at the picture again, thinking he had missed something. He was a bit embarrassed he knew so little when Ben thought he should know so much.

"Sorry, I forget. You hardly know anything," Ben said, throwing one hand in the air, clearly annoyed. "And it doesn't help that you're surrounded by ordinary people living in an ordinary world. Surely your father would have prepared you."

"Ordinary people?"

"Yes. They dress ordinarily, act ordinarily, and most definitely think ordinarily. There is nothing special about them. I am certainly not ordinary. I daresay I could figure out almost anything, if I had the right tools. And that is what the thinking cap is: a tool."

"A tool to help you think?" William asked. He raised his tone, trying to make it sound like he was following along. Really, he was confused as ever.

"Precisely!" Ben said. He clutched his hand into a fist and brought it down quickly, thinking he was getting through to William. "It could make you smart enough to do anything you wanted."

William had no idea what to say. How could a hat help you know everything? Then again, he had wondered how a watch could keep him from getting lost just moments ago. He fumbled his words for something to say. "That would be nice."

"You certainly wouldn't have any trouble finding your father," Ben said. He wiggled his fingers at William, trying to amaze him.

William realized how right Ben was. If there really was a hat that could tell him everything, it could lead him straight to his father. Furthermore, it could tell him what in the world was going on.

Ben held one finger in the air and shook it back and forth. "But we don't have it. The point I'm trying to make is we need it again."

"Why don't you open the puzzle organ again if you did it before?" William held the picture toward Ben.

"That would be simple if I knew how. Your father is to blame for that. He locked the thinking cap back in that infernal puzzle organ because . . ." Ben took a long pause like he was thinking over his words carefully.

"Because why?" William probed.

Ben narrowed his eyes sinisterly. "Because thieves tried to steal the thinking cap. We needed to keep it safe. The only way to protect it was to put it back." Ben grinned, satisfied with his witty answer.

"It seems safe to me," William said. He shuddered at the thought of being blasted backwards again.

"I assure you that it isn't safe!" Ben nearly yelled. He folded his arms commandingly. "I've guarded the thinking cap for years from bandits. They're getting smarter. Every time they break in, they get closer to solving the puzzle organ. The house has been destroyed by those vandals. There is little to stop them from finding everything they need to steal the thinking cap." Ben dramatically put the back of his hand against his forehead. "I can't do it alone anymore. Soon the thinking cap will fall into their hands and all will be lost." He theatrically walked to a nearby couch and sat down.

"Isn't there anything that we can do?" William asked with as much sympathy as he could muster.

"I was hoping to get your father's help. After all, he was the one that locked the thinking cap inside again," Ben said hunching his head down crossly. "He thought it was locked away forever. If only he knew how dangerously close it was to falling into the wrong hands. I tried to tell him, but he wouldn't listen. He was already gone, leaving me in a precarious situation. If only I had help, I could move the thinking cap to a new, safer location where no thief would be able to get it. If only there was someone to lend a hand. I'd do it myself, but I'm limited in more than one way." Ben pointed to his short legs. He lay back dramatically.

William felt like he was watching a B-rated drama. Was Ben being serious? Still, even if Ben had a flare for the dramatic, he had at least expressed a desire to find his father, even if it was secondary to opening the puzzle organ. That was more than William could say for most of the adults he knew. If opening the puzzle organ was the key to finding his father, Ben's drama was something he could put up with. "Maybe I could help," William began, but he was interrupted before he could finish.

"Perfect!" Ben nearly shouted, jumping from his seat. "You could help. Even if you don't know much, McFaddens are quick learners. Your father was the second fastest learner I know--next to myself, of course. I bet you know more than you think. Tell you what. You help me open the puzzle organ, and I promise to find your father."

It was an exciting proposition. The very thought of being free from Mrs. Burbank filled him with excitement. It was also the first time that anyone had offered to help him find his father. He nodded.

"Fantastic!" Ben shouted, throwing his arms in the air.

From around a corner, Jay's large figure came into view. William, now seeing his full height without having to look under a doorway, was amazed at his size. Jay didn't quiet reach the height of the ceiling, more than thirty feet up, but he was still the largest person William had ever seen. William was increasingly convinced that giants were real, and Jay had to have been one of them. Moments later, Charley came trailing into view panting profusely.

"How . . . how . . . did you . . . get . . . here . . . so fast?" Charley asked gasping for breath between each word.

"Mr. Millner showed me a shortcut, I guess?" William shrugged. He honestly had no idea.

"Shortcut . . . *shortcut*!! You didn't say . . . anything about . . . a shortcut, big guy." Charley looked at Jay crossly.

Jay didn't say anything. He looked emotionless under his big bushy eyebrows and beard.

Ben stuck his hand out. "I am Uncle Ben."

Charley tried to lift his hand in a terrible attempt at an exhausted handshake. "Nice to meet you. Glad William found you." His hand flopped into Ben's like a wet fish.

"I'm sorry about the long walk. Can we get you anything?" Ben asked.

Charley plopped down on a couch. Dust filled the air, billowing up from the seat. He seemed too tired to care. "I'm hungry. Do you have any sandwiches? The fancy kind cut up into little squares? And please put lactose-free cheese on them. I'm lactose intolerant. If I eat real cheese, I get gassy. I'll avoid the dairy products for everyone's sake."

William would have thought Charley would want water. Who wants a sandwich after jogging, anyway?

Ben nodded at Jay, who stamped his feet in irritation on his way to get sandwiches. Ben looked hesitant to ask Charley if he was comfortable. "Anything else?" He said, raising his eyebrows.

Charley lay down. "Car parts? My van broke down."

Ben looked confused, but only for a moment. "Oh, a car," he said, and his eyes opened wider. "Yes, I know about those. How peculiar that ordinary people get around in them, don't you think? I've always wanted one to try."

Charley slumped deeper. "Can you help me fix it?"

Ben shook his head. "I don't have car parts; however, I might know where to find them--Mr. Wyatt's store in town. As it happens, I'm passing near it tomorrow. I have special business nearby."

"Is that like an auto parts store?" Charley asked.

"No, it's more of a knick-knack store."

"I'm not sure I can fix my car with knick-knacks. Maybe some duct tape would work." Charley nodded his head, convinced that he could fix anything with duct tape.

"Who knows, you might find something you like too. Like some new clothes?" Ben suggested, looking up and down at Charley.

Charley looked down at his shirt, which was covered in soot from fixing his car. "This is my favorite t-shirt. I doubt I can find a replacement."

"Suit yourself." Ben looked down at a watch on his wrist. "It's getting late. I have some beds made up. The two of you can stay the night and we can head to town tomorrow."

Jay's footsteps thundered on the ground as he arrived with square sandwiches. Charley scarfed down a handful. William ate a few too. When they finished eating, Ben stood up and hopped onto Jay's leg, standing comfortably on his gigantic foot. As Jay walked down the hall, his foot carried Ben for the ride. William and Charley followed.

William had never seen such a thing, a short person riding on a big foot. He would have liked to ride on the other foot if he had the chance.

After passing a few halls, they stopped in front of a door and Ben climbed off Jay's foot.

Catching his breath, William examined the door. Like before, there was no door handle in sight. He shook his head, confused all over again. "Why don't you have doorknobs?"

"I've never seen a lock that couldn't be broken. On the other hand, a door puzzle can only be opened by a sharp mind. It keeps people locked out who are too foolish to solve it. The way I see it, if someone can solve the door puzzle, they should be able to go in any-way," Ben explained. He looked satisfied with his explanation.

William didn't like that answer at all. "I opened one of these doors and was nearly eaten by a purple tiger!" he blurted out. His face flushed red. He hadn't meant to seem so angry.

"No way! I knew they were real!" Charley exclaimed. He nodded his head up and down in big waves. "Righteous!"

William shook his head. "No, not righteous. It had huge fangs and everything."

Ben waved his hands in the air to calm William down. He chuck-led a little. "Oh, yes. I suppose there are some doors that you shouldn't open. You see, animal transfiguration used to be a required course for every student here at the institute. I've tried to round up the leftovers, but a few stragglers remain. I'll make sure that one doesn't bother you again."

"Animal trans-fig-ur-what?" Charley asked, dropping his bottom lip downward.

"It means they change animals, right?" William looked to Ben for confirmation.

"Right you are!" Ben said, nodding his head in satisfaction. He looked down at his watch and shook his head. "Look at the time! I am sure that you have many unanswered questions that we can address later, but for now, do you care to give this door a try?" He gestured toward a picture puzzle. "Rest assured, there are no purple tigers in there."

William looked at the puzzle intently. The scattered pieces didn't look like a tiger. He hesitantly moved the picture to reveal a comfortable bed. There was an audible *click* as the door opened.

"Genius!" Ben smiled and clapped his hands. "You are definitely a McFadden."

William took two steps into a well-lit room. The door started to close behind him.

Ben looked inside. "Might I give one suggestion? Keep this door closed. Thieves break in all the time. They're not the friendliest bunch," he said.

"Wait. What?" William asked.

It was too late. The door was shut.

Chapter 6

STRANGERS IN THE DARK

William rolled in bed. The soft mattress consumed him like a marshmallow bean bag. All he could think about was his father. There were so many questions. *Why did my father not tell me about this place? Who is Uncle Ben? Am I supposed to open the puzzle organ?* The list of questions snowballed, buzzing around in his head like a hornet's nest keeping him awake. Alas, thinking about them didn't bring any answers. It only added more questions to the swarm. He tried to tally them like counting sheep to fall asleep, but nothing but a horse tranquilizer would get him to close his eyes right now.

He slapped his hand down, flattening the poufy mattress on one side, and sat up. His feet dangled over the edge. A lamp gave enough

61

light to see the overwhelming lumpy comfort behind him. He tried pounding down on it to make it more relaxing.

As one arm came down, the Never-Lost Watch on his wrist snagged. He had nearly forgotten about it with so many things on his mind. He had only used it once, and it had worked like a charm. Curious, he wondered if it really could lead him anywhere. "Take me to Australia," he whispered into the watch. The arrow came to life, spinning in a circle until it rested, pointing out his door. "Take me to the moon," he spoke softly. The arrow spun around in circles madly until he turned his wrist to the side, allowing it to point directly at the ceiling. He leaned closer, hopeful his next directions would take him where he wanted. "Take me to my father." He eyed the watch carefully, but the arrow went limp, toggling around the watch with however he moved his hand. "I guess you can't take me to a person," he sighed, talking to the watch like it was a person. Still, there had to be somewhere that it could take him to get answers. He couldn't wait until morning.

William flopped back onto the bed, consumed in covers, thinking. *What is the puzzle organ?* He couldn't shake the idea that the puzzle organ could help him find his father. He didn't know how all the handles went together, but the feeling wouldn't leave him. He was beyond restless. *Where is my father? Why didn't he tell me about this place?* Ben wasn't very forthcoming with answers, which meant one thing: he needed to get them on his own. This couldn't wait until morning. He jumped from bed and ran for the door.

It didn't take long to solve the picture puzzle again, though the pieces made a terrible scratching noise shifting into place. When it was solved, it revealed a darkened hallway. The door opened to reveal the same. He raised his wrist and said, "Take me to the puzzle organ." The arrow on the watch dangled loosely. He wondered if it was broken—until it began to spin. Round and round it twirled, like it would never stop. Then the arrow came to an abrupt halt, vibrating in place like a spring. William's heart fluttered with excitement.

Broken oval windows allowed moonlight to come in at regular intervals as he walked down the hallway. It struck the fragmented floor, making circles of light up and down his path. Walking was like passing through a slow strobe: light, dark, light, dark. It was just enough to see the arrow on the watch.

He followed through the dark, determined to find answers. Finally, around another corner, golden tassels from a curtain were lying on the ground. He parted the curtains and tied it open to let the light in. There it was: the organ. At night, the pipes from the organ cast an eerie shadow on the ground, sending chills up William's spine. He didn't care how spooky it was. He needed to investigate.

The night was silent around him; not a creature was stirring. Dust floated through the air when he sat on the ground between broken floorboards, thinking. He crossed his legs in front of him. At first, he just stared, thinking about his father. Somehow, he felt a connection with his father and the puzzle organ. He couldn't explain it really. It wasn't that his father had told him about the organ; it just felt like a lost memory. The institute was no different. *But why is it a maze?* He knew his father would have loved the labyrinth. He was always having William solve different puzzles, and mazes were no exception. Come to think of it, his father used to tell him that "puzzles are meant to keep the mind sharp; without them, you will surely dull." His father had a motto that went along with it: "Tell me and I forget, teach me and I may remember, involve me and I learn." -Benjamin Franklin. To William, it meant that you had to be involved to learn. It's why his father used to tell him that puzzles themselves would make the greatest school because you had to constantly be thinking, learning. A student in such a place could never let his or her mind dull. It dawned on William that this place was a school. It had required coursework; at least, Ben had said as much. He smirked at the thought of this being a place where his father might have taught. It made sense, but it didn't answer all his questions. He took the picture of his father from his pocket and held it in front of him. "I can do this," he said into the night air.

William approached the puzzle organ. The shadows from the handles combined with the pipes, swirling on the ground around him, making it look like he was walking into the open jaws of a ferocious beast. He rubbed his hand across the handles, wondering which to pull. He didn't want another episode like before, being shot backwards. He rubbed his elbows remembering how painful it was, but he was no chicken. Yesterday, he was making fun of his friend Andy for being scared of his paper boomerang. He wasn't going to be that guy.

Minutes passed as he stared at the handles, searching for a clue on which one to pull. It was a mess before his eyes. One handle looked exactly like the next, worn wood with poorly applied varnish that had dried dripping downward. There were no marks, no symbols to guide him. It might have been easier to win the lottery than to pick which handle to pull first. But he wasn't going back to his room without trying something.

He stood on his tiptoes and reached. His arms were out as far as he could get them, but it wasn't far enough. His fingers scraped against a handle just out of his grasp. There were plenty of other handles closer, but his gut told him this was the right one. He had to pull it. He bent his knees and leaped into the air. It was only high enough to flick the handle an inch; it didn't flip all the way.

He bent his knees again, ready to flip the handle the rest of the way, but then he heard it. A deep rumble from the puzzle organ was brewing. The pipes moaned and creaked in the dark, and William knew what was coming. He straightened his knees—not to jump, but to *run*. Past the curtains and around the corner as fast as he could. He jumped against the wall and covered his ears.

Boom sounded from the puzzle organ. A blast of wind came rushing down the hallway, ruffling through his hair. It had been a loud noise, but not like before.

William stood up. His ears were okay. He looked to either side to see if anyone was coming, but the night stood still. He was glad that he had only nudged the handle; otherwise, he might have lost his hearing again.

He stared at the puzzle organ, hoping for more answers. But it was an empty hope. His thoughts pushed him later into the night until he started to nod off. His quest for answers hadn't yielded what he had hoped and staring longer wasn't bringing them either. He told the watch to take him back to his bedroom and started to follow the arrow.

After several halls, he pulled the watch close and squinted to check its navigation when a noise came out of the dark. If the hallway hadn't been so quiet, he would have missed it. He listened carefully, wondering if Mr. Millner was spying on him.

There it was again. It was the sound of footsteps tiptoeing across the ground. He used to make the same noise going past Mrs. Burbank's room late at night, but these footsteps weren't trying to sneak away. They were getting louder. He peered into the darkness, looking for a source. Ben's words of warning telling him to not leave his room seemed more serious now. He'd thought Ben was joking.

William tried to move quietly, but the floor creaked under his weight. It echoed off the walls in the darkened hallway, making his heart pound. He looked to see if anyone had heard him. Suddenly, the darkness in front of him came to life. No further than one of Jay's steps, an enormous cloak unfolded, and a figure raced in and out of the patches of moonlight at a dead sprint toward him.

Filled with terror, William turned to follow the watch. His room couldn't have been far off. He pushed his feet as fast as he could, headed back to the safety of his locked door. Behind him, the creaking floor was getting louder as the figure drew nearer. He didn't dare look. Nightmares of being caught by the hooded man in black that roamed his neighborhood flashed before him.

Around a bend, he let out a small sigh of relief as he caught a glimpse of his door in the moonlight. He raced to the door, crashing into it. Panicked, his fingers fumbled to solve the door puzzle, and he jumped inside. He pushed the door almost shut and stopped. Call it curiosity, but he had to know who was chasing him. He looked beyond the open edge of the door. The minute he looked out, he wished he hadn't. It filled him with terror seeing a figure not more than an arm's reach away. He pushed with his might against the door until it clicked shut in the nick of time.

William scrambled to get away and waited. Under the door frame, he could see the moonlight. It darkened as the shadowy figure paced back and forth. He was just outside the door.

William half expected his door to be broken down, but instead, he heard a soft knock. "William," a woman's gentle voice called out. "William." Aside from being unexpected, it was creepy.

"Go away!" his shaky voice called back.

There was no response.

"I don't want to hurt you," said the voice.

"Leave me alone," William yelled back.

There was a moment of silence before the door puzzle started moving.

William sprang for the door. Weak with terror, he held the pieces in place like his life depended on it.

"You have to listen to me," the woman insisted.

"No," William answered, quivering.

Loud footsteps thundered down the hall. *Thump, thump, thump.* William felt the tension on the door puzzle release. Had the figure left?

The thumping stopped outside his door.

William held his cheek to the floor to look under the frame. When Jay's feet came into view, he hurried to opened the door.

Uncle Ben had positioned himself on Jay's back, clutching Jay's suit like reins on a horse.

"Come on, boy!" Ben shouted excitedly. "We're on the hunt!" He whipped one finger in the air and pulled on Jay's suit as they dashed away.

William couldn't keep up with Jay's running. Fortunately, Jay's booming footsteps echoed through the hall. He chased after them, turning corner after corner until he didn't think he could take another step. Panting, he bent over his knees to take a breath and heard voices around the corner. A few steps later and he was back at the puzzle organ.

On one side of the room, a figure in a hood was backed against a wall. Almost instantly, William recognized him. It was the same person who had been roaming his neighborhood. Rumors about the figure had spread like wildfire: he eats snakes, he flies, he has four arms. Obviously, none of them were true, but he wondered why he was here. *Did he follow me?*

Suddenly, the hood dropped from the figure to reveal a trim wom-an dressed entirely in black leather standing her ground. Tight-fitting clothing went from her shoulders to her ankles and matched her short black hair, which swung in front of her face. It was the kind of face that Charley would like. Her eyebrows were drawn with anger and her lips curled defensively. She was cornered. She held her hands up in fists like a boxer readying for a fight.

On the other side of the room, Ben and Jay were circling. Jay crouched forward with his knees bent. Ben had taken off his green suit coat and hat. They hovered like cats ready to pounce on their prey. The tension between them was thick.

"It's over!" Ben shouted angrily across the room.

The woman reached toward her ears to adjust something. William squinted to see a pair of hearing aids fastened to either ear. Flashing back, he recalled what Mr. Millner told him: people had gone deaf trying to open the puzzle organ.

"You never should have brought the boy here," responded the woman. "I only came for him."

"You don't know anything!" Ben replied. He circled the room, getting closer while Jay circled the other direction. They looked like a pack of hyenas. This was not their first hunt.

"You're a traitor. You betrayed your closest friends. Don't deny it," yelled the woman.

"You're a fool! I did what I had to. I can't change the past. You can't have the boy," Ben shouted back.

"Will you betray him too?" asked the woman.

Ben threw his hands down, almost throwing a tantrum. "There's only one traitor here, and you've run out of places to hide!" he bel-lowed.

Jay threw his hand toward the woman. A strange white ball flew through the air and struck the ground, erupting in a cloud of smoke that engulfed the woman. She dived to get away, but there was no avoiding it. The cloud enveloped her.

Jay and Ben moved away from the smoke as it followed closely at their feet.

The woman looked desperate. Frantically, she held her breath and raced to the puzzle organ. In her flight, she ripped her hearing aids from her ears. Then, smiling heartily, she pulled as many handles as she could.

The puzzle organ rumbled deeply like it was clearing its throat. The metal organ pipes shook as a disaster tumbled through them, then all at once it erupted in a deafening blast. The walls of the room shook on all sides.

William clapped his hands over his ears. The sound came rolling over him, knocking him from his feet and throwing him into the hall- way. He toppled along the ground like a tumbleweed. Bits of debris broke from the floor, windows, and walls and followed along next to him. Somersaulting over and over, he struck the floor, going around in a circle like he was rolling down a hill. Somehow, he managed to keep his hands against his ears.

When he stopped, all was silent. He took his hands off his ears and went back to the puzzle organ. His elbows were beaten from hit- ting the ground. Dazed, he looked around to see that everything was covered in fragments. A couch was overturned. The only thing not damaged was the puzzle organ, which stood steadfastly as if nothing had happened.

Ben and Jay got to their feet, pushing rubble out of the way. On the ground, on the far side of the room, covered in debris, the woman lay motionless.

William stumbled over debris, his ears ringing. He figured he knew how a tumbleweed felt now, and he never wanted to become one again. He was glad that he hadn't been any closer to the puzzle organ; his elbows might have been torn off. "Uncle Ben, are you, all right?" he called out.

Ben glanced in his direction and nodded. Limping like he had a broken leg, he climbed aboard Jay's foot.

The next thing he knew, William was being placed on Jay's other foot. It was easy for Jay to pick up William by the back of his shirt and set him down.

William didn't argue. It was a comfortable spot. He clung tightly to Jay's pants so he wouldn't fall off.

Jay grabbed the paralyzed woman with one arm and carried her like a dangling shopping bag. The woman didn't move. She was as stiff as a board. Had William not seen her move before, he might have been convinced that she was a statue.

William watched the woman swing back and forth like a briefcase. Was this a burglar coming to open the puzzle organ? He was hoping he would have answers soon enough.

When the ride ended, Jay pulled a string dangling from the middle of a room. A bulb with no covering turned on, casting a soft yellow glow around them.

William looked about uneasily and gasped. Every inch of the wall was lined with coffins. Each stood upright.

Ben hobbled off Jay's foot, cringing with every step. "Don't worry. There's nothing to be afraid of, but we must hurry. Jay, quickly!"

Jay spun around one of the coffins. It toggled from its base and fell to the floor.

Ben reached down the front of his shirt, and out came a key hanging from a chain. He threw it into a lock on the coffin and the top half sprung open. He switched keys for another lock, and the bottom half did the same. "Quickly. Before it wears off," he said urgently.

Jay plunged the woman into the coffin.

As the woman landed, she jerked and her fingers moved. Her eyes, once stony rigid, blinked and darted in either direction. Progressively, each body part started to shiver. She was thawing.

Ben shut the bottom part of the coffin, covering her from the waist down, and turned the key. "We're safe. She's trapped," he declared with a gasp. He slumped back against Jay's foot to support himself.

Straining with effort, the woman screamed through the upper part of the coffin that was still open. "Don't listen to him, William. He's a traitor. He betrayed your father. He'll betray you—"

Ben slammed the top of the coffin shut and locked it. "You can't trust a thing out of her mouth. She's a thief, a vagabond. The moment the paralyzing powder wore off, I had no doubt she would start spouting lies. Trust me, she would say anything to be free of this lockbox."

"Paralyzing powder?" William questioned.

"Yes. It's very effective. That smoke will stop a raging bull in its tracks, but it's only temporary."

William leaned over the coffin. He looked down like he could see through the lid. The woman's image was burned into his memory. "Who . . . who is she?" he stammered.

"Like I said, burglars break in all the time. I've never had one get away from me for so long though," Ben said as his face expressed concern. "The regular deterrents aren't enough anymore. That is the problem."

"She came to my room. Why would she do that?" William asked. His voice was filled with anxiety.

Ben put his fist to his chin like he was thinking over his words carefully. "Obviously, she wanted to get rid of you. She knew, just as I did, that you might help us open the puzzle organ." He shrugged his shoulders.

"But I don't know anything about the puzzle organ," William protested.

"That may be true now, but you're Arthur's son."

William put his hand over his mouth in shock as he took in this information. It made him wonder how long he had been followed. Maybe that's why she was lurking about his neighborhood? The dark stranger had more than once looked in through the mansion windows. It made him shiver to think that he had been unknowingly observed by a dark thief dressed in black leather. "What should we do with her?" he asked hesitantly.

"Tomorrow, we'll take her to town. She needs to be locked up properly with the other burglars."

"Will she be all right?" William asked.

"Of course. She's safe enough she could be buried," Ben answered with a laugh. "Now then, I think I broke my ankle," he said holding out his right leg. From out of his pocket, he took a bottle of Mr. Spirin's Miracle Medicine. In one gulp, he swallowed the hairy pill down his throat. With a hand outstretched, he offered one to William too.

William rubbed his elbows. They ached along with his ears, but the thought of forcing a hairy pill down his throat made him gag. He politely declined. He wasn't hurting badly enough.

Ben offered a pill to Jay too. Jay's large hands had trouble rolling the small pill between his fingers, but with a toss, he managed to throw it to the back of his throat.

William leaned over the coffin. He could hear quiet screams from inside. This wasn't right. But before he could say anything, a tug lifted him from the ground and sat him on Jay's foot. Off they went, leaving the coffin in the distance. The screams gradually faded away.

Chapter 7

INTO TOWN

William stood in his father's office back at the mansion.

"There you are, William. I've been looking all over for you. I have a new quote to show you," said a friendly voice.

William blinked his eyes several times. His father was sitting behind his desk. "Dad, I can't believe it. How did you get here? Where have you been?" he exclaimed. He stumbled over his questions, unable to ask them quickly enough.

"I've been here the entire time," his father replied. He shrugged and got up from his desk, throwing his arms around William. "Look at this quote," he said excitedly, holding up a small piece of paper. "'Ninety-nine percent of failures come from people who make excuses.' – George Washington. I was going to add it to the wall. What do you think?"

William didn't know what to say. He was caught completely off guard, wondering how his father was standing in front of him. "It's great, Dad," he finally muttered.

"Come on, we have to put it on the wall," his father announced. He pulled William over to the wall of quotes. His hand moved to one of the few blank spots. "I think it fits here, wouldn't you say?"

"Yeah, Dad, I guess." William shrugged.

"You guess? It's perfect. Don't you see the puzzle? It's all about the pattern."

William knew the wall of quotes backward and forward. He had never seen a puzzle in it. Even now, it looked like a haphazard, scrambled wall of papers that pinwheeled outward. "Sure, Dad." He shrugged again in agreement.

William's father held his hands out, disappointed. "What's wrong?"

William couldn't hold back the questions. "Where have you been? Why didn't you tell me about Uncle Ben? Or the puzzle organ?" He didn't mean to sound so annoyed; it all just burst out of him like a firecracker.

His father shrugged and reached high on the wall to pin the quote. "I told you lots of things. If you don't remember, it's not my fault; it's yours," he replied. He looked satisfied with the placement of the quote.

William took a step back, his jaw nearly dropping to the floor. "What are you saying? It's *my* fault that I don't know about any of this? You never told me anything."

"Are you sure? I told you plenty, but how could I trust you? I mean, you ran away from a burglar. Did you even stop to ask yourself if she really was a burglar? For all you know, she could have been there to help you. What if Ben betrayed me and you're next? It doesn't matter. You should have been braver." His voice lowered as he shook his head disappointedly.

William thought for a moment. "Yes, but Ben said—" He shrugged his shoulders, confused.

"Do you believe him?" his father interrupted, throwing his hands in the air.

"I don't know. What does it matter? You're here."

"You don't think it matters? I am trying to prepare you. That's why I can't tell you things," his father said as he started to pace.

William wrinkled his forehead. This didn't make any sense. It wasn't like his father to be so blunt. He was normally understanding and as gentle as a church mouse. "I care. I do. I just don't understand," William replied as convincingly as he could.

"You're important, William. More important than you realize. Don't you know that?" His father let out a woeful sigh.

"But I don't know anything about puzzle organs or this place. You just vanished. I was left with Mrs. Burbank," William said, dumbfounded.

His father paced up and down. "I told you everything you need to know." He folded his arms and put his head down.

How can that be? William wondered if he'd misunderstood. *What about Ben? the mysterious woman? I hardly know where I am.* His eyes welled with tears. "I don't remember."

"You will," his father said. He turned to face William. "You know everything about the puzzle organ. Give it time and you can figure this out. I know you can."

William buried his face in his hands.

"Talk to the burglar," his father began, but his voice faded into the distance.

"Okay, I'll speak with her," William said uncovering his face. His father was gone. The room was silent. "Dad," he called out, but the room was empty. "Dad!" he called again.

Running from the office, he flung the door open and ran into the hall, frantically looking for him. Sprinting down the stairs, his feet drifted between the steps. The stairs stretched beneath his feet until he couldn't stand. Falling, he stumbled downward. He braced himself and his hands jutted forward. "Daaad!" he yelled at the top of his lungs.

The ground never came. William opened his eyes in darkness. The space around him was motionless. In pitch blackness, there was nothing he could see. He felt walls on every side of him. It felt like a box, trapping him. The realization came quickly. This was no box; it was a coffin. He let out a scream that was nothing but a deafened cry. The claustrophobic surroundings horrified him. He panicked as the air grew thin. It made him shriek at the top of his lungs until his head felt dizzy. Spots raced before his eyes, and he slipped into unconsciousness.

William jumped awake in bed, sweat beading across his forehead. Vivid images from the nightmare were fresh. A strange mix of panic, remorse, and loss for his father aroused him. He rolled over. Unable to sleep, his thoughts wandered, thinking about the burglar. He knew that his father's words were just part of a dream, but it didn't make them less impactful. Something wasn't sitting right. Not to mention, it hadn't felt right watching Ben lock someone in a coffin. The burglar didn't steal anything as far as he could tell. The situation bothered him like a pea under his mattress, keeping him awake until the wee hours of the morning.

When the sun came through his windows, William was still staring at the ceiling. He wanted to get out of his room again, but with the events that happened last night, he was more diligent listening to Ben's warning. He thought about waking Charley; however, Charley was not a morning person and probably wouldn't be awake for a few more hours. Waking him up too early made him act like a zombie. Not that he would eat people, but he would drool from his mouth and mind-lessly walk around moaning incomprehensible sentences.

William sat up in bed surprised when a knock came at his door. He was taken back even more when he saw that it was Charley standing there doing the knocking.

Mouth slumped open, with drool falling out, Charley was hang-ing his head, staring at the floor, his fist still in the air knocking even though the door was open. It didn't look like he had slept through the night either. "I accidentally locked myself out of my room looking for the bathroom. There is no way I can open that door again. Can I just stay with you for a bit?" he asked.

William nodded. He was glad to have the company with his in-somnia. It would give him a chance to talk to someone. He moved aside for Charley to come in.

Charley wasn't interested in listening. He slouched forward, walked to the bed, and slumped face-first into the covers while William dic-tated his account of the puzzle organ. It wasn't until William got to the part about an attractive burglar that Charley perked his ears up to listen. Charley was attracted to dangerous women, or so he said. This was followed by a tale of a girlfriend who ate habaneros like candy—apparently, Charley thought that was dangerous. Truthfully, William didn't think there was a woman in the world that Charley wouldn't be attracted to.

When Charley said he didn't hear anything last night, William threw his hands onto the bed. *How could anyone sleep through all that noise?* He'd forgotten that Charley slept with headphones on, blasting alter-native rock music all night. Truthfully, William didn't understand how Charley could snooze like that.

Another knock came at the door and Jay hunched into the room. The smell of fresh fruit and pancakes wafted from a silver platter in his hand. Ben followed closely behind. He had bags under his eyes and his suit was wrinkled. His hair, yesterday combed at the sides, was now nested in knots. It looked like he'd had a hard night too.

"Is everything okay?" William asked.

Ben tapped his foot on the ground and checked his watch. "We need to go to town as soon as possible. I cannot be late."

Charley stuffed pancakes down his throat. He didn't use utensils. Famished by the lack of his usual midnight snack, he was determined to get as many down as possible. He had a philosophy: if he folded the pancakes in half, he could fit more in his mouth. It grossed William out, but it was impressive to see three pancakes bulging from his mouth at once. The butter and syrup ran down Charley's cheeks, making a dripping syrup beard. William recalled why Mrs. Burbank didn't invite Charley over for meals.

Ben didn't eat; instead, he pulled a pack of papers from his pocket and flipped through them mumbling to himself. "Mr. Millner, Mr. Millner," he repeated shaking his head.

"Is everything all right?" William asked again.

Ben broke from a trance. "I need to meet with Mr. Millner to straighten things out," he gruffly replied. "Nothing for you to worry about." He gave a crooked smile.

William knew he wasn't telling the truth—or at least not all the truth. That smile told it all. Mrs. Burbank would do the same thing when she was angry but didn't want to talk about it. "Is there anything I can do to help?" he asked, trying to pry out more information.

"Unless you can recall if your father told you anything about the puzzle organ—even the slightest detail could make a difference—then not really." Ben raised his eyebrows and pushed his chin forward, waiting for an answer.

William thought it over. *Why is he asking me again?* "Sorry, I don't know anything." He was getting tired of not knowing anything. He put his head down and poked at his pancakes.

"Did he ever mention Mr. Millner? Or perhaps the thinking cap?" Ben asked, pushing his head forward and shaking it.

William felt like he was being probed. He searched his thoughts, looking for any piece of information. There was nothing. Honestly, he was pretty sure he would have remembered if his father had told him about a man who stunk like manure, had different colored eyes like a calico cat, and had flies buzzing around him. How could he forget something as odd as a puzzle that can kill, or a little man dressed in green? No, there was nothing. He shook his head without making eye contact with Ben.

Ben rolled his eyes and tapped his watch, accepting William's answer. He put the papers back into his pocket and paced the room, mumbling.

At the end of breakfast, Jay offered his foot to William, who gladly accepted. Of course, Charley was jealous.

"Are you sure you don't have a third foot tucked under those coat tails?" Charley asked.

Jay wiggled his bushy mustache back and forth. He didn't find the question amusing.

On Jay's foot, Ben glanced at his watch. He pushed Jay like he was commanding a dog sled. "Get a move on," he demanded. They moved quickly through the hallways. Truthfully, William didn't think that Jay knew how to travel slowly. It was his long legs that made him fast.

It didn't take long to return to the burglar. William had an eerie feeling that made his spine crawl when he saw the walls lined with coffins again. Charley cringed at the sight. Charley didn't want to know if the coffins were filled with bodies because he was terrified of dead things. Ben was completely unfazed by Charley's whimpering and commanded Jay to get the coffin with the burglar. Jay picked it up without flinching, carrying the coffin effortlessly like he was casually strolling through a park. He barely wrinkled his suit.

William listened carefully, expecting to hear the woman screaming. Not a peep could be heard. His throat tightened at the thought of being trapped inside himself. His dream had been too real. He never wanted to experience what it was really like, nor did he think anyone else should have to suffer it. Burglar or not, he empathized with her situation. Part of him wanted to let her out, not just because it was cruel to lock someone up, but because he needed to speak with her. Nothing felt right. She would probably give him answers he was desperately craving.

The hallways were like a labyrinth. Turning in all directions made William feel like they were going in circles. He couldn't tell where they had begun or where they were going. Up three flights of stairs, through countless hallways, past hundreds of doors and pictures, until finally they came to a stop. Jay turned his head, looking in either direction, pausing at each as if confused.

William wasn't sure if they were lost or not. Either way, he was thankful for the stop; he was nauseated. He never did well on carousels either.

"He always gets lost here," Ben said as he climbed off Jay's foot. He was shaking his head, disappointed.

"We're lost?" William asked. He closed his eyes to get rid of some of his queasiness.

Charley was panting loudly. "You've . . . got to . . . slow down . . . big guy." He bent over his knees to rest.

Jay smirked with all the pleasure in the world.

"Where . . . are we . . . anyway?" Charley asked. He threw one hand in the air like he was asking a question in a classroom.

"We are almost to town. You don't want to get lost here. You could die," Ben said, looking in each direction.

"Die? What do you mean die?" Charley asked, his voice quivering.

"If you can't find the way out, what do you think happens?" Ben raised his tone, shaking his head at Charley.

"Do you know where we are?" William asked, calming the shakiness in his voice. He raised his Never-Lost-Watch to his mouth, hoping he didn't have to use it.

"Of course! I've never gotten lost," Ben said. He licked the tip of his finger and lifted it into the air. "Eenie, meenie, miney, mo," he said, pointing in one direction. He looked satisfied. "There it is. Simple as that," he said firmly and without reservation.

"For real?" Charley replied in an exaggerated high pitch, making his dumb-face. "*Eenie, meenie, miney, mo.* Are you kidding?"

Ben looked impatiently at his watch and climbed back onto Jay's foot. He held his finger out and told Jay to mush. Jay followed Ben's finger without question until they came to a door.

William jumped from Jay's leg, seasick—or in this case, leg sick—and stumbled unsteadily.

The door opened and a ray of sunlight blinded William. He gripped Charley's shirt instinctively and followed behind him. His eyes had a hard time adjusting as he emerged from the dimly lit hallways of the institute. When his eyes cleared, he was standing on the edge of a street bustling with people.

There were people walking in the middle of the road in neat lines. Some went this way and others went that, minding their own business, following the person in front of them like rows of ants. Men read the daily headlines and women put on their makeup as if there was a conveyer belt moving them forward. No attention was required. Men's top hats, bowlers and fedoras bobbed up and down in sync with one another. Prim ladies in fashionable dresses kept to themselves under high umbrellas shading them from the sun. Shoulder to shoulder, stacked like sardines, they kept their spots in line.

On the edge of the street was another matter. Crowds toppled over one another, getting in and out of the lines as if entering a freeway. They pushed and elbowed, securing their spot in line. That explained the occasional black eye that passed by.

Shops lining the street were filled with merchants chanting their daily routine. They called, "Fifty percent off, today only!" People clambered over one another to be the first in line. When they didn't get their way, men puffed out their chests demandingly. Women stomped their feet and rattled off ultimatums. It was pandemonium.

William looked in either direction, taking it all in. He had been to his fair share of places around the world, but he had never beheld a place such as this. He almost wondered if they had gone back in time;

the clothes were anything but modern, and not an automobile was in sight. Yet, there were other parts that didn't seem old at all. High above the streets was a grid of ropes zigzagging across the skyline, swooping in and out of buildings with neatly folded letters strung along them. Falling from their perch, the letters zipped downward to be delivered into waiting hands. It made for a continuous stream of paper floating through the air.

"What is this place?" William asked, turning his head every few seconds to behold something new.

Ben shook his head in disappointment. "I would have thought you would at the very least know your own birth place," he replied, placing one hand over his face.

William took a step back. How could this be the place where he was born? "I didn't know," he muttered, embarrassed.

"It would seem there is a lot that you don't remember. Welcome to Fairhaven," Ben said, waving his hand lazily at the scene in front of them.

William looked around the crowd again. On one corner, he saw invisible clothing for sale; of course, the racks looked empty. On another, a weather manipulation device. Things didn't make sense here. *How can I not remember a place like this?*

Ben continued, "Since your father has clearly shirked his fatherly responsibility, I suppose it falls on me to give an explanation. Would it come as a surprise to you that most of the people in this world rely on a small fraction of extraordinary minds? After all, ordinary people don't invent; they just buy."

William shook his head. He didn't understand why that mattered in the least. It wasn't that he was agreeing or disagreeing; he just didn't understand what Ben was talking about.

Ben continued, "Ordinary people are content to purchase things, hardly considering how someone smarter than them made it all possi-ble. Yet, when a genius invents something as extraordinary as a purple tiger-walrus hybrid or a bubble that can carry you into outer space, he is considered a madman by them. Some have even been rejected for things as simple as suggesting that washing hands prevents disease. But not in Fairhaven!" He threw his fist into his open palm commandingly. "Ordinary people don't belong here. They wouldn't accept this place. It's more of a magical place to them than a reality. There are things here that seem very magical indeed but are really the product of a brilliant mind at work. That is what Fairhaven is: brilliant minds that have been rejected by *ordinary people*. They come together here, creating extraordinary things that the outside world wouldn't appreciate. They come here for acceptance."

"So, rejects live here?" Charley blurted out. It sounded rude.

Ben hung his head low and massaged his forehead in frustration. "That depends on how you look at them. For example, some accepted Frankenstein for who he was, not a hideous monster. Others cast him out as a demon. Depending on how you view it, Fairhaven is filled with Frankensteins. Not because they're an experiment come to life, but because they have been cast out for their ideas and their creations; inventions that could only be considered magical. Whether you accept them or despise them is up to you."

"So, Frankenstein lives here?" Charley asked, looking up and down the street with his jaw open in amazement at the splendor.

Ben slapped his forehead with his open palm. He pointed at Charley. "William, do you see what I mean? This is why ordinary people don't belong here."

Nodding his head, William thought he understood. He could see how different this place was, but somehow he felt comfortable. It was like he had been here before. Now, he was wondering how so many people came together in one place. "What about the institute?" he asked.

"Great minds need a place to study and learn, wouldn't you say? At least, that's what it used to be—a school."

William felt like his feelings were confirmed about the institute. He leaned forward, eager to ask more, but Ben's attention was immediately directed toward a letter that fluttered toward him like a kite on a string. When it stopped, Ben plucked it quickly from the air and ripped it open. The minute he read it, his face reddened with anger. Tapping his foot on the ground, Ben mumbled, "Blast that Mr. Millner." It reminded William of Mrs. Burbank again, whose face turned red in a dirty scowl whenever she became irritated. Even the pressure mounting on Ben's face looked the same.

"We need to get a move on!" Ben suddenly blurted out. "There is no time to waste." He crumpled the paper into his pocket, and in a few short steps, he entered the crowded streets, disappearing in a sea of legs.

Jay didn't hesitate to follow. He hurdled over vast portions of the crowd, following Ben.

William ran into the crowd, trying to follow. He pushed with his elbows, nudging people until he found a comfortable spot. No one tolerated his line-butting very well. They even became tighter to keep him out.

When his elbows had made enough bruises wrestling his way between people, he was finally allowed a space, wedged between a potbellied man, whose stomach pushed him forward, and a feathered dress in front of him. The feathers tickled his nose when he got too close, but it was hard to stay away with the big belly pushing him forward. He was swept along unable to see Charley.

A shift in the line changed the man behind him to a scraggly-looking woman. At first, he was glad to be rid of the fat belly—until the scraggly woman became impatient. If the line slowed, she screamed and yelled at the top of her lungs, her face purple with intolerance.

When his line came to an unexpected stop, William looked far ahead at Jay lurching over the crowds off in the distance. Not wanting to be lost, he tried to get through the wall of people, but it was no use.

He wasn't as small as Ben; he couldn't scurry between legs. Pushing didn't help either. It only enraged the scraggly woman behind him, who sharply pushed him forward, causing William to take a nasty fall and land on the feathered dress ahead of him. Feathers flew into the air.

"I'm sorry," he exclaimed, but it was no good. Like a plucked chicken, the feathered dress had been ruined.

The lady in the feathered dress turned abruptly, and one glance at her bare dress sent her fiery gaze alight. She glared at the scraggly lady, whose arms were outstretched from pushing William.

"I've had just about enough of you!" shrilled the woman in the dress.

"I beg your pardon!" screeched the scraggly woman. She plucked a feather from the nearly naked dress and threw it to the ground.

Before William knew it, he was in the middle of a fight. Feathers flew and clothes were torn.

The orderly lines miraculously swerved to miss the excitement. Neatly shaped lines formed on either side of the scuffle. Gentlemen lowered their newspapers at the day's excitement. Ladies turned their noses up in disgust. It was a riotous event and everyone had an admission ticket, yet no one stopped to help. They were content to keep their spot in line, minding their own business.

William bent down while the two women exchanged arguments over the top of him. Feathers came falling from the sky. He had to get away. He braced himself and rushed the edge of the crowd. It was no use. The crowd was nestled like a wall. There was no amount of elbowing that would get him through.

Curiously, a hand came waving out of the crowded legs. William couldn't see who it belonged to. He wasn't sure that he cared either if it was going to help him escape. The fingers tightly wrapped around his arm and pulled forward. Twisting and turning, William was dragged away.

Chapter 8

MR. WYATT INC.

Bumping between people, William lost all sense of direction. He grasped at the hand that held fast on his arm, pulling to free himself. Whoever was pulling on him wasn't about to let go. He was grateful he didn't have to deal with a fight over a feathered dress, but honestly, dragging him away probably wasn't necessary. He hoped it wasn't another of his father's *friends*. He didn't want to deal with another Mr. Millner with his wild emotions right now. The moment he was free, he thought about using the never-lost-watch to run away.

William, finally slowing down, glanced upward to find in front of him a pair of hairy legs attached to short khakis that were well above mid-thigh. They led him up a staircase and through a door. *Ting* sounded a bell as they went through. When the hand let go, William dropped to the floor. He held his watch up, ready to run, and turned quickly. He couldn't see anyone. He straightened his shirt and ringed his arm uncomfortably where the hand had been. He wondered who would drag him away, but even more so, he wanted to know why.

William turned, looking for his captor. Around him, rows of trinkets with price tags littered aisles of shelving. They were arranged in categories. A row of hats lined the aisle next to him. One shelf was labeled *Happy Hats* and another *Smart hats*. No matter where he looked, everything had one thing in common: a mark that read *Mr. Wyatt Inc.* Posters on the wall bore the same insignia. Each had the picture of a man in short khakis well above mid-thigh, a safari shirt, a monocle covering one eye, and a hat with one side curled. William had to admit the posters made the man look dashing, showing him stepping on top of a lion or atop a great mountain.

Looking from poster to poster, William nearly missed his hijacker. When William first spotted him, his eyes brushed over him, thinking he was another poster. It wasn't until the man snorted and moved his legs that he realized it wasn't a poster after all, yet he was the spitting image of the poster's heroic character.

The man stood with one leg propped high in the air like he was modeling for his next photo shoot. He appeared much shorter than his posters advertised. William wondered what this meant about his ego.

Chewing on a reed, the man went to the windows to close the blinds.

"Do we know each other?" William asked, wondering why the stranger was so eager to close the windows. He looked in either direction for a weapon in case he needed one.

"No, mate," the man said in a thick Australian accent. "But there's no time for long intros. My name is Mr. Wyatt."

"I'm William," he said. His hands brushed a shelf, grabbing something that looked like a spork.

"Yes, yes, I know. Did you get the message?" Mr. Wyatt questioned. He started chewing the reed more quickly, bouncing it along his lips.

"Message? I didn't get any message," William replied. His fingers held the spork tightly behind his back. If he needed a weapon, it was going to have to do.

"Vanessa came to give you a message. Didn't she speak with you?" Mr. Wyatt said, raising his tone anxiously. His head bobbed in between the blinds in the windows, looking out suspiciously at the crowded streets.

William shook his head. "Vanessa? What? No, there was no message."

"A girl dressed in black, wears hearing aids. Probably came late at night. Did you see her? We haven't heard from her since she came to talk to you, mate," Mr. Wyatt pressed more intensely. Convinced that no one had followed them, he turned around and stared at William through his monocle.

William's eyes widened. "You mean the burglar? I saw her, but there was no message. Ben locked her in the coffin."

Mr. Wyatt paced up and down nervously. "This is bad, very bad." He bit the reed in half and chewed his fingernails.

"I'm sure we can tell Uncle Ben," William tried to explain.

"Nooo!" Mr. Wyatt half-screamed. He placed a finger over his lips. "That is the worst thing you could do," he whispered. He turned toward the window.

"Why?" William questioned.

"Listen carefully. Uncle Ben cannot be trusted. Not after what he did," Mr. Wyatt said. His eyes were exaggeratedly wide.

William looked puzzled. "Are you sure?" he asked, squinting one eye and turning his head.

"That is exactly what your father said too—until he betrayed him," Mr. Wyatt replied. He bit down hard on one nail.

William wondered if his fingers were going to bleed. Mr. Wyatt was gnawing at them firmly. "Are you sure we're talking about the same person?" he asked. Ben was no angel, but he wasn't sure Ben had betrayed his father.

"As sure as I know shrimp cooks on the barbie, he's the reason your father is missing."

William shook his head. "But he told me—"

"Forget what he told you, mate. Vanessa would have told you as much if Ben had let her. It's not the first time he has ruined someone's life. He got rid of your father. Now he has his sights set on you. Go figure." Mr. Wyatt said. He stopped chewing his fingers and turned toward William with his hands together.

"What do you know about my father?" William asked. He wondered if Mr. Wyatt might be able to help him find him.

"Not as much as Vanessa. I think she almost found him."

William nearly jumped through the roof with excitement. "Where is he!?"

"I don't know, mate. She was worried you were in danger. We were supposed to talk about that after she delivered her message to you, but that obviously didn't go as planned."

"Why should I believe you?" William asked squinting both eyes suspiciously.

"Why would I lie? I'm no dingo," Mr. Wyatt replied. "I'll prove it." He pulled a hat from the shelf labeled *Truth Hat* and threw it on William's head.

The hat was far too big, sinking down over William's eyes. "What's the hat for?" he questioned, turning his head from side to side as it toggled.

"With this hat, you can't lie. Try it! Tell me you're a hyena." Mr. Wyatt put his hands on the sides of the hat and straightened it on William's head.

William thought it was ridiculous. "I'm an hy. . ." His tongue tied in knots. "I'm a hy. . . hye. . ." he tried again. He opened his mouth in surprise. *How can a hat stop me from saying something?* Regardless of how big it was, an item like that could come in handy. Deep down, he wanted-ed to throw it on Ben's head and ask a few questions.

"Now, put it on my head," Mr. Wyatt said gesturing with his hands.

William threw the hat on his head. "Are you telling the truth?" he asked.

"Cross my heart and hope to die, I did not tell a lie," Mr. Wyatt rhymed with one hand over his heart.

The stairs leading up to the door creaked as a customer climbed them.

Mr. Wyatt looked over his shoulder quickly to see who was coming. He tensed his fingers into fists. "There's no time. Trust me. Uncle Ben twists the truth. Just like he manipulated your father, he'll manipulate you. If you care about your dad, help Vanessa escape. Most importantly, don't speak a word of this to anyone. It could endanger you!" he said.

Ting, the bell on the door rang, Mr. Wyatt threw the hat back on the shelf and jumped behind a counter. "An excellent selection, mate. I couldn't have picked it better," he said to William in a tone that reeked of poor acting. He took a package from under the counter and handed it to William. "Don't forget to come back to Mr. Wyatt's store for all of your needs," he said proudly. He winked at William and brushed his hand at him like he wanted him to leave. Turning his back, he started to blurt out a high-energy sales pitch to the customer at the door.

William fumbled with the package. It read *Mr. Wyatt's Animal Whistle.* It was light and square, just the right size to place in his pocket. The bell rang as he went outside. To his surprise, at the bottom of the stairs, Charley was looking through the crowd with one hand shading his eyes. He was scanning the bobbing heads in the street. William felt a sense of relief seeing a familiar face.

Charley didn't seem surprised to see William. He casually looked at him and kept scanning the crowd. "I knew you'd find us. I told your

Uncle Ben he didn't need to worry, but he gets anxious."

Ben suddenly grabbed William from behind and twisted him about. "There you are!"

William wasn't sure what to say. Having been told that Ben was a traitor, he wasn't sure that he could trust him anymore. Mr. Wyatt seemed serious when he told him not to tell anyone. "I guess I got lost in the crowd," William said, shrugging his shoulders.

"You're not the first," Ben said. His bowler hat pulled low over his brow didn't hide his frustration. "For as smart as all these nincompoops are, I wonder why they're so crowded going about their daily routines." He pointed a chastising finger at the crowd. The tension was only broken as a note floated through the sky and stopped over Ben.

Ben ravenously plucked it from the air and tore it open like he was taking his frustration out on it. William hoped it won't be another letter like before that had sent Ben running into the crowd.

After reading it, Ben announced, "I have to go see Mr. Millner." He snapped his fingers and Jay bent down on one knee, still holding the coffin in one hand. By the back of his shirt, Ben was hoisted up to sit on Jay's leg like it was a bench. The next moment, William was being lifted to sit alongside him.

From Jay's knee, William towered over the crowd. His view was only obscured by the occasional large feather in a passing hat. He lapped up as much of the view as possible. The variety of people was amazing, but none so much as a woman across the street, covered with keys. She had key earrings, key necklaces, key hair clips, and keys hanging from every inch of her clothing. She sat on a pillow in front of her shop in a serene pose with incense burning next to her. She had a headband decorated in keys holding her long, flowing hair in place. As customers came, she would pluck a key off her clothes and sell it to them.

Ben saw William staring. "That's Miss Lockit, a curious person. I suggest you stay away. She's a con artist who sells junk, like the rest of this lot." Ben waved his hand over the crowd. "But, there's no time for that. Do you see over there?" Ben pointed to a large building with a police symbol. It wasn't hard to recognize even in a place as different as this, but had they not been high on Jay's knee, they wouldn't have been able to see it. "Listen carefully; I have other urgent matters to attend. Take these keys." He pulled the keys from a necklace hanging around his neck. "They unlock the coffin. Deliver them with the burglar to the police station. They will know what to do."

William nodded, taking the keys from Ben. His fingers wrapped around them tightly. Mr. Wyatt had told him to help Vanessa escape, and now he was holding the keys to do it. His father's dream had even told him to talk to the burglar, yet he felt guilty betraying Ben, who trusted him enough to give him the keys.

"Before you go, Charley may find some parts for his van in that shop," Ben said, pointing at Mr. Wyatt's shop. "Don't delay." Ben snapped his fingers, and Jay's large hand hoisted him to the ground. Seconds later, he vanished in the crowd.

Chapter 9

COFFIN DELIVERY

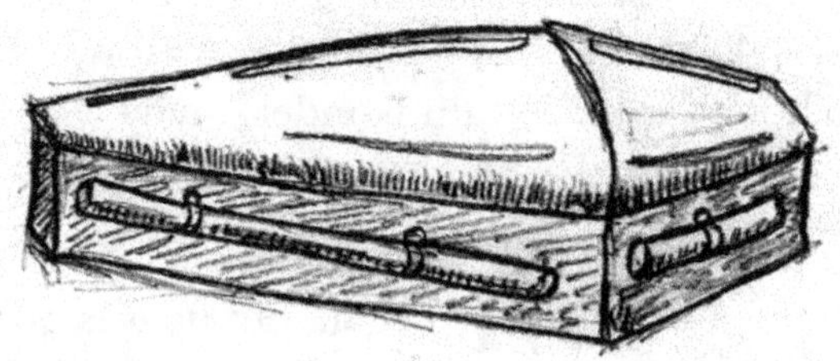

William rubbed the keys between his fingertips. *Now what?*

Jay gently lowered him to the ground. He moved his hand toward William and Charly as if he was brushing them along like a broom, insisting they follow Ben's directions by going into the shop.

Not wanting to raise any eyebrows, William didn't put up a fuss. He didn't want Jay's big hand to push him along either. He followed Charley up the stairs and into the store for a second visit.

Jay kept a close watch from outside, leaning against the windows and peering through them. He was obviously being an overprotective babysitter.

Mr. Wyatt enthusiastically turned to greet his customers. "Welcome to the outback's toy box," he advertised. As the words came out of his mouth, he locked eyes with William. No amount of bad acting could hide his astonishment or the way his enthusiasm drained straight from his face as he slumped down.

William knew that Mr. Wyatt hadn't wanted him to tell anyone about their meeting. He was sure that was the reason Mr. Wyatt was so unenthused to see him so soon. Trying to explain, he pointed over his shoulder at Jay.

Mr. Wyatt's eyes widened. His glance went back and forth between William and Jay.

William didn't dare say anything else with Jay overseeing their every move. Though it made him wonder—why was Jay being so overbearing? *Does Ben not trust me?* He decided to play along and let Mr. Wyatt act his part as the salesman.

"I have this van," Charley began, but he was quickly interrupted.

"Don't worry, mate," Mr. Wyatt said. He nervously wrung his hands and glanced at Jay. "I know exactly what all my customers need."

"No, I need van parts. That's all," Charley tried to interject.

Mr. Wyatt spoke as quickly as possible trying to hurry them along. "What are *van* parts?" he twisted his head at an angle looking confused.

"You don't know what a van is?!" Charley put his hands on the counter and leaned back in shock and disgust, hyperventilating. Most people wouldn't have reacted the same, but Charley was in love with his van. He even participated in a club called Vans for Life, whose members believed that the roomy comfort, cargo space, and reasonable gas mileage of a van meant it was the only vehicle that should be driven on the road. It was clearly offensive to Charley's ears to hear that someone didn't even know what a van was.

Mr. Wyatt jumped back at Charley's outburst. He waved his hands to calm Charley down. Nervously, he looked at Jay again and reassuringly winked at William. "Right, is it some kind of transporter?"

Charley might have started hyperventilating, but he handled the response well considering he saw Mr. Wyatt's wink. Mistakenly, he thought Mr. Wyatt had winked at him. "Oh, I see, you don't have them." He winked his eye a few times. "Gotcha." *Wink, wink.* He leaned forward on the counter. "No worries, I won't let it look like you are a pushover," he whispered. Charley looked around the store at other customers and loudly exclaimed, "You drive a hard bargain, but I'm not leaving until I get van parts." He slammed his fist down on the countertop.

William went red with embarrassment. People were staring, including Jay. This wasn't the first time that Charley had publicly humiliated him. He punched Charley in the arm.

"Ouch," Charley yelped, rubbing the small bruise that William had given him.

Jay squinted his eyes and moved closer to the window, suspiciously looking in.

Mr. Wyatt froze in place. His back was as straight as a pole. "Right, well I can't have an unhappy customer. Maybe there is something else I can interest you in." He hunkered down and started into one of his sales pitches. "Gentleman, have you ever asked yourself what the best way to conceal something is? A hidden pocket? Under a hat? NO! It's a concealed compartment that sits in plain sight. Welcome to the world of Wyatt's Disguise Dentures," he said, proudly producing a pair of dentures from under the counter.

"That's great and all, but I don't really need dentures" Charley said with a disgusted look on his face. "I have all my teeth." He smiled widely, showing his pearly whites.

Mr. Wyatt pressed harder with his sales pitch. He continued to glance nervously at Jay's head bobbing from window to window. "With these Disguise Dentures, you will have the ability to conceal anything in your mouth. I dare say, they once saved my life when I was captured by a cannibalistic tribe of aborigines. There I was, stark naked in a pot of boiling water, with only my teeth to save my life," Mr. Wyatt continued with dramatic hand-swooshing.

"I think I'd rather not hear what happens when you're naked and in a pot of warm water," Charley replied, trying his best to stop Mr. Wyatt's aggressive sales pitch.

"I dare say, this is the best concealment device ever. You can hide anything you want. Put a bit of paralytic powder in there, and you have a right deadly weapon. Put in a piece of Mr. Spirin's Miracle Medicine, and you have yourselves a dandy first-aid kit that goes everywhere. It sits right in your mouth. You might ask, 'What is the secret to the dentures, Mr. Wyatt?' The secret lies in its patented ability to open false teeth. You can hide small objects inside the teeth. Plus, you can only release the teeth by kissing. One kiss releases the first tooth; two kisses releases the second tooth and so on, up to five teeth in all. All this can be yours for just three easy payments of thirty-nine nine-ninety-nine ninety-five, and if you order right now, I'll throw in the Miracle Medicine that can cure anything for free. You heard right, mate, absolutely free," Mr. Wyatt said persuasively, finishing his pitch with enthusiasm.

Charley didn't seem interested, nor did he catch on to subtle hint that Mr. Wyatt was pushing them out the door. "I'm sorry, are you saying you can conceal things in the false teeth? The teeth fall out when you kiss someone?" Charley asked rhetorically. He made his dumb-face to express how stupid it was.

"Yes," Mr. Wyatt said, leaning forward.

"I see, but I just need VAN parts," Charley replied, emphasizing one word.

William could see Jay peering through the window so intently he was fogging the glass. He could tell that Charley wasn't leaving until he found something either. That's just how Charley was sometimes. This happened once before when he wanted to rent a DVD from a pet store. Charley had never gotten his DVD but was content with a goldfish that William bought for him. The goldfish helped William get back home without spending the entire evening in a pet store arguing over proper protocol for rentals. He was worried this was another goldfish situation. "Maybe you should look at it more closely. It looks neat," he suggested. He couldn't believe that he was encouraging Charley to buy Disguise Dentures.

"Tell you what. You buy two of them right now, and I'll throw in a Forgetful Hammer. You can only use it once, but it does the trick," Mr. Wyatt said, pulling a small hammer out from under the counter. He was sweetening the deal to get them out the door. He obviously wasn't comfortable with Jay staring at them, and he didn't want Jay coming any closer. "Hit anyone in the head with it, and I promise that they'll forget anything that happens for about twenty minutes."

Charley nearly burst out chuckling. He looked at the small hammer in front of him with his eyes watering from laughter. "Isn't it obvious? If you hit someone in the head with a hammer, they're going to forget a lot. You're hilarious!" He clearly had no intention of buying.

William looked over his shoulder at Jay, who was walking up the stairs. He was surprised that the stairs could even hold Jay, probably bowing under his weight. He needed to get Charley out of the store with or without parts.

Mr. Wyatt leaned in close. He was a salesman at heart. It was time to close this deal. "If I do say so, I have convinced quite a few pretty lady friends to kiss me to demonstrate how the dentures work." Mr. Wyatt grinned.

Charley abruptly stopped laughing. A light bulb went on. It was pure genius. Mr. Wyatt's words sunk into him like teeth that would never let go. Whether Charley needed the dentures was irrelevant. He was sold hook, line, and sinker. "How many can I buy!?" he asked. He had forgotten about his van.

William let out a sigh of relief. Charley had found his goldfish. He turned toward Jay to see him hunched at the front door. He waved at him as a gesture that everything was okay. Jay nodded and stopped partway up the stairs.

"That's what I thought, mate," Mr. Wyatt said with tense wrinkles fading from his face. He took out a piece of paper to write down Charley's order. It included the Miracle Medicine, the Forgetful Hammer, and a pair of Mr. Wyatt's genuine Disguise Dentures.

William waited while Charley was fitted for the dentures. It was disgusting watching him try on several pair. Slobber dripped down his chin when he tried ones that were too big, making William turn away from the grotesque sight. He looked at the ground to divert his eyes and noticed the keys in his hand. He thumbed the keys in his fingertips, wondering what to do.

"What do you think?" Charley asked with a big grin.

William was still rubbing the keys between his fingers. His fingertips had gone white from pressing too hard. "Sorry, what?" he asked.

"The teeth. What do you think?" Charley asked. He opened his mouth to show his dentures.

Truthfully, William couldn't tell that he was wearing Disguise Dentures at all. "They look great," he remarked. He wouldn't have cared even if they were hideous. He was too preoccupied considering his next move.

Having parted with nearly every cent he had, Charley was ready to go. He was so excited about his new dentures he had nearly forgotten about his van. William didn't want to remind him either. It's not that William didn't want the van fixed, but now just wasn't the right time.

Mr. Wyatt let out a sigh of relief as they departed and Jay's face disappeared.

At the bottom of the stairs, Jay was waiting like a good babysitter. He narrowed his eyes suspiciously at them when they arrived. Charley didn't seem to notice. He was preoccupied with his dentures: licking them and practicing air kisses while whispering sweet nothings into the air. Jay was not amused, and he seemed a little disturbed. He wasted no time watching Charley flirt with the air and pushed them through the crowded streets toward the police station.

It was much easier traveling through the crowd with Jay as long as they stayed close on his heels. People moved out of Jay's way, creating a path for them right to the police station. It easily turned a 20-minute walk through a crowded street into a five-minute venture. Moments later, William had arrived.

Standing in front of the station, William wouldn't have known it was a police outpost without a sign. The windows were barred and looked more like a jail than anything. He didn't like prisons, nor did he like police all that much. At least, he hadn't liked them since the day he reported his father missing and couldn't get the detective to do much more than eat a donut. He had even offered to help find his father, but he was dismissed as a boy. That had been months ago. At one point, he'd wondered if the police had locked his father up without telling him. His father never would abandon him; he was sure of that. It didn't seem right that he was about to deliver someone to a mysterious jail. He rubbed the keys between his fingers. If he was going to do something, he was running out of time.

William approached the front door. "Should we knock?" he asked, shrugging one shoulder.

Jay nodded his chin.

William tapped softly on the door, hoping no one would answer. To his dismay, someone did. Halfway down, in a much smaller door in the bottom half of the first, a peep hole opened. It would have been the perfect peep hole for someone as small as Ben. Through the opening, two beady brown eyes peeked out.

"Yes?" the eyes quickly shot a look left and right scanning the area.

William got to his knee to line up with the peephole. "I'm here to deliver a coffin," he said awkwardly, shrugging his shoulders.

"Delivery? I'm not expecting a thing." The eyes narrowed suspiciously.

William was following Ben's instructions so far, but it didn't sound like they were going to let him in. "It's a burglar," he said raising his tone and wondering if that was what he was supposed to say.

"Ah," the voice said in a long, drawn-out breath. "A burglar." The peephole slammed shut.

William, convinced that he was locked out, looked at the keys in his hand in relief. He could return the coffin to Ben. Even if he never helped her escape, he could at the very least have more time to talk with Ben about all this.

"I don't think they are going to let us in," William told Jay. He stood up and stepped away from the door. "Who are these people anyway?"

Jay didn't say anything, but that was no big surprise. William knew Jay wasn't much of a talker. Most of Jay's responses were wiggling his mustache and grunting. "Should we head back?" William asked, pointing toward the main street.

Jay nudged William aside and bent down with one hand. It made William's feet scoot along the ground until he was no longer standing in front of the door. Jay lowered himself to the floor and gave a loud knock that could have broken the door down.

The peephole slid open again. "Ah," the voice said, startled. The eyes jumped backwards. "Jay! Give me one moment."

Seconds later, William was horrified to see the door open and a short man, only slightly bigger than Uncle Ben, dressed in a blue police uniform and round hat, jump out.

"And where is Ben?" asked the short man, pacing the ground around Jay's feet.

"Dude, you're just as short as the other guy! You must be midget brothers," Charley exclaimed. He stretched out his arm with his thumb up, sizing him up.

William kicked Charley in the shin. "Shhh." He couldn't be publicly embarrassed again so soon. Addressing the police officer, he answered, "Ben is gone."

At first, the short man looked disappointed, but when he noticed the coffin, a smile came across his face. He walked over to the coffin and put his arms around it. "Could it be? Did you catch *the girl?*"

Jay nodded silently.

"Come in. I have just the place to lock up that villain," the policeman said excitedly, waving at them to follow. The regular size door opened as he passed through the small one.

Inside, William was surprised to see that Jay was coming too. He supposed that he had to because no one else could have carried the coffin. How Jay was going to get through the door was beyond him, yet Jay found a way. He contorted his body like a gymnast wrestling through a keyhole. Unfortunately, once inside, he was much too tall for the room and had to sit on the ground with his knees up against his chest.

Charley thought it was amusing that he could touch Jay's forehead with him sitting on the ground. "It's good to see you down here. You know, I don't think I knew what you looked like with your head so high."

Entering from the other side of the room, two short policemen wrestled a burly, handcuffed man between them. He was twice their size and dragging his feet. It looked like two men trying to move an ox that didn't want to go. With some difficulty, they pulled him near a jail cell. "Get in there, you brute," threatened one policeman, but the burly man didn't budge. The other policeman gave a firm push, but it didn't move the prisoner any more than it would have moved a brick wall.

Enraged, the prisoner furiously twisted free. He flung about and ran like an unstoppable train. Police officers shouted and blew their whistle as flocks of officers came out of nowhere. Loud prisoners cheered.

"Excuse me a moment," the short policeman next to William said in a calm, proper tone. He took a small pellet from his pocket and moved directly in front of the charging prisoner.

"Look out!" cried William.

"Don't worry," he replied. "You have to show them who's boss."

With that, he flung the pellet.

A puff of white smoke erupted. When the smoke cleared, the prisoner was frozen in place. Four midgets ran alongside him, but it took one extra to tip him over and move him to his jail cell. Inmates rattled the bars of their cages, making an immense racket.

"I need to attend to other prisoners," said the policeman. "It takes a good ten minutes to calm them. Please wait here. We'll lock up your burglar the moment I return." He walked down a hall, shouting at jail cells.

Jay's eyes followed the policeman down the hall. He bent his head down low to the ground to see around the corner.

No eyes were on William. Even Charley was preoccupied with watching the policeman. William knew that if he let them lock up the woman in the coffin, there was no telling if he would ever hear from her again. *What if I get caught?* Questions tumbled around in his head. There were too many of them to count. He resolved that if the woman in the coffin knew where his father was, even a few seconds of talking to her would be worth any consequence. He grabbed Charley by the shirt collar.

"What?" choked Charley, strangled by his neckline. He didn't even look at William, enthralled watching the inmates.

"I need you to distract Jay," William said, his heart fluttering frantically. He grabbed Charley's cheek and forced him to look at him.

"What? How?" Charley asked, confused.

"I'm not sure," William said, starting to sound desperate. He looked around the room for something that could help. "I need to open the coffin." He held up the key.

"Are you crazy?" Charley shook his head lazily back and forth like it was a wet noodle.

"I have to," William grabbed Charley's shirt tighter with one hand.

"I'm attracted to dangerous women too, but maybe you need to let this one go. I mean, she broke into your uncle's house. The point is, she's a criminal. If you like her that much, I bet this place has visiting hours, so you can come see her."

"No," William blurted out. "I don't have time to explain." Every second he was debating was another moment of opportunity lost.

Charley shook his head. "Fine! I've done some crazy things for women, but you owe me one." He took the Forgetful Hammer out of his pocket.

"That's not going to do anything," William said, looking at the pitifully small hammer.

"I paid good money for this thing. It better work!" Charley flipped the hammer over in his palm, sizing it up. He looked at Jay's head, wondering if it really was going to work. The hammer was like a child's play thing. Without hesitation, he walked bravely over to Jay, holding the small hammer above his head ready to strike. "Hey, Jay," he shouted.

Jay turned his gruff beard toward Charley. Without warning, Charley swung the tiny hammer around. It landed square in Jay's forehead. Stunned, Jay had a bright red ring where the hammer had smacked a welt.

Charley stood motionless, processing what he had done. Either he was going to be clobbered or the hammer was going to work.

Jay didn't move an inch. It didn't matter that Charley waved his hand in front of his face either; there was no response. Charley fluffed Jay's beard like a pillow just to make sure Jay was out cold, and Jay sat motionless, the red ring swelling in the middle of his forehead.

"It worked!" Charley exclaimed.

"How long do we have?" William asked frantically running to the coffin, hand stretched outward, aiming the keys for insertion.

"Better act fast," Charley said, flicking Jay in the nose with his finger.

William slid the key into the coffin.

Chapter 10

CATCH AND RELEASE

William was about to open the coffin. In fact, he would have had it opened by now if it wasn't for Charley making squeamish noises. William kept looking at Charley to make sure he was okay. Obviously, something was making Charley uncomfortable. William wasn't sure he wanted to know what was so disturbing. He had little time to dilly dally.

"Wait," Charley yelled. "You think she's dead?"

William turned his head toward Charley and paused momentarily. "No . . . I mean . . . I don't think she's dead," he replied without a shred of confidence.

"Think about it. She's been trapped in a coffin this whole time. There can't be much air in there," Charley pointed out.

"Why don't we just look and see," William said. He had come this far. No dead body was going to stop him now.

"You want me to look at a dead person!?" Charley exclaimed, raising his tone. This was definitely outside his comfort zone.

"Suit yourself. But she's really attractive," William said temptingly, raising his eyebrows.

Charley let out a sigh and mumbled under his breath. He folded his arms tightly and nodded, giving the okay.

William pushed the upper part of the coffin open. It left the lower part of the coffin locked tightly. His heart was fluttering with anxiety. He kept telling himself that the woman in the coffin was going to lead him to his father.

As soon as the lid open, William thought the woman was going to try and jump out. Instead, he saw her lying motionless with her eyes closed.

"Well?" Charley asked, reluctantly inching closer on his tip toes trying to look over the edge of the coffin.

"I don't know. She isn't moving."

"Well, check for a pulse," Charley said.

If she was dead, William didn't want to touch her. "Be my guest. You check for a pulse."

"Me? Why me? I hate dead bodies," Charley protested.

"It was your idea," William reminded him.

"It's just medical knowledge 101, the basics of life. Therefore, not my idea," Charley argued. He was standing firmly, not moving an inch closer to the coffin.

"That's the dumbest thing I've ever heard. There's no time. Jay could wake up any second."

Charley looked at Jay. "Fine," he said, stepping closer and grudgingly reached into the coffin. With his arm inside, he looked disgusted with his nose crinkled and starting dry heaving. When his arm came out, he said, "Nothing," and shook his head. "Unfortunately, she's dead. She might even be decomposing, because she smells terrible." He placed his hand over his heart and plugged his nose.

"What!" William said in disbelief. He leaned in to check for himself. She wasn't moving for sure, but there was no malodourous scent of her body decomposing. He reached down to check her heartbeat.

"Like I said, d-e-a-d."

Suddenly, the burglar opened her eyes.

Terrified, William pulled his hand out and tripped over Charley, stumbling backwards. They both tumbled to the ground.

"Yeah, she's a babe," Charley remarked as he stood up with William.

The burglar, lying flat on her back in the coffin, looked directly at them. Her short black hair fanned outwards from milky white skin. "I'm Vanessa, and if it isn't the boy that got me caught," she said, staring at William.

"What!" William said, half-insulted. "I'm pretty sure you got yourself caught."

"I never should have come to find you. What a fool I've been. What's worse? I got chased down the hall and locked in here."

"Hi . . . My name is Charley." He batted love-struck eyes.

William paid no attention to Charley. "I hardly think you can blame me. What did you expect?"

Vanessa drew her eyebrows, frustrated. She angrily breathed in and out through her nostrils. "You're right. I never should have come. I was only doing what your father would have wanted."

"Don't worry, pretty lady. You can come to my room at night to deliver messages any time," Charley said, desperately trying to be noticed.

It seemed like everyone knew William's father around here. Vanessa spoke about him like she knew him as more than an acquaintance. "And what would my father want?" William asked.

"He wanted me to help you. He said you were the key to the puzzle organ," Vanessa replied.

"Would it surprise you if I told you I hardly know anything about it?" William asked. He shook his head, wondering if his father would actually send someone like Vanessa to help.

"Regardless, Ben thinks you can help him. Call me loyal to your dad, but I came to warn you."

"Warn me about what?" William shook his head. He failed to see the immediate danger.

"There is no time for me to explain here," She turned her head to look toward Jay. "Suffice it to say, Ben betrayed your father and is obsessed with getting the thinking cap. He knew he couldn't do it alone. When you father refused, Ben got rid of him. He gets rid of anyone in his way. That's why I can barely hear anymore." She turned her head from side to side, showing her ears.

William grabbed the side of the coffin so he wouldn't fall over. He knew Ben was offbeat, but he'd never imagined that he was the reason his father was missing, neither could he imagine that he would have caused Vanessa to go deaf. He rubbed his ears, remembering how badly they had been hurt from the puzzle organ's blast.

Charley tapped William on the shoulder. "She's in black leather," he whispered. "Ladies in black leather can't be trusted, no matter how good looking they are. I know from experience."

"There is no time here!" Vanessa argued. She struggled from side to side, trying to get out of the coffin but to no avail. "Just know that if you can't help Ben either, he'll do the same thing to you. You'll be in a coffin just like me." She raised her head up to peek out toward the prisoners. The noise from the inmates was dying down. "Now, if you don't mind," she said, looking at the remaining lock on the coffin, indicating that she wanted to be set free.

William was still trying to process the situation. Stunned like a deer in the headlights, he felt like he was having an out-of-body experience. Time slowed down as he looked upon himself trying to make his next decision. *Should I help Vanessa?* She seemed genuine, but then again, he would have said anything to get out of a coffin too. Letting her out would definitely get him in trouble with Ben. Frankly, there was only one reason to let her out. The thought of it made his heart skip a bit, and he jumped back to reality. "Take me to my father," he demanded with his hands gripping the side of the coffin.

"Are you insane?" She replied, wide-eyed.

"If you want out of here, promise to take me to my father!" William leaned over the coffin and held the key in front of Vanessa. He felt cruel teasing her in such away, but the situation called for it.

"You don't understand." Vanessa drew her brows angrily. "It's dangerous."

William put the key into the lock, preparing to turn it with his fingers.

Jay let out a grunt, rubbing the welt on his forehead, which was turning purple. Time was running out.

Drawing Jay's attention, Charley moved away from the coffin. "Looks like you hit your head on the door," he said, pointing at Jay's forehead. "You might want to have a doctor look at that."

Vanessa struggled again, thrashing about in the coffin. Finding she was still stuck, she finally said, "Forgive me." In a flash, she jerked upward. She was surprisingly strong enough to jostle the coffin so that it turned slightly. William's hand didn't move, but the coffin turned under the key nonetheless. It was just enough. The coffin sprung open. As free as a bird, Vanessa jumped out.

William felt a sense of panic, which worsened when he saw Jay snap out of his daze. He was surprised at how quickly Jay awoke. It was like he was waking from a nightmare.

Jay immediately glared at the open coffin and snatched at Vanessa with his hand as it whooshed unsteadily in the air. It flung back and forth until it bumped the coffin, tumbling it over. The crash rang through the prison. An audience of prisoners clung to their jail cells, cheering. "Run, run, run!" they chanted.

The short policeman came running into the room. "What is that racket?" The moment he saw Vanessa, he flushed white and reached into his pocket. His short arms flung pellets like a machine gun.

Vanessa sprinted around the room, ducking behind William and then Charley as the pellets flew through the air. Each missed its mark. The room erupted in white powder as Vanessa hurdled desks, chairs, and counters.

Surrounded by the white cloud, William stumbled with his arms stretched out, trying to feel his way through the thick white. He held his breath until his face turned blue from lack of air. There was no escape; his lungs were screaming. When he couldn't stand it anymore, he took a deep breath, and instantly, his lungs turned an icy cold. His muscles felt like they had been plunged into a frozen lake. A brain freeze like a polar ice cap melting on his head flushed over him. He could have passed as an ice statue.

Charley and Jay were motionless—Charley with his hands out in front of him, and Jay still trying to grab Vanessa. A horde of policemen was stuck in mid-stride racing around the corner. The short policeman's arms were still in the air, ready to launch another volley of pellets. Prisoners were stuck against their bars. Their cries had been silenced. Even flies that had been buzzing around the room fell to the ground. Like a museum of statues, the room stood still. The only piece missing was Vanessa.

Chapter 11

ON THE HUNT

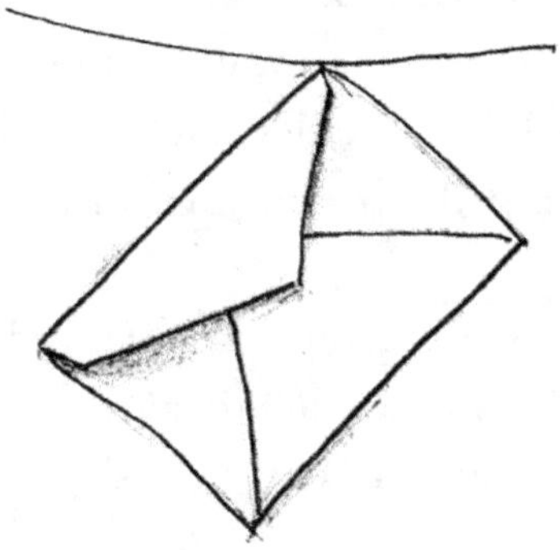

Waiting to thaw, William heard steps. At first, he wondered if Vanessa had come back, but he was certain that it wasn't her when he overheard angry grumbling. Out of the corner of his eye, he saw Ben stomp into view. His brow was drawn crossly, making large furrows in his forehead that looked cartoonish. He mumbled unintelligibly, "That infernal . . .How did this . . ." He stormed to the short policeman and nodded disappointedly. It didn't take a detective to figure out what had happened, and Ben was putting all the clues together. When he finally looked like he'd figured out what occurred, he approached the coffin and slammed the lid closed in frustration.

William knew the scene told the whole story. Well, almost the whole story. Obviously, the burglar was missing. The real question was:

how would he explain it?

Ben produced a gold glitter from his pocket and sprinkled it on William and Charley. It fluttered through the air until it landed on them.

As soon as it brushed up against William's skin, he immediately felt the warmth run over him like a hot shower. By the time it hit his toes, he was sweating like he had been in a sauna. His arms and legs released from their frozen state.

"What happened to your forehead?" Ben asked Jay, staring at the circular welt above his eyes as he sprinkled the same glitter on him.

"He hit it on the door," Charley interjected in a quirky tone.

"Yeah, he just bumped it coming in. I mean, the door is so small," William agreed.

Jay felt the bump on his brow and shrugged uncertainly.

William held his breath, waiting to see if Jay remembered, but Jay never said anything. He just started the task of wiggling through the front door.

William finally let out the deep breath that he had been holding. He normally wished Jay would talk more, but this time, he was glad that Jay had stayed silent.

"That's not like him," Ben said. "I've never seen Jay hit his head on a door. Even in the tightest of spaces he maneuvers so well." He rubbed his chin, thinking.

"Keep your head down," Charley yelled as Jay passed under the door. "Even monkeys fall from trees."

Between William's nervousness and Charley's big mouth, it was a wonder that Ben didn't know what had happened already. "Ben, I'm sorry. I didn't think that . . ." William stammered.

Ben held up his hand. "I know what you're going to say. But there's no need crying over spilt milk. What's done is done. My idiot brother was always a poor police officer. I should have known he would underestimate the burglar; he never does anything right. You can't blame yourself."

A tidal wave of guilt and relief washed over William when he realized Ben blamed the policemen. Surprised, he looked back and forth between the policeman and Ben trying to compare the brotherly similarities. They both were short, but other than that, they didn't resemble one another anymore than Charley and he.

"There isn't a minute to spare," Ben said seriously. He held his hand over his brother, ready to sprinkle the glitter, but hesitated. William almost thought he wasn't going to free his brother until Ben finally let the gold flakes fall from his fingertips.

"We need to find the burglar and capture her," Ben said, turning to William. "It's that simple. She can't have gone far. If she escapes, we will be in grave danger."

William had a pit in his stomach thinking about looking for Vanessa. *Will she tell Ben that I opened the coffin?* The nagging voice in the back of his head said he couldn't trust Ben.

Ben seemed to sense William's reluctance. "She came for you in the night, and she is coming for the puzzle organ. There is no telling what will happen if we don't stop her." Ben threw his fist down in his hand, making a slapping noise.

William wasn't trying to show his hesitancy, but his acting abilities weren't up to the task of concealing it. His stomach twisted in knots.

The short policeman was moving again and fumbling his words trying to explain what had happened, but Ben wouldn't have it. Repulsed at the excuses, Ben marched out of the police station and mounted Jay's leg like it was his steed. Moments later, Jay was marching them through town.

Ben's frustration was apparent. He took a lot of it out on Jay telling him to "get a move on". He even commandingly yelled "mush" like they were being pulled by a pack of dogs on a slay. William thought it was kind of rude, but Jay didn't seem to mind. It was effective too. Each time Ben let out a command, Jay stepped a bit further. They moved so fast that riding on Jay's foot, William's hair was blowing in the wind. It reminded him of driving on the freeway with his head out the window in a sports car. It was amazing that Jay didn't step on anybody. His agile feet hopped and skipped around every ally and street corner just as skillfully as he had managed to slip into the door at the police station.

Luckily there was enough room on Jay's foot for Charley too. There was no way that he would have been able to keep up. Charley nearly giggled with delight the moment he stepped on Jay's massive foot with William. Like a dog, he hung his tongue in the wind. William got the sense that Charley felt like he was hanging his head out of fast-moving car too. Of course, Charley would have likely been thinking about a van window rather than a sports car. Either way, the sensation was the same: they were moving rapidly. In no time flat, they were back to the door they had come through when they first entered town.

Ben jumped off Jay's foot. Even though they had made great time coming back, it didn't seem to quell his frustration. The moment his foot touch the ground, he charged Jay with standing in that very spot. His tone was very authoritative. "Don't move!" he ordered.

Jay took a formal stance, peering over the crowd. He wasn't very military-like in his suit; it looked more like he was waiting to serve someone. However, his general appearance gave William the distinct impression that Jay was guarding the door. It was likely to keeping Vanessa from getting through. At least, that is what William assumed.

Ben glared at Charley. It looked like Ben was trying to make up his mind about him. Finally, he said, "Keep Jay company while William and I flush out the burglar."

Charley didn't seem to like what Ben was asking. He looked up at Jay's face and immediately saw the big purple welt where he had struck him. He swallowed hard. "You might not have noticed, but me and Jay don't get along," he told Ben, keeping his voice down so Jay wouldn't hear. "There's really no connection. In fact, I think he hates me. He doesn't even want my advice on women, and believe you me, everyone wants my advice on women." Charley lifted his eyebrows and nodded with certainty.

"Build a friendship then," Ben demanded. "We have a burglar to find." He grabbed William by the arm and pulled him into the street.

Weaving through people, William dodged arms to avoid getting a black eye. It was surprising how nimbly Ben move between people, hopping and skipping around boots and high heels. William had a hard time keeping up. When William stumbled, Ben pulled him upright by the waistband, dragging him along. He followed that up with nagging comments about how William wasn't moving fast enough.

William's stomach twisted with a sense of unease. *What am I doing here? Where am I?* Ben hadn't been forthcoming about many details. *What about the puzzle organ?* With all these questions, it was hard for him to want to find Vanessa. He didn't know who to trust—certainly not Ben. He needed answers, and he needed them now.

The growing frustration turned from a small seed into a giant cactus, poking at him. Ben pulling him along was the biggest thorn of them all. He tried to brush it off, but it was driving deeper under his skin. At first, when Ben's hand nudged him to keep up, he shrugged it off. Of course, Ben responded by pulling harder. It turned Ben's badgering into nothing short of a hot poker. It felt like Mrs. Burbank belittling him all over again. In fact, he could have replaced Ben with Mrs. Burbank, and he wouldn't have known the difference.

William finally met his boiling point when he tripped face forward over someone's leg and struck the pavement. The tip of his nose scraped on the ground. Turning over, he thought he was going to be trampled. He jumped upright to find Ben's hand gripping his arm, ready to pull once again. William wasn't having this anymore. He dug his heels into the ground, hard. "Stop!" William demanded. "Where is my father?!"

Ben didn't turn around, likely sensing the frustration. His hand let go of William's arm, letting it fall. He looked to the ground and shook his head disappointedly. "I'm trying to help you," he said, his voice filled with annoyance.

William wasn't letting up. "Help me? Help me? The way I see it, you have done nothing to *help*. All I hear about is the puzzle organ, which hasn't helped me get one bit closer to my father. In fact, the only thing it's done is nearly kill me. What does it matter if you open it or not?" William breathed heavily. "What are we even doing here?" he said with his voice shaking.

Ben turned on his heels, scowling at William. He tipped his green bowler hat over his eyebrows, which were drawn in irritation. This was clearly testing his patience. "You have more of your father in you than you realize. He was silly too."

William's frustration turned to anger. "What do you even know about my father?"

"If you must know, your father is the one who put us in this predicament. He is the only reason that you are even here!" Ben snapped back.

William shook his head, not believing a word that was said.

"Don't believe me? Well, here is some food for thought. The thinking cap has been safe for years. Years! Fairhaven was one of a few places that we called home, away from the world. Mind you, there aren't many places left. There were no burglars then, and we were happy letting the outside world know nothing about this magical place—until your father. He left us; he broke our secret. He told others how to open the puzzle organ. Now look at this place! It was an Eden that has been turned into a perdition, and we struggle to hide the magic that lives here every day from people that want to steal it. If your father had kept his mouth shut, none of this would have happened." Ben's temper was red hot.

Stunned, William's mind was blank. He couldn't believe it; he didn't believe it. He shook his head in doubt.

Ben continued furiously spitting into the air with each sentence.

"Try this on for size. Your incompetent father was stupid enough to let it slip that he had the four things needed to open the puzzle organ, and do you want to know what the fourth one is?" Ben breathed heavily. "It's you!"

William wasn't angry anymore. He put his hands up to his ears, not wanting to listen. *No, no, no, that can't be true.*

"Now that your father broke every rule, everyone thinks they can open the puzzle organ, and for whatever reason, you, his incompetent son, are needed to do it. Why do you think I brought you here except to keep you safe? Every thief this side of Fairhaven was about to come after you, the key to the puzzle organ, and I can't decide if you are a key or an idiot."

"You liar!" William yelled at the top of his lungs.

"Oh, a liar, am I? If I hadn't gone to stop Mr. Millner today, he would have snatched you away himself. The loon is convinced he can strap you to the puzzle organ and leave you there until it opens. Now that I have talked sense into him, this is the thanks I get?" Ben shouted.

William couldn't take this anymore. He didn't care what Ben said; it wasn't true. He couldn't believe it.

Ben tried to compose himself. He lowered his arms to his sides and cleared the anger from his face. He sighed, "I'm sorry."

It was too late. William had heard enough. He turned on his heels and ran.

Chapter 12

DRINK UP

Running uncontrollably through the crowd, William twisted and turned every chance he could. There was no way to keep a sense of direction as he dodged newspapers and bustles on lady's dresses. He was only hoping it was good enough to lose Ben.

He was exhausted and utterly disoriented. He ran into a nearby building and nestled himself in a shadowy corner, out of the way, where he wouldn't be noticed. With his knees up to his chest, he threw his face into his hands. Minutes passed as he sat softly sobbing, with no sign of Ben.

When his tears dried, he wiped them from his face and adjusted his position against the unpadded ground, feeling a lump in his pocket. It interrupted his thoughts and reached in to find the package that Mr. Wyatt had given him. It seemed like ages ago he'd received it. The inscription across the front read: "Mr. Wyatt's Genuine Animal Whistle. USE WITH CAUTION. Impersonate any animal call and SEEK SHELTER!" He didn't want to think about Ben right now, and the package was a welcome distraction. He opened it to find a bamboo shoot with cutouts along the top like a flute.

Scoffing, William wondered if it worked. The forgetful hammer from Mr. Wyatt might have worked on Jay's head, but it was a hammer. Charley had been right; if you hit anyone with a hammer, they are likely to forget a few things. *Maybe I should try it?* He puckered his lips, ready to blow, thinking of an animal call he could impersonate. Nothing came to mind, at least nothing he could impersonate. Come to think of it, he couldn't impersonate anything except for a cow, but any kindergartener could do that. Practicing, he blew into the air to sound like a cow. What came out sounded more like an angry goat than a cow, with grunting noises and snorting. When enough slobber came out of his lips, he was too embarrassed to continue. His sickly animal cries were drawing strange looks from people passing. Self-conscious, he wondered if he needed to brush up on "Old McDonald" before embarrassing himself again. He decided to put the whistle away for now.

He looked about, trying to figure out what to do next as masses of people began to gather in the room. Luckily, their attention wasn't on him. Instead, it focused on the center of the room.

Curious, William wiggled through the crowd to get a better view. It was hard to see unless he knelt on the ground. Between a pair of legs, he saw three men ruthlessly staring at each other. They each had a glass of black fluid that was boiling over resting in front of them. A gong sounded and each drank his glass without flinching. The room fell silent, waiting in anticipation.

Before too long, one man had a small blister erupt on his face the size of a penny. At first it was just one, small and red, but soon there were two, growing like water balloons. It didn't take long for his body to erupt into blisters that swelled to the size of a softball. In one stunning finish, the blisters burst open, sending him flying backwards. Flat on his back, he was dragged away as the crowd cheered and set their sights on the next two victims.

The next man succumbed to a horrific rash. It spread from his nose to his cheek, then to his arms, until it covered every inch of him. The itching was ferocious. He clawed at his arms and legs, trying to appease the cursed skin, but it was like a spreading wildfire. Desperately, he tried to stay seated. When the rash raised into hideous red bumps, there was little hope left for him. Scratching, he went running from the room. His exit was followed again by applause from a pleased crowd.

With one man left, the crowd cheered. People congratulated one another on their pick of the winner and a few bets were paid, but that didn't save the last man standing. He started to laugh. From a chuckle to all-out hysterics, the roar burst out until he could hardly breathe. When he turned blue in the face and fell to the floor, he was dragged away.

Confused why anyone would get near the black fluid, William got to his feet when a note fluttered down and hung over his head, dangling on a string in front of him. He plucked the note out of the air and read:

William,
> *Come see me tonight at Mr. Wyatt's shop.*
Your Friend,
> *Vanessa*

His eyes searched the crowd, curious. When he finally caught sight of Vanessa's slender figure, mixed in a hundred faces cheering and laughing, their eyes locked for a moment. William held the note high and nodded.

Vanessa nodded back and disappeared into the crowd.

No sooner had her face vanished than Ben's bright green suit appeared. He couldn't have been more than a few feet from where Vanessa had vanished into the crowd, and it looked like he was on the prowl.

William's blood ran cold. He looked at the letter in his hand. *Can I trust Vanessa? I can't rely on Ben, not after what he said.* Panicked, he looked to the door to see Jay standing in the way, filtering the crowd as they left. There was no way for Vanessa to escape. The minute she left, Jay would likely grab her and toss her into another coffin. Vanessa couldn't have stayed here either. Before too long, Ben would have produced one of his white pellets and froze her in place; William was sure of it.

A jolt shot through William. He knew he had to do something. *Would Ben lock me in a coffin too if I help Vanessa?* He was determined not to let that happen. He wasn't sure if it was adrenaline or panic, but his feet started to move. Running through the crowd to the center of the room, he found a set of glasses full of black liquid. He picked them up and grabbed tightly. His heart was racing as he wound his arm and hurled black fluid through the air.

The mass burst into hysterics; everyone went running to the door to escape. They thronged against Jay's legs. People jumped over one another. There wasn't an orderly line of any kind.

Ben turned and somehow found William, locking eyes with him. He yelled, but his voice couldn't be heard above the riot running for safety.

William saw a large barrel full of the black liquid. He leaned his foot against it. Holding his eyes on Ben, he kicked. The container rolled on the ground, sending black fluid gurgling across the floor.

The crowd shrieked in terror and the riot turned to a stampede as they burst toward the exit.

William looked about at the chaos he had created. He couldn't see Vanessa, Ben, Jay, or anybody for that matter. A satisfaction came over him. Vanessa was sure to escape. Then, he heard a hissing on the ground. His gaze darted downward to find the predicament he had put himself into. Boiling as it rolled across the ground, the black fluid had surrounded him on every side. Small bits of smoke were rising from it and burning his nostrils. For a moment, William wondered if he would end up with blisters, a rash, or a malignant fit of laughter like the men that drank a full glass. None of these options seemed very pleasant.

To one side, William spotted a table within reach. He jumped on top of it and looked for the next one. It was close enough that he could leap to it. Bounding through the air, he landed. He once thought he might fall short, but that wasn't the case at all. In fact, he overjumped. He was falling forward from the edge of the table about to fall face first onto a black boiling mass when a hand grabbed him about the leg. He shrieked and tugged as he looked at his leg. It was Charley, one hand holding William's leg with his own legs spread across pools of black that were hissing toxic gas.

"Me and Jay didn't get along so well. Doesn't look like you're doing so well either," Charley commented.

William was grateful that it wasn't Ben. Grabbing Charley's hand, they worked together to hurdle pools of black liquid and raced for the door. As they exited, they were inches from Jay's feet, but with so many people running for safety, Jay couldn't sift through everyone. William and Charley slipped past between Jay's legs, into the crowd and vanished into the street unnoticed.

Chapter 13

MEETINGS IN THE NIGHT

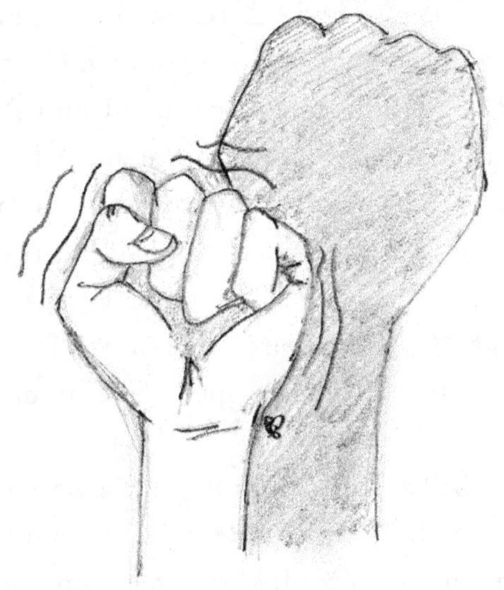

The sun set in the distance. William shook his head, thinking about Ben. Ben must have been lying to me. My father never would have done some things that he told me, would he? There must have been an explanation for what happened. The dark night set in around him, precipitating his darkest fears: What if I never see my father again? He was the only person who could tell him the truth about the past. William longed for his father now more than ever.

William took another look at the note from Vanessa before putting it in his pocket. "Take me to Mr. Wyatt's store," he whispered into his watch, and the arrow on the face sprang to life.

The streets in town were different in the dark. Once teeming to the brim with orderly lines and market shoppers clamoring over one another, they were now almost devoid of life. The only light flickered from lamps along the side of the road. Anything passing in front of them cast an eerie shadow. Dark figures ducked into alleyways to avoid being detected.

William was glad he had Charley with him, even though Charley was less than enthused about missing dinner. Charley dragged his feet until he found something that entertained him. Next to an oil lamp lining the street, he put his hands in the air. A large outline darkened across the buildings like a shadow puppet as he twisted his palms to make a figure that looked suspiciously like Jay. It danced and grunted while he moved his hands. "I don't like lactose-intolerant people. I hate square sandwiches. I despise welts on my forehead," Charley said, cheerfully waving his shadow puppet while mimicking Jay's voice the best he could.

Chuckling, William tried to join in. He wasn't the best at shadow puppets, but it was fun anyway. He made a round fist and tried mimicking Mrs. Burbank's voice. It distracted him enough that he barely noticed a short, dark figure off in the distance, directly in front of him. At first, he figured there was no reason to be concerned; several other people lurked in the shadows, and this person was far away. William expected him to disappear into an alley like the rest of the strangers, but that was not what happened.

As he came progressively closer, the figure didn't deviate course. Instead, he walked in a straight line at them. Uneasy, William moved to the other side of the street, dragging Charley along the way; he was hoping to pass by at a distance.

To his surprise, the stranger jumped across the street to be un-swervingly in front of them again.

William felt the hair on his neck stand on end as he tried to move away. The moment he stepped aside, the stranger followed as if he wanted to stay on a collision course. As closely as they were being mimicked, he didn't think it would make a difference if he ducked into an alleyway, nor did he want to encounter other dark figures that might be waiting for him away from the protection of the streetlights. Ten yards became five and five became two, until they were about to collide.

William's stomach turned over and he clenched Charley's arm tightly. It didn't seem like Charley even noticed the small stranger. He was too interested in creating his next shadow puppet.

Within reaching distance, the figure held a dark hand up toward them. William reached to push it away, but the stranger snatched his wrist out of the air. William tugged back quickly and the stranger's grip released. He was free. Without another word, the stranger bumped past Charley and rushed away.

Finally taking notice, Charley turned. "Excuse me," he said. "If you want me to do a shadow puppet of you, you'll have to get in line."

The figure didn't respond. As quickly as he had appeared, he dashed into an alleyway and vanished into the shadows.

William rubbed his wrist, but there was no injury. He didn't know what to think of the curious encounter. It was no good trying to pursue the stranger, who was long gone by now. Chills ran up and down his spine, and he wiggled to brush them off. With the stranger gone, almost as quickly as he had appeared, William looked into the distance, at the end of the road. He almost thought they had gotten off course, but he was wrong. Sure enough, he recognized the stairs to Mr. Wyatt's store. A shimmer of hope came back to him as he grabbed Charley's arm and raced ahead.

The bell rang as the door swung open. William could hardly see a thing with all the lights turned off. Glancing about, he caught sight of a single flame flickering at the desk. He barely noticed that Mr. Wyatt was the one holding it. Mr. Wyatt greeted them quietly and made a motion for them to follow.

Walking along the aisles of the store, William was amazed at how many things he passed. He didn't dare ask what they were right now. It's not like Mr. Wyatt had asked him to be quiet; it just seemed like the right thing to do. Mr. Wyatt had greeted them with a hushed voice, and he didn't want to break the silence of the night. Still, he found it amusing to look at all the trinkets they passed. It was too dark to tell what they were, but just looking made him all the more curious. After all, the forgetful hammer had worked. He wondered what else might. He was sure that he could burn a couple days rummaging through all the items.

Around an endcap with tiki torches, Mr. Wyatt led them through a back door. The shelving lined with trinkets vanished and was replaced with rifles that adorned the walls. Their barrels were polished to a shiny silver that made them look like a prized collection standing at attention. Above them were ferocious-looking stuffed animal heads, which were, no doubt, another of Mr. Wyatt's valued assortments.

Scattered about the room were boxes labeled Mr. Wyatt Incorporated, filled with contraptions that William had seen throughout the store. In the middle of the boxes, a woman that William had seen earlier, dressed from head to toe in keys, was sitting on a pillow with her legs crossed. Her long hair, held by a headband, flowed onto the floor behind her. Her hands rested on her knees with her fingers posed in circles. She hummed gently and swayed from side to side. Like wind chimes, the keys hanging from her clothes made a pinging noise. Smoke from burning incense was ripe with the scent of cedar wood that pooled over her head and into a light fixture.

"By jiminy, why are you burning that stuff in here?" Mr. Wyatt said angrily.

"I could feel the lack of energy in this room. You have been out of touch with Mother Earth for too long," the woman said in a mellow tone.

"Crikey, Miss Lockit, that is the last blooming thing I need. If Mother Earth wants to come in here, she's gonna have to come through me like everyone else," said Mr. Wyatt. He grabbed a nearby shotgun and pumped the action.

"Don't let your negative vibes influence the atmosphere. It brings too much undesirable energy. Why don't you have William sit while we wait," she said, swaying from side to side again.

William and Charley looked at one another, then took a seat on the floor.

Mr. Wyatt looked irritated as he paced the wall, rubbing his fingers across the barrels of each rifle as he went by.

"I'm William and this is Charley," William said trying to sound upbeat.

"I know," Miss Lockit replied serenely.

"Vanessa told me to come," he explained.

"I know," Miss Lockit said, still swaying.

"I'm looking for my father."

"I know."

"You have lots of keys," Charley said pointing at them hanging from her hair.

"I know."

Charley leaned over to whisper out of the corner of his mouth, "She seems to 'know' a lot."

"Give her a minute; she gets like this sometimes with all her hippy garbage," said Mr. Wyatt, admiring his guns.

"So, are you close friends to Vanessa?" Charley asked Mr. Wyatt. "Cause I was just wondering if she's single or not."

"You want to date her? Good luck, mate. She is a little nutty, like a frog in a sock," Mr. Wyatt replied, putting a gun to his shoulder and looking down the sight.

"A frog in a what?" Charley asked, making his dumb-face.

Just then, Vanessa came stumbling through the door, breathing heavily. Behind her, she was dragging Mr. Millner, flies pooling over his head. The minute he entered the room, the air reeked, a powerful stench reminiscent of fermented cow dung.

"Where have you been?" Mr. Wyatt asked impatiently. "You're harder to keep track of than a beetle under a rock."

"I've been busy," Vanessa retorted sharply.

"Yes, I can see that," Mr. Wyatt said, acknowledging Mr. Millner.

Charley grabbed his nose. "You need some cologne or something, because whatever you're doing right now isn't working."

"What's he doing here?" William asked. Having Mr. Millner in the room made him feel uncomfortable. The last time he spoke to Mr. Millner, he was thrown from the puzzle organ. It didn't make him feel any better that Ben had mentioned Mr. Millner was after him—the key to the puzzle organ, apparently.

Vanessa tapped Mr. Millner. "Why don't you tell them," she demanded.

"I don't know what you're talking about," hissed Mr. Millner. The flies orbited his head.

"He knows where your father is," Vanessa said, pushing Mr. Millner to the ground.

"No, no, no I don't!" shouted Mr. Millner, standing back up and stomping around the room. "Ah! I'm a good boy. No, No, No! All I need is the thinking cap!" Mr. Millner said, going into a full-blown tantrum. He grabbed his face and pulled at his hair.

Miss Lockit broke her meditation pose. She walked across the room in bare feet, her hair dragging behind her on the floor. Gracefully, she put an arm around Mr. Millner, whispered in his ear, and took his hand.

Mr. Millner stopped pulling at his hair. He followed Miss Lockit to a pillow near the burning incense, where he quietly sat. It helped the rotting smell.

"Why would she touch him? He's filthy," Charley asked, trying to keep his mouth shut to prevent a bad taste from coming in.

"It always amazes me how she has a way with him. He's made a lot of progress. Sometimes we even see a little of the old Mr. Millner," Mr. Wyatt said, producing a black bowler hat with a dark ribbon tied around the top from one of the boxes lying about the room. He proceeded to slip the hat onto Mr. Millner's head.

Mr. Millner didn't flinch. In fact, the hat made him look refreshed.

"It's a Truth Hat, just like the one I showed you," Mr. Wyatt remarked. "If he has it on, he can't tell a lie. We use it to help him remember."

Miss Lockit sat on her pillow next to Mr. Millner. "Do you know where Arthur McFadden is?"

William tensed all his muscles. Finally, it was the question that he was dying to have answered.

Mr. Millner twitched forcibly as words came out of his mouth. "N . . . N . . ." his mouth twisted. "N . . . Ahhhh," he yipped.

Miss Lockit softly rubbed his shoulder. "Mr. Millner, do you know?" she calmly asked again.

Mr. Millner fought the truth until he soberly nodded.

"This whole time. You knew. Why didn't you tell me?" William questioned. His gut turned over with emotion. He was ready to jump out of his seat.

Mr. Millner recoiled with tears in his eyes. "I'm sorry. I couldn't. Besides, he's trapped," he cried.

"Trapped?" William said, jumping back with surprise. "What do you mean? Like in a prison?"

Miss Lockit looked at William and subtly whispered, just like she had done with Mr. Millner. "Not all prisons are the same, especially in Fairhaven, but if he is trapped, we will find his captor and help him."

William's anger didn't dissipate, but a sense of calm swept over him.

"Do you know how to free him?" Miss Lockit questioned further.

In response, Mr. Millner shook his head. "I can't. Not without the thinking cap. He sleeps. I don't remember. It's all jumbled."

"Where is my father?" William cried, but Mr. Millner was boiling with so much emotion that he choked up. The only response that William received was a tearful one.

"We need the thinking cap. It's the key to everything," Vanessa declared. Her frustration showed across her face as she paced the room. "Mr. Millner is useless. He can hardly remember what century it is, much less how to free Arthur. I've told you a thousand times, if you want to help Arthur, you need the thinking cap."

Miss Lockit sat on her pillow and swayed. Ping, the keys sounded, gently tapping together. "Look what the thinking cap did to Mr. Millner."

Mr. Millner shuddered and rocked back and forth. "He knows who I am. I know who I am. I know who I am. I am Mr. Millner," he repeated.

"What happened to Mr. Millner is a tragedy. I won't let Ben do this to someone else. Look what he did to me." Vanessa pointed to her hearing aids.

"What's wrong with Mr. Millner?" asked William.

"It's personal hygiene, if you ask me," Charley said, now holding his mouth and nose tightly with his fingers.

Miss Lockit said, "The thinking cap did this to him. His memory is like water through a sieve. He can't remember a lot of things."

"I don't understand," William said. He stared at Mr. Millner. "How did Mr. Millner get the thinking cap?"

Vanessa toyed with her hearing aids. "You can thank Ben for that. Long ago, he had the thinking cap, along with your father. Obviously, Ben didn't know how to use it, and he experimented at Mr. Millner's expense, who ended up being a lab rat. Now look at him!" She clenched her teeth. "We need to focus on getting the thinking cap before Ben, or there is no telling how many more Mr. Milliners there will be," Vanessa said throwing her arms out.

Mr. Wyatt placed his gun against the wall and turned sharply, raising his voice. "Now hold on! Let's not forget we had a deal. We are trying to find Arthur, and if you want this arrangement to stay alive, you'll need to fulfill your end of the bargain first."

Vanessa shook her head, annoyed. "What does it matter if we find William's father if you can't free him? I don't think anything but the thinking cap will do that."

Mr. Millner smiled crookedly. "Yes, yes, yes, get the thinking cap. That will make it all better," he snickered. His schizophrenic emotions pushed him to tears. "I'll help Arthur. All I need is the thinking cap. Then it will be all better," he mumbled.

"That's a load of rubbish," Mr. Wyatt said. His voice was tense and irritated. "You never said anything about the thinking cap. You are supposed to help Miss Lockit and myself find Arthur and we will help get Ben out of the institute. That's the deal, plain and simple! Now you are telling me that we need to get the thinking cap?"

Vanessa turned and crossed her arms. "It's like I told you. It's not just about finding Arthur. What good does it do if he is still trapped when you find him?"

It didn't look like Mr. Wyatt was going to let it go. His eye winced tightly around his monocle. Things were going to turn into an argument, but Miss Lockit didn't flinch. She calmly rocked back and forth comforting Mr. Millner.

"Take me to my father," William suddenly demanded. He stood from the ground and threw his hands down in fists. The room fell silent and all eyes centered on him. He didn't care if he needed the thinking cap or not. He had to know that his father was safe before he would lift another finger.

Vanessa shook her head. "Too dangerous. We could be caught by Ben, and I am not about to be locked in another of his coffins."

William shook his head, disappointed. It felt like Mrs. Burbank was telling him that he wasn't allowed to find his father. Then it struck him. "Ben said I was the key to the puzzle organ," he said, breathing heavily. "And until I see my father, I'm not helping anyone."

Miss Lockit stopped swaying. "It would seem that young William is a lot like his father, and he is determined. If he is indeed the key to the puzzle organ, it seems that we don't have much of a choice in the matter," she said, smiling at William.

Vanessa blew hot air from her mouth, annoyed. She paced a few steps before coming to a stop, holding her fingers pinched across the bridge of her nose. "Fine!" she concluded. "We can use Mr. Millner to find Arthur if that is what you want, but after that, we open the puzzle organ. And another thing: I won't take everyone. We'll be caught for sure."

Mr. Wyatt started to object, but Miss Lockit held her hand up to keep him silent. It seemed to work since Mr. Wyatt turned in frustration without saying a word. He shook his head back and forth in protest.

"I'm going!" William insisted. He wouldn't take no for an answer.

Charley raised his finger in the air. "I guess I'm headed out too." He shrugged his shoulders.

Vanessa started to object to have Charley come, but she was interrupted by William.

"He's coming!" William declared, stamping his foot on the ground. As far as William was concerned, Charley was the only person in Fairhaven not selling peculiar items, meditating by incense, chasing down burglars, or downright being insane. He needed him there, even if just to keep him grounded.

Vanessa shook her head in irritation. She stamped over to Mr. Millner and struggled to pull him upright as he protested. Vanessa commanded Mr. Millner, "Take us to William's father!"

Mr. Millner struggled against the Truth Hat. "I . . .I . . .I . . ." He pulled against Vanessa's grasp and fell to the ground limp. When he struck the floor, the truth hat shifted on his head. No one noticed it wasn't resting flush against his brow. He rolled his tongue like it had been let loose. "Yessss," he hissed.

Chapter 14

THE WYATT WHISTLE

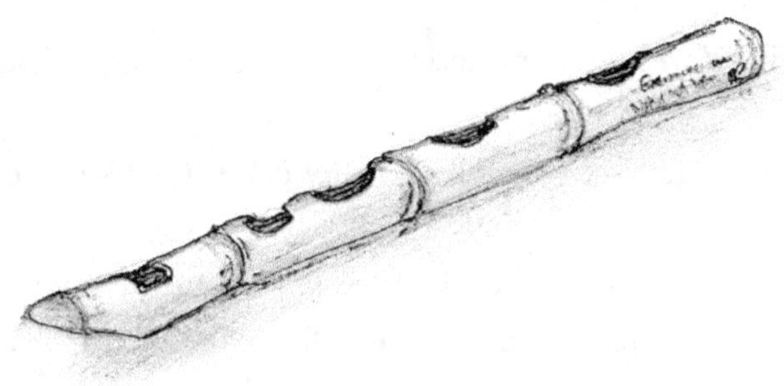

"Left, right, yes, this is the way," Mr. Millner mumbled, guiding them through the halls of the institute.

William anxiously followed. He had to agree that he was more comfortable with a smaller group, but they still made a lot of noise walking across the broken floorboards. Mr. Millner's constant yammering wasn't discreet either. Mr. Wyatt had wanted William to bring one of his prized guns for protection, but William wasn't even sure that he could hold the weight of one. Plus, it seemed odd trying to carry a large firearm that shimmered like a reflector in the moonlight. Charley had volunteered to hold it, but in the end, thankfully, Miss Lockit wouldn't allow it.

"Are you sure he knows where he is going?" asked Charley with a quiver in his voice.

"Mr. Millner might forget a lot, but he never gets lost," Vanessa replied, but she seemed anxious letting Mr. Millner out of her sight for one reason or another. She kept calling him unpredictable. "Don't trust anyone, especially Mr. Millner. He's as crazy as a wild animal," she remarked.

"I was a wild animal myself back in the day," Charley said. "Of course, my hygiene was a lot better than Mr. Millner's. I at least showered nearly every day."

"Nearly? You mean you didn't shower every day?" Vanessa asked, repulsed.

"Not with my sweet-smelling body odor. It's like a cologne. I call it Musk Bonjour. It's French."

"Ha! I'd call it more like Musk Bidet," Vanessa snickered.

"That sounds nice. Okay, we'll call it Musk Bidet," Charley said, naively satisfied.

William chuckled. He thought he heard Mr. Millner chuckle too.

Walking through the hall, William began to think about what Ben had said. "Vanessa, is all this my father's fault?" he asked. He held his hand up and pointed at the broken hall.

Vanessa rolled her eyes. "Did Ben tell you that?" she scoffed.

William shrugged. "He said that my father broke the rules and that's why all this happened."

"First off, you can't trust everything that comes out of Ben's mouth. Ninety-nine percent of the time, he's trying to manipulate you." She paused and kicked at a splintered board on the ground.

William gave a sigh of relief, thinking there was another explanation.

"But in this case," Vanessa continued, "there may be some truth to it."

William's heart sank. He hadn't believed Ben even for a second. The realization that Ben might have been telling him the truth hurt.

"Does that mean you're a real-life burglar?" Charley asked. "Cause that is my number two on my hotness-list, right under Amazon women."

Vanessa shook her head. "I hardly think that I am a burglar. Ben tries to maliciously label everyone against him as a burglar, but that doesn't mean we are all stealing something."

William nodded. "It's because of my father, isn't it?"

Vanessa twisted her head and scratched like she didn't want to answer. "I can tell you that your father might have let it slip that there are four things needed to open the puzzle organ. Ever since, people have thronged the institute like a pack of 49ers searching for gold in hopes of finding them. The institute hasn't held up that well to the abuse." She shook her head, looking at the splintered hallway. "Whoever finds the items and uses them will have the thinking cap."

William hung his shoulders downward. "Did my father really say that I am the key to the puzzle organ?"

Vanessa didn't reply right away. She looked almost intimidated by the question. Finally, she answered, "Why don't you ask him yourself when you can?" She walked past William, catching up with Mr. Millner.

Around a bend, another door appeared. Mr. Millner solved the door's picture puzzle and held it open. "Thirty-three," he said. "He's in thirty-three."

William had no idea what Mr. Millner was talking about, but something told him that they were close. He passed through the door.

Mr. Millner clicked on an overhead light, and a hazy glow cast shadows across coffins lining the walls.

"Ahh!" Charley shrieked in a high-pitched tone. "I hate coffins. I was hoping I never had to come back here again." He shrunk his shoulders downward.

Mr. Millner paced the walls. He started at one end and counted, "One, two, three . . ." Halfway through his count, he stopped. Looking confused, he mumbled to himself. "This is it. Thirty-three. I . . . here he is . . . no, no, no."

"Is everything all right, Mr. Millner?" asked William. He was so close to seeing his father he could taste it.

"This can't be it!" Mr. Millner shouted. He hunched forward and counted his fingers: "One, two, two, two, three . . ."

"Mr. Millner." William tried to get his attention. He tapped Mr. Millner's shoulder. "Are you okay?"

Turning sharply, Mr. Millner's eyes darted in either direction, welling with tears. He screamed at the top of his lungs. "NOOO! NO, I didn't do it!" He picked up his feet and dashed out of the room with his arms above his head.

William couldn't believe Mr. Millner could move that fast. The flies could hardly keep up.

"Wait. Mr. Millner!" Vanessa shouted furiously. It was too late; Mr. Millner was halfway through the door.

Vanessa sighed. "Wait here, I'll get him," she said as she ran out of the room.

William eyed the coffins. His eyes followed the path that Mr. Millner had counted. It wasn't hard to continue where Mr. Millner left off. "Thirty-three," he said after following down the rest of the line.

"What are you talking about?" Charley asked.

"He's in thirty-three. That's what Mr. Millner said." He steadied himself to open the coffin lid.

"Wait," Charley said suddenly.

"What's wrong?"

"Are you sure this is the right one? I mean, it's a coffin. There could be a dead body in there." Charley flinched uncomfortably.

"Are you serious?"

"You should never mess with death. It's a scary thing."

William wasn't about to stop. "There's only one way to find out." With his heart racing, palms sweating, he pulled and twisted. The lid swung open. He peered over a silky cloth lining to find it empty.

Charley cautiously opened his eyes to a slit.

"He said thirty-three," William said, dumbfounded. "This has to be it." He went to the end of the room and counted off the coffins again to make sure he hadn't miscounted. Then he started to open all the coffins one by one. Each lid made a swooshing sound as its door swung open.

Charley kept opening and closing his eyes, scared that a dead body would fall out.

When William had opened every coffin, Charley let out a sigh of relief. "Well, I'll be a monkey's uncle. Not a single dead body."

William couldn't express his feelings. He was more than disappointed. Nothing like getting your hopes up only to have them come crashing back down. He might have been happier if a dead body had fallen out. He stared into coffin thirty-three. There was an emptiness inside him much deeper than the coffin.

Charley put his arm around him. "Hey, you okay, buddy?"

"Yeah," Williams voice quietly quivered. "I was just hoping."

"I know." Charley squeezed. "We'll find him."

"Thanks." William drooped his head.

"And what kind of a friend would I be if I let you hang around in a room full of empty coffins? It's super creepy. You wanna get out of here?"

"I guess," William half-heartedly answered. He lifted his hand to whisper into the Never-Lost Watch for directions, but there was nothing but bare skin on his wrist. He held up his arm to the light overhead. A feeling of panic swept over him.

"What's wrong?" Charley asked.

"The watch is gone!" William anxiously replied in a destressed high tone. He was turning his pockets inside out, frantically searching. Had it fallen off?

Charley got onto his knees and searched the floor. "Where did you put it?"

"Nowhere. It's been on my wrist the entire time."

"When do you last remember it?"

"When we went into town. That guy bumped into me and then . . ." A cold fear swept over William with the realization of what had happened. "He stole it from me!" he loudly exclaimed.

Loud footsteps echoed off the open coffins. These weren't just any footsteps. They were unmistakably thunderous footsteps, which were getting louder. It wasn't Vanessa coming back.

"I'd never forget those footsteps," Charley said. He reached overhead, pulling the string attached to the lightbulb to turn it off, and quickly pulled William behind an empty coffin.

William breathed slowly. On his knees, he peeked between coffins to see a flashlight break the darkness. It bobbed up and down high above their heads, passing the open coffins one by one. It finally came to a stop and the room light came back on.

Ben got off Jay's leg. "What happened here?!" he shouted, glancing around the room at the open coffins. "Mr. Millner must have told them. That weak-minded fool. I have had enough of this. He must be dealt with quickly."

Jay mumbled and nodded.

"It's about time that we find William and open the puzzle organ!" Ben shouted. He looked around the room filled with scattered coffins. "I asked Mr. Millner to get me one box so that we could lock up Vanessa, but that idiot doesn't seem to know how to count. Stay here and clean this mess up. I don't think that we can count on Mr. Millner to get rid of all these empty boxes. In the meantime, I'll see if my brother and his brilliant police force have found anything yet." He ran his fingers along the open coffins, leaving in a fury.

Jay started at the top of the line, closing the coffins and stacking them against a wall in his attempt at cleaning.

"We have to get out of here," Charley whispered. "Do you remember how to get back to our rooms?"

William looked at the empty spot on his wrist. "Not without the watch."

Jay stacked another coffin against the wall.

"We don't have long before Colossus over there finds out where we're hiding. He's moving all these coffins."

William's thoughts were racing. "Think, think," he said.

Charley was wracking his brain for ideas too. "I got it. What about one of your origami things you make? Like that boomerang."

"And throw it at him?" William questioned. It sounded like a ridiculous idea, but he was open to anything. Unfortunately, Charley didn't always handle pressure that well. This was noticeably one of those times and throwing a paper boomerang at Jay did not sound sensible.

"Hit him in the forehead. He already has a big welt. It could give us just enough time to slip by."

"Do you have any paper?" William asked as he rolled his eyes. His voice was filled with sarcasm.

Charley reached for his pockets. His hands darted in and out of each until he held his palms up empty. "No."

"That's not going to work, then," William replied nodding his head like it should have been obvious in the first place.

"Note to self: always carry paper." Charley looked out into the distance and seemed to jot a mental note.

"Any other bright ideas?"

Charley was straining. "Sometimes if I squeeze my stomach it helps me think. Pushes the ideas up to the brain." He wrenched his abdomen tightly and his face turned red.

Jay cleared another coffin from the lineup. They were running out of coffins to hide behind.

"We could hide in a coffin," William said. He thought it was a good idea.

Charley looked mortified. "I'd rather die," he firmly stated.

There was no way they could make it to a door. The minute they moved, they would be spotted.

A hop, skip, and jump away from being discovered, William frantically dug into his pocket. He didn't know what he was looking for. Anything would help right now. Even if he found a piece of paper it might have satisfied him, but he was sure there was no paper in his pocket no matter how deep he reached. It was a grab at nothing until his hand came across a lump. He pulled at it to reveal the whistle that Mr. Wyatt had given him. He quickly recalled the instructions: impersonate an animal. It was a problem. Under normal circumstances he could barely impersonate a pregnant cow. There was no chance he could do better with Jay about to find them. He thrust the whistle at Charley. "Quick, blow an animal noise into the whistle."

Charley looked confused. "What is this?"

"There's no time. Just do it," William pleaded.

"Okay, what animal?" Charley asked.

William said the first thing that came to mind "A . . . fox."

Charley put the whistle on his lips. "What does a fox say?"

Jay picked up the coffin next to them. It was now or never.

Truthfully, William had no idea what a fox said. "Anything!" he demanded.

Charley pursed his lips. Choking in fear, he managed to blow a tiny squeak into the whistle just as Jay picked up the coffin in front of them. Stuttering, he stopped blowing. Any sudden noises now would alert Jay. They had run out of time.

Jay turned around without noticing them. He carried the coffin to stack it with the rest.

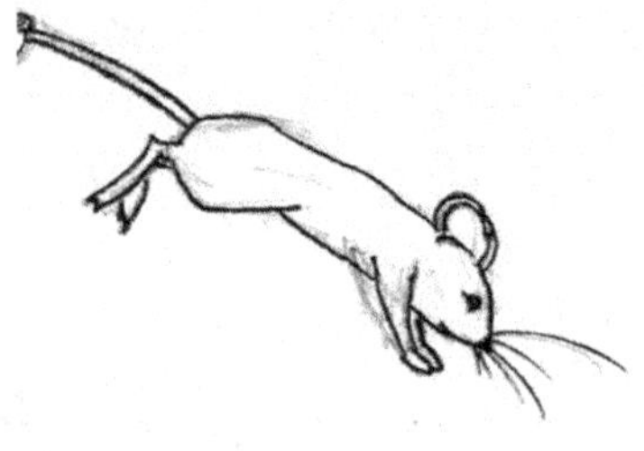

Just then, a furry ball ran past William. It had a tail that scampered behind it and whiskers out front. It was the cutest mouse that William had ever seen. It let out a squeaking noise just like the one Charley had blown into the whistle. In fact, they matched almost perfectly. Who knew Charley could impersonate a mouse so well? He was glad to know the whistle worked, but what good was one mouse? Just as William thought their demise was imminent, the first mouse was followed by a second, and the second by a third. The mice scampered from out of nowhere. Their fuzzy bodies ran past William like a moving rug. They piled on top of one another, running over William until they covered him.

Startled, Jay turned. In no time, the room looked like a mouse plantation. There wasn't a square inch of floor to stand on. The squeaking grew to a harmonious orchestra that resonated across the coffins.

Jay let out a deathly shriek. Terrified, he fell backwards. Coffins tumbled to the floor with a crash, but that didn't stop the mice. They surrounded him on every side. They crawled over his head and up his pant legs. Jay dashed toward to the door, yelling and stomping his feet frantically.

William let out a sigh of relief.

"Who would have thought he didn't like mice?" Charley remarked. He had mice hanging from his arms and sitting atop his head.

William was in shock. It didn't matter that rodents were hanging from every part of his body. He and Charley were safe.

Chapter 15

LOST BUT FOUND

William and Charley were utterly lost. Navigating the halls was an impossible task. Charley resorted to licking his finger, holding it up in the air, and using "Eenie, meenie, miney, mo" to pick where they were going.

"What are you doing?" William asked after one such event.

Charley was concentrating hard on his wet finger in the air, like it was prophetically going to tell him which way to go. "It worked for Ben," he declared.

William waited for the revelation. "Well, did it work?"

Charley licked his finger again. "There's a slight breeze coming from the north."

"Which way is that?"

"I have no idea. Maybe I should try saying 'Humpty Dumpty' instead."

"It's no use, Charley. We're lost," William said, slumping against the wall.

Charley recited, "Eenie, meenie, miney, mo" again and pointed left. "It's that way," he said, waving his finger about.

"Why not? That way is just as good as the other," William said. He had given up trying to figure out where they were headed. He couldn't even say whether or not they were turning in circles.

The halls were all the same. One after the next came and went. Portraits on the walls changed, but there were too many to keep track of. He wondered how Mr. Millner kept from getting lost.

Off in the distance, a sound broke the silence. William strained to listen. "Ahhhh!" a cry wailed past the portraits. It broke the maze of halls, giving a sense of direction, a destination.

"Did you hear that?" William asked, excited.

"Yeah, what was it?" Charley craned his neck and tilted his head to listen.

William pushed his ear out too.

"Ahhh!" the cry sounded again.

"I think it's coming from this way."

As they carefully made their way down the hall, the cries grew louder. William had to strain his hearing to make sure that he was going in the right direction. Following the cries led them straight to a door with an edge ajar. He snuck to the edge and peered inward.

Beyond the door, he saw a coffin. On one side was Ben. On the other, Mr. Millner was on his knees groveling, wailing loudly.

"You idiot! How can I trust you?" Ben shouted at Mr. Millner.

"No, no, I'll be good," Mr. Millner sniveled.

"Really! Do you think I'm a fool?" Ben snapped. He pulled a watch from his pocket and swung it in front of Mr. Millner's eyes.

William stared in disbelief. It was the Never-Lost Watch that had been stolen from him.

"Look what you've made me do!" Ben yelled. "You gave this to them and told them about the coffin. Didn't you?" Ben shook his head angrily and flipped the watch in the air. "Whose side are you on? I told you to leave William alone. I will help him open the puzzle organ!"

"No, I'm sorry," Mr. Millner sobbed, putting his hand on the coffin. "I want it to be like before."

Ben laughed through clenched teeth. "After all we have been through, you think we can just go back? Those days are gone."

Mr. Millner shuddered.

Ben shook his head like a disappointed father disciplining his child. "I know what you want."

"But Arthur! What about Arthur?" Mr. Millner shrilled.

"Yes, of course. You want to look at our mistakes, don't you?" Ben unlatched the coffin and the lid sprung open.

William gasped, almost collapsing in disbelief. His father was lying motionless inside.

Mr. Millner was beside himself. He reached into the coffin and shook Arthur, but Arthur didn't wake.

"Oh, contain yourself. What did you expect? We did what needed to be done. You of all people should know that. You cannot undo the past," Ben said.

Mr. Millner shrank back, ashamed. "I didn't mean to."

"Of course you did! We all did. Crying about it won't make it any better," Ben said, then he narrowed his voice cunningly. "I need your help. You have to promise me you'll help."

Mr. Millner stared at Arthur with tears rolling down his cheeks.

"We have the boy. This is our chance to make things right. Help me," Ben bargained.

William was ready to burst through the door. He turned to regain his composure, and when he looked back, Mr. Millner wasn't pleading any longer. He was standing on his feet with his eye patch removed. His blue and green eyes were puffed red from crying and he was shaking hands with Ben like they had come to an agreement. Ben was smiling from cheek to cheek.

William's muscles tightened with frustration. He was about to run inside when he felt a hand slip over his mouth and pull him backwards. He tugged at the fingers to pry them away, but they were quickly dragging him. He kicked outward at Charley and nicked his shoe.

Charley, looking a little confused at William's frantic behavior, realized what was happening and leaped toward William, missing his shoe by inches. He quickly jumped to his feet and dashed to help.

With Charley out of reach, William was being dragged away mercilessly until three doors down, when a finger fell between his teeth, and he bit down hard. He was set free almost instantly and he turned sharply to see his captor. Instead of seeing Jay as he'd expected, Vanessa stood before him. "Why did you do that?!" he yelled.

Vanessa rubbed her bitten finger. "Be quiet!" she demanded.

"How did you find us?" William said, lowering his voice.

"I told you to wait at the coffins."

"Jay came. The watch, Ben stole it from me. We were lost," William said, flustered. He was so worked up he could barely collect himself.

"Yeah, but you should have seen us," Charley said in a manly tone, his chest puffed out. "Scared Jay off with some mice. Worked like a charm."

"And now you're lost," Vanessa pointed out.

"My father, he's in there. Quick, we have to stop them!" William said, hysterically waving his hands.

"We can't," Vanessa argued.

"Can't?!" William was beside himself again. "What do you mean we can't?"

"Ben is the one who put your father in there in the first place, so unless you want to end up in a coffin yourself, I suggest you listen to me."

William paced back and forth. His body wouldn't let him hold still. He had finally found his father. Not only that, but he had no doubt that Ben was to blame for his disappearance. "I have to do something. I have to," he said repeatedly. His eyes teared up.

"I know you're upset, but it's not that easy. Your father is in a dark place. if I could wake him, I would, but without the thinking cap, it's useless," Vanessa explained.

"How do I get the thinking cap? Ben knows ten times as much as I do, and he still can't open the puzzle organ. They might as well ask Charley to do it."

"Hold on there, little buddy," Charley said. "I drive a sweet van and know a thing or two about women, but I don't know anything about puzzle organs."

"Are you sure you know a thing or two about women?" Vanessa interjected.

Charley strained his stomach again to bring the ideas to his head. "I know they are attractive." He stopped to take a breath. "And I like the way they smell." His face became a bright shade of red.

"Don't use both of your brain cells thinking about it," Vanessa replied. "I wouldn't want you to be reduced to a single-celled organism."

William didn't think he could feel another emotion without his heart bursting from his chest. How could his father be within reach, but he couldn't do a thing? The helplessness threated to suffocate him. Each breath was laborious just to fill his lungs with air. "You mentioned four things to open the puzzle organ, right?"

"Yes, but burglars have turned this place over looking for them."

"Who knows where they are?" William demanded. "Or what they are?"

"Ben probably knows, and perhaps Mr. Millner. But you can't trust Ben, and there is no telling what is rattling around inside Mr. Millner's head."

"Do you think Ben could open the puzzle organ?" William asked, leaning forward with his fists clenched.

Vanessa shook her head. "I'm not sure, but the only people who have ever done it are in that room back there." She pointed one finger down the hall.

William nodded and backed away from Vanessa. No matter how much he hated Ben, avoiding him wasn't the answer, nor was turning a nose up at Mr. Millner's madness. There was no telling how long his father would be trapped unless he did something. The answer was as clear as day.

Far enough away from Vanessa that she couldn't grab him again, he turned on his heels and ran back to the door.

Chapter 16

A DEAL

"William, wait!" Vanessa lunged for William as she cried out, but he was out of reach.

William refused to look back, determined to get to his father. His heart fluttered with a strange mix of fear and excitement, making him press harder.

Nearly to the door, he could see a halo of light around the edge. He lowered his shoulder and sent the door flinging wide open. The force of the blow caused him to stumble forward, and he tumbled to the ground. When he came to a stop, he jumped to his feet expecting Ben and Mr. Millner to be staring at him. At the very least, he expected to hear a surprised reaction from one of them, but nothing. He quickly turned about, surveying the room. It was empty.

Charley came running into the room. "Wow, you really showed that door who's boss. Are you okay?" He looked around, noticing it

155

was empty too. "Where did the coffin go?"

William shook his head, dumfounded. He walked to where the coffin had been located and put his hands out. "It was here. It was right here." He half wondered if it had been a hallucination. "Maybe we are in the wrong place?"

"You're not," came a voice.

William knew that voice, but instead of a warm greeting, Jay's hand swept through the air, seemingly out of nowhere. The fingers tightened around his waist and stopped him in his tracks.

Charley ran to William's aid and stretched his arms out, ready to karate chop. "I didn't want to have to do this, big guy, because I am a skilled martial artist," he cried. Thump. His hand sliced through the air and struck Jay's hand.

Jay's fingers didn't budge.

"Hi-yah!" Charley whirled his leg around, trying to roundhouse Jay, but his feet never made contact. Jay's other hand swept downward and grabbed him.

"Time to break some bricks. Hi-yah!" Charley's hand again came down on Jay's hand like he was karate chopping a block in two.

Again, Jay didn't flinch.

William kicked his feet as Jay raised him and Charley into the air. William's feet were dangling. "Put me down," he said, prying at Jay's hand. "Where are you Ben?" he shouted.

"I'm right here," Ben replied as he walked under William's feet and looked up.

"You liar. Where is he? Why would you do that to my father!?" William's feelings were spouting off like a firehose.

Ben walked over to Jay and sat on his foot. He gazed at William while calmly propping his elbow up and resting his head in his hand. "I didn't want it to be like this."

"Neither did my father!" William belted. It was exhausting struggling against Jay. He could feel his muscles aching.

"You know, for what it's worth, this is what they want you to believe. I never lied to you."

William wondered what Ben meant by "they". He looked out the door, hoping Vanessa was about to rescue them.

Ben looked at the door too. "She's not coming. Thieves, especially those as manipulative as her, don't have friends. She can't help you or your father, nor does she care."

William was fuming. "She's helping me more than you ever have."

Ben gritted his teeth. "You have no idea what you're talking about. That is what she wants you to believe." He shook his head. "This is much bigger than you think, William. There are forces at work that you cannot comprehend. I know you don't believe me, but I can help you free your father."

"Had enough?" Charley asked, panting. He was still karate chopping Jay's hand over and over again.

"Listen to my proposal," Ben said. He held his hands out and leaned forward. "I don't know how to free Arthur without the thinking cap. If I did, I would have already done it, and we wouldn't be in this mess. Whether he will sleep in there for another fifteen minutes or fifteen years is a mystery to me. If you want him back, we can open the puzzle organ together. You can do it for your father, and I can do it to stop Vanessa and any other would-be thief."

William stopped to mull over his decisions with a fine-tooth comb. Without Ben, he was convinced that he was never going to see his father again. No matter how much he didn't like it, it wasn't a choice at all.

"Don't be a fool," Ben urged. He got off Jay's foot and approached William.

William looked at the empty door behind him. Vanessa never came, and deep down, he knew she wasn't coming. She had warned him about Ben. He looked at Jay's fingers gripping tightly around him. If he didn't agree, he would end up in a coffin, locked up at the police station.

Ben rubbed his hands together and nodded. "We can open the puzzle organ if we work together. There are three pieces to the puzzle organ that we need to collect." Ben shook his head and bit down angrily. "We already have the fourth piece—you." His eyebrows pulled downward and he threw his hands outward frustrated. "Apparently, you know what I don't," he said through clenched teeth. "I guess your father found it funny to keep secrets from me." He tilted his head to the side and gave an irritated grin.

William shook his head, confused.

Ben continued, "You can use the thinking cap to help your father first thing, I promise." Ben held his hand over his heart.

William felt nauseated at the idea of working with Ben. There must be another way! He looked again at the fingers gripping his waist. He couldn't escape. He hung his head and reluctantly nodded in agreement.

Chapter 17

DOWN THE CHUTE

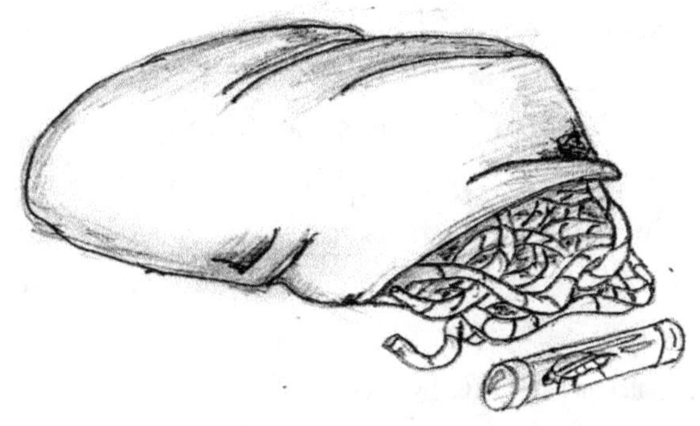

Mr. Millner couldn't hold still, bouncing from side to side. He led them through the halls muttering, "No, I can't. It's not right. Yes, of course. This will work."

William shook his head back and forth. You didn't have a choice. You had to agree to help Ben. He kept trying to convince himself that this was the only way. He felt a sense of uneasiness looking at their guide, Mr. Millner. Ben had more or less commanded a cowering Mr. Millner to lead the way. Mr. Millner had shriveled at first, like he was going to crawl into a ball and die, but the minute Ben mentioned the puzzle organ, Mr. Millner perked up. It seemed that Mr. Millner wanted to obtain the thinking cap just as much as Ben. William thought it was likely that Ben want the puzzle organ open for power and probably to fill his narcissism, but he hadn't quite figured out why Mr. Millner wanted it. Would it restore his mind? He chewed over the question while they walked until they came to a crossroads of seven different halls. Mr. Millner licked his finger and held it in the air.

"Okay, does that really work? I mean, for real. There has to be some trick," Charley said. He licked his finger and held it in the air too.

Mr. Millner chuckled and followed his finger down one of the halls to a door with thick, rusty hinges. Dark moss ran along its edges. At eye level, there was a filthy knocker barely visible under the overgrowth.

Jay took ahold of the metal latch and pulled. The mossy edges gave way like weeds being pulled from a garden as the door screeched open. Clearing the edge, a burst of wind came flying outward. It blew over William's hair, ruffling it. It had a dark, musky odor that filtered through the hall.

William looked past the door. "Where does it go?"

"Does it matter?" Ben replied sharply. "If you want to rescue your father, we are headed in no matter what. Suffice it to say, it goes down."

William didn't like the sound of that, nor did he like how curt Ben was being. Still, Ben was right. If it meant helping his father, he would have gone despite the danger.

Jay took a bag from his shoulder and it slumped to the ground. The contents spilled onto the floor, including a long rope. Taking one end, he promptly handed it to Ben.

"Everyone grab a light. Give it a shake to turn it on," Ben instructed.

William reached into the bag to find an abnormal-looking flashlight. To his surprise, neither end had a bulb. It looked like a glass tube shaped like a glow stick. He gave it a shake, as instructed, and a bug trapped inside fluttered into the air and glowed a fluorescent green. Its wings hummed and twirled as it spun.

"Mine has a bug in it!" Charley exclaimed as he shook it like he was trying to get the bug to come out.

"Yes, no batteries required," Ben said. He looked at Charley trying to dump the bug out and shook his head. "As long as you don't kill it," he sneered at Charley. He proceeded to hand part of the rope to Mr. Millner.

"No, no, no. Too much. Too much for me," Mr. Millner said. He paced back and forth then suddenly dashed into the halls. Flies streaked after him in his general direction.

"I don't think Mr. Millner will be joining us past this point," Ben said. His hand slumped downward, still holding the rope.

Leading the way, Ben held a large coil of rope over his shoulder. He let parts of it fall off, leaving a trail behind them. Jay was holding the other end. William wasn't sure what the rope was going to be used for, but it looked like Ben knew what he was doing. He moved past the door and began to descend a set of stairs. In no time, he was out of sight.

Entering the stairwell, William was met with a winding staircase descending into darkness. The bug in his light cast a bright green haze onto slippery moss covering the stairs and walls. No wonder it smelled dark and damp. He braced himself against the wall and inched downward. Each step seemed steeper than the last. The wind came rushing up from the stairs in waves. With each wave, he held his hands up to protect his eyes.

"Ouch!" Charley yipped after hitting his head on the ceiling. "Is it just me, or is the ceiling shrinking?" he asked, rubbing his head.

"It's not you," confirmed Ben. The words echoed up the stairs.

"Why is a big buff guy like me coming down here at all? I could clog this staircase like a toilet," Charley pointed out.

"You'll fit—I hope," Ben mumbled.

The walls narrowed as the vertical steps gave way to a mossy slide.

William steadied himself to stay upright as he grabbed at the rope that Ben was leaving behind. He could see the ropes utility now. This whole thing reminded him of a time he'd tried to go up a waterslide, which hadn't ended well; he'd fallen flat on his face. He was hoping he wouldn't repeat that experience, but the further he descended, the more certain he became that he would. He grew progressively more nervous following Ben when the ceiling came downward, forcing him to sit. "Are you sure about this?" he asked in a quivering, high-pitched voice.

"Everything will be fine," Ben reassured. It would have been more comforting if they could at least see Ben, but he was too far off in the distance.

"That's easy for a midget to say," Charley mumbled. He was wiggling like a worm on his back as he slid downward, holding on to the rope.

William grew desperately concerned lying on his back as flat as a board when the walls touched his chest and back at the same time. He could hardly breath. *How am I getting back up?* He desperately scraped his feet against the floor for traction. When a burst of wind came upward, he instinctively reached to shield his eyes, letting go of the rope. Instantly, he slid downward on his back and collided feet-first into Charley.

Charley jutted forward, losing his grip. Unable to stop their momentum, they slammed into Ben. The rope uncoiled from Ben at a blinding pace, whipping past them.

William closed his eyes tightly. The walls brushed up against his cheeks, crushing him on every side, until pop, he plummeted into darkness.

Chapter 18

ANTIGRAVITY

"I thought we were only supposed to be born once," Charley said, popping out of a tunnel. He sat up in a panic and shook his flashlight. It hummed as it gave off a fluorescent glow that illuminated a pile of moss and goo that he was sitting on.

William was breathing heavily. He felt himself up and down to make sure every piece had come out intact. Aside from being a little scraped, everything was in order.

Ben was the only one who didn't react. He casually got to his feet, brushed off the filth from his arms and took a giant step out of the moss pile that had traveled down the stairs with him. He shook off each shoe in turn trying to clear them of green slime before placing them solidly on stone ground. Like he was headed out on a daily stroll, he walked to the edge of an area covered in light and stopped just shy of it.

William saw a smile appear across Ben's face. Once, he might have liked to see Ben smile from ear to ear, but now it only made him curious about what Ben was up to. He wondered what could make him so happy. He looked out, hoping to find what had caught Ben's attention.

The light was ghastly bright, like a spotlight being shone from high above. But William couldn't see any spotlight; in fact, he couldn't tell where the light was coming from at all. As far as he could tell, there was no ceiling in that area of the room. It was hard to say though, because the opening above him had to be at least as high as a skyscraper. It seemed a little absurd to have a room with no ceiling. What if it rained?

Peculiarly, the light coming from above didn't shine on anything but the center of the room. Its outward glow cast just enough light to see. Sheer rock walls, covered in moss, surrounded them. They enclosed the circle of light on four sides like they were guarding it, trapping it between its slippery rock faces.

Looking upward along the rock walls, if William didn't know any better, he would have thought he had been thrown to the bottom of a pit. There would be little hope of escape. In fact, now that he thought about it, he wondered how they were going to get out at all. He looked back at the rope they had used. He gave off a sigh of relief, seeing its coils running out of the small hole in the wall and snaking across the ground, ending near his feet. There was plenty of it. Just knowing that Jay was hanging on to the other end, high above in the safety of the halls, gave him a bleak ray of hope that exiting this place was possible.

Already at the bottom, he focused his attention back to the circle of light. It couldn't have been more than a few yards wide, too far to jump in a single bounce but still small enough it could have been run across quickly. He thought about moving to the other side of the circle, but he could already tell it didn't have much to offer other than moss-covered rock. Then he saw it: something resting in the center of the light. He narrowed his eyes. From what he could tell, it looked like a small harp, no bigger than the palm of his hand. He couldn't be certain from this distance, but it had strings. "What is it?" he asked, squinting his eyes harder.

Ben's eyes gazed hungrily at the object; it had his full attention. "That is one of the keys to the puzzle organ."

"Is it a tiny guitar?" Charley asked. He was squinting his eyes too. He held his hands up and strummed his fingers in the air like he was playing music.

Ben clenched his teeth; he wasn't in a friendly mood. Sliding on his backside down the tunnel had obviously given him a gruff attitude. "It's a tuner. Every instrument needs a tuner," he said, pointing toward the small harp. "Without it, we cannot open the puzzle organ."

William found it odd that Ben referred to the puzzle organ as a musical instrument. Up until this time, he had seen it as nothing more than a destructive machine, yet Ben referred to it like it should be at home in a philharmonic orchestra. It seemed peculiar that it would need tools just like a real instrument.

Charley threw down his air guitar. "What are we waiting for? Let's get it," he exclaimed.

Ben burst out yelling frantically. "Stop, stop!"

No sooner had Charley stepped into the light than his leading foot swooshed out from under him. It pulled the rest of his body into the light, and in a matter of seconds, he was upside down with his feet over his head, floating in mid-air.

It took Charley by surprise, having the blood rush to his head, but he was otherwise all right. He grasped at the bare ground, trying to turn upright. "What just happened!?" he exclaimed.

Ben, looking shocked, ran into the shadows like he was desperately trying to get something.

"That looks kind of fun," William said, laughing at the sight of

Charley hanging in mid-air.

"I guess if I get the hiccups, I know where to come," Charley said. But then suddenly, he wasn't just floating in mid-air. He steadily glided upward, floating away. It started slowly, but like a stream turning into a rapid, the momentum was building quickly. The fun was over.

Charley scrambled to get back down. "Quick, help me down!"

William looked for something to hang on to. "Give me your hand," he yelled.

Charley dropped his flashlight and reached outward, grabbing William's hand. In seconds, his flashlight floated upward, steadily gaining speed until it was a streak of light bursting away like a rocket.

William held Charley's sweaty hands just outside the light. His fingers clenched, but he could barely hold on. The light was pulling Charley harder by the second. "Why are your hands so sweaty?"

"I'm sorry," Charley said, trying to hold on. "Hyperhidrosis is a medical condition, okay?"

"Fine," William replied as he tried to adjust his grip. It was no good. Charley's fingers slipped away. Frantically, he leaped to grab Charley by the hair. It was the only thing that he could get a good grasp on, and Charley's excessive hair gel made it somewhat easier to hold onto. William's arms strained to keep him down. He couldn't anchor him for long. Every inch of him that entered the light was floating away with Charley too. Half of his body already in the circle, William dug in his heels with all his might. His shoes skidded across the floor and lifted into the air. He stretched his tiptoes to touch the ground as he lifted off. It did no good. There was nothing but air now.

Charley was blowing in the opposite direction and swimming with his arms in a vain attempt to get back to the ground. It didn't do anything, of course. They were going to streak through the sky like Charley's flashlight.

Gaining speed, William was at a loss. He looked upward into the light, hoping that their inevitable demise would be quick, until he suddenly stopped in mid-air. A sudden jerk almost made him lose his grasp on Charley's hair. He gripped with his might, letting a few strands slip between his fingers. What happened? Looking down, he saw the rope around his foot. On the other end was Ben, pulling them to safety.

The moment they exited the light, William and Charley fell to the ground.

William sat up and rubbed his hip where he'd struck the floor. In his hand, he was holding a tuft of Charley's hair.

"Oh, no. Am I bald?" Charley moaned, feeling the top of his head.

"That was not a bright thing to do," Ben said. He scornfully crossed his arms and frowned at Charley.

"Tell that to my hair. I probably have a bald spot. Do you have any idea how expensive my hair gel is?" Charley cried. "I can't use it if I'm bald!"

"You're lucky you didn't die," Ben pointed out.

William looked back at the circle, now realizing how dangerous the situation was. "So how are you supposed to get that thing?" he asked. He threw Charley's clump of hair on the ground.

Charley rubbed his head again and whimpered when he saw the hair fall to the ground.

Ben slumped his shoulders disappointedly as if William should have known the answer already. "We have to work together, for starters." He raised his voice for emphasis as he glared at Charley. "If I could have done it alone, do you think I would have brought you here?" His voice had an arrogance that made William feel foolish. "I've tried doing this with Mr. Millner, but dark, cramped spaces don't seem to agree with him. Trying to bring Jay down here is more than laughable. Ben shook his head and cursed under his breath. "It never works out, and this time seems to be no different thus far." Ben took a deep breath. "Let's just say it takes a motivated person to risk their own life for something so small, which makes you the perfect candidate. Besides, your father is the one that put us in this mess anyway, which makes it feel like poetic justice that you're here undoing this predicament. To your father's credit, after we opened the puzzle organ, how he secretly got all items for the puzzle organ back in the same place still eludes me. It is another of the few insignificant areas that he may have bested me." He rubbed his chin with his hand, concentrating. "Of course, he added a few caveats to protect them. This light circle, for example," Ben said gritting his teeth. He paced the edge of the circle, being careful not to enter the light. "Although, it's just like him to leave a solution to the problem so simple that even a child could have figured it out, and I think that I have the answer." He handed William a piece of paper seemingly out of nowhere.

William looked at the white sheet in his hand and turned it over. It was blank on both sides. He shrugged his shoulders, "What do you want me to do with this?"

Ben folded his arms. "I thought the McFaddens were smart. At least your father used to tell me so. Is this what their legacy is?" he mocked.

William shook his head, almost angry. What am I supposed to do with paper? He eyed it again, flipping it over. What can I do with this?

The question was answered almost as quickly as he asked it. He had done it a thousand times.

He sat on the ground and line after line intricately creased the paper. When he was done, he had masterfully crafted a boomerang.

Ben didn't congratulate him. He merely smirked and nodded. "Whatever you do, don't miss."

William grinned at the boomerang in his hand. Ben didn't seem to have much faith in him. It didn't matter; he could knock an apple off someone's head; he was sure he could pelt a small harp in the middle of a circle of light. Holding the boomerang in his hand, he warmed up his arm with a twist.

Ben narrowly informed William how perfect the throw needed to be. The way that Ben spoke was as sharp as a knife, reminding him that his father's life was on the line. The knife twisted even deeper, making his gut fill to the brim with anxiety when Ben told him that he only had one chance because there were consequences to missing. Ben didn't elaborate any more. Suffice it to say, his emphasis on throwing once was impressionable to say the least. It made William's stomach twist on itself with the added pressure. He had thrown the boomerang a lot, but this time was different. What if I don't miss? Ben didn't go into detail on this either. However, it was easy to assume that this was the safest course of action to help his father.

Working as a team, Charley positioned himself on the far side of the light as William aimed. Ben seemed to do the same on another side of the circle.

Looking at Ben and Charley, positioned like outfielders on a baseball field, William tried to not focus on all the things that could go wrong. Did it really come down to this? One miss and I'll never see my father again? He took a deep breath and tried to pretend like this was nothing but hitting another apple. He drew his arm back. "Please, please, please," he yelped as he zipped his arm forward with all his might.

The boomerang spun through the air, twirling end over end on a collision course. It made contact and the harp tumbled away.

Charley crouched, ready to catch.

Halfway to Charley's hands, everything was looking good. It was going to make it!

William jumped for joy, waiting excitedly for Charley to grab it; however, that moment never came. Nearing Charley, the object slowed in mid-air, tumbling awkwardly end over end. The joy faded quickly. He watched helplessly as it moved upward into the sky, gaining momentum into the light. Fear replaced his anxiety looking at the harp that was about to streak into the sky.

With a running start, Charley leaped forward like he was catching a fly ball. "I got it!" he yelled loudly as he stretched his arm outward and plucked the tuner from the air. It was a play that would go down in history; however, he was floating away too.

"You imbecile," Ben yelled. His eyes darted to William, "I said you had one throw." In a scramble, Ben grabbed Charley's feet, but his dwarf-sized body didn't have a chance at anchoring Charley. His stubby arms were quickly pulled into the light, dragging the remainder of his body until he was floating unsupported beneath Charley.

William didn't know how to respond to Ben. There was no time. Ben was grunting trying to hold Charley to the floor, and Charley was cheering that he had grabbed the key like a fly ball and made the perfect play for the game. In fact, Charley didn't seem to care much other than admiring his hall of fame potential.

William needed his head on straight. He dashed into action and grabbed the rope nearby. There was no time to think, no time to come up with a smart solution. He was going to have to make his own theatric move. Letting his mind go blank, he held the rope and dove into the light from the other side. His arm stretched in front of him and swept through the air, grabbing at anything. Luckily, his hand found Ben's foot. By some miracle, he held tightly to the rope. It floated upward with them until the slack ran out and stopped them with a sudden jerk. His muscles were straining to hold to the lifeline. He could see the rope stretching to the wall and into the small hole. He hoped that Jay wasn't going to let go on the far end of the rope any time soon.

"Hang on buddy," Charley yelled as part of the rope floated upward toward him. It seemed that Charley had finally come around to the danger they were in yet again.

"Grab the rope together," Ben yelled. His tone was commanding and frustrated, and it got to the point.

All three of them grabbed ahold of the free end of the rope dangling next to them. Working together, one heave-hoe at a time, they pulled themselves to safety. The moment they came out of the light, they tumbled to the ground in a pile, one on top of the other.

Charley moaned, "What is it with falling in this place? You'd think they would at least put up a warning sign."

William breathed a sigh of relief. He had never been so grateful to have two feet on solid ground.

"I'll take that," Ben said, snatching the tuner from Charley's hands. He didn't seem to care one bit if they were injured. With a big smile, He put the object into his pocket. His hand caressed the top of his pants where the tuner lay. It made his grin grow three sizes.

"I want a new van when all this is done," Charley replied. "Maybe something super nice, like a Town and Country."

"You can dream about a van later," Ben flippantly replied. You could tell from the callus reply that he was getting tired of Charley's nonsensical responses. He flipped his hand in disregard. "Let's get out of here," he commanded.

The stairwell they had come through was nothing but a hole in the wall, and it was anything but inviting. Nevertheless, Ben instructed them to hold the rope tightly. He pulled it in rapid succession and wiggled it up and down. "That should signal Jay," he said. "Whatever you do, don't let go."

Moments later, the rope came to life. In a line, it pulled them up the slimy staircase.

Chapter 19

DOOR NUMBER TWO

The top of the stairs was a welcome sight for William. No matter how grumpy Ben was, or how much moss and grime covered him, William was satisfied knowing that they were one step closer to saving his father. Of course, it would help if Ben would lighten up a little. During their climb, Ben didn't hold back his disappointment about how clumsily things had gone. Charley, in particular, got an earful. Ben's rant reminded William of Mrs. Burbank. There was no telling when she would fly off the handle. *I wonder if they know one another?*

At the top of the stairs, Mr. Millner was waiting nervously, twirling his thumbs. When he saw William reach the hall, his fingers stopped and his face brightened like he was more surprised to see them alive

173

than happy they had returned.

Charley had been wishfully talking about a new van to try and keep his mind occupied as they made their ascent. "I can see it now. Extra room in the back, maybe a sunroof, and I'm considering a racing stripe. It is gonna be a babe magnet."

Ben didn't seem amused. In fact, he quickly marched past the door and onto Jay's foot. He fidgeted his fingers nervously, almost as jumpy as Mr. Millner. "Time to move to our next task." He twirled his finger in the air, signaling Jay to get a move on.

William was hoping for more of an explanation about the tuner, but he wasn't sure that he was going to get one. He had loads of unanswered questions. For starters, he wondered why his father would have put the items to the puzzle organ back at all. Who was he trying to keep the thinking cap protected from? It was nagging at him. More than once, he tried to talk to Ben on their way up the stairs, but Ben didn't answer with more than a grunt about how this was all his father's fault. He thought about asking again, but Ben, sitting atop Jay like his trusty steed, didn't look like he was in a mood to explain things.

As William's eyes stared at Ben, he could see his hand rubbing the outside of his pocket that held the tuner. He wondered if his father had made the obstacles to stop Ben. In fact, they could have been specifically built against him. He could see how Ben would have had little chance at getting the tuner alone. He nervously thought about getting the next key to the puzzle organ. What obstacles lay ahead? If they had to go down another dark, dingy staircase, he wondered if Charley was going to develop an acute case of claustrophobia. "Where is the next key?" he blurted out. He was hoping he would get more than a grunt as an answer.

"Oh, wait and see. William can figure it out," Mr. Millner said as he jumped up and down, clapping his hands. "He can open the puzzle organ. He can!" He quickly ran away, nearly stumbling with enthusiasm.

"It's not far from here," Ben snickered. He looked at William, who had a concerned look about him. "Don't worry. Being a Mcfadden, you shouldn't have any trouble with it," Ben said, but his words gave no comfort.

Jay turned on his heels and followed Mr. Millner, who was already off in the distance.

William brushed off as much moss and grime as he could from his arms and legs and hurried to catch up.

They traveled rapidly; Jay saw to that. The halls passed in a blur. Charley gave off his usual grumbling that didn't stop until they slowed in front of another door. It was nothing like the first. This one was made of metal and had rows of solid-steel bolts. Otherwise, it was nearly featureless except for an oval window near the top. It made it look like a door from a submarine. William wished he could peek inside the window, but the glass was hazy; he wouldn't be able to see much even if he could get high enough. The door was big, but still, the window was no higher than Jay's waist. William reckoned that this door was smaller than the one at the police station in town, which had barely fit Jay. It didn't seem likely that Jay was going to fit through easily.

Jay pulled on a large steel beam that somewhat resembled a door handle, but the door didn't budge.

For a moment, William wondered if they were going to get in at all. If Jay can't open it, who can? It wasn't until Jay buckled down with both hands that a loud screech rang through the hall as the door gave way and lights just beyond flickered on and off.

William desperately hoped that there wasn't a mossy staircase. He squinted into the dancing light past the door and a sense of relief washed over him. Instead of a windy staircase, there was a small hall-way.

Ben turned around with a concerned look on his face to address everyone. "This needs three of us. How about you, Mr. Millner?" Ben asked, obviously trying to avoid Charley's help this time.

Mr. Millner sheepishly tucked himself behind Jay's leg.

"Fine," Ben said, gritting his teeth angrily. "Coward," he whispered under his breath. "Let's not be so hasty this time," he said, turning his gaze to Charley. "We don't want to be as awkward as last time."

"Thank you for that vote of confidence. Can I just say that my self-esteem has greatly improved because of you," Charley said sarcastically? Ignoring Ben, he put his foot over the threshold of the door as confidently as he could. He took each step like the ground might fall out from underneath him.

Ben snickered and walked past Charley. William followed.

Inside was nothing but cold, hard metal. Like the door, the walls were made of steel, connected by rivets. Flickering lights made them look like polka dots on the wall spread out in straight lines, running the length of a corridor until stopping at another door. Unlike the first, this one sat wide open. Beyond it, another hallway revealed itself. It was nearly identical, rivets and all. It even ran to another door just like the first.

Passing the third door, William was starting to wonder if they were going down a hall that repeated itself over and over. Fortunately, that wasn't the case. Beyond the third door, they came to a room. Knowing that danger could be eminent, he longingly turned and looked back at the safety of the hall, yards away. Jay was bending down, peeking in at them. He looked like a giant staring down a mouse hole, and William felt like the mouse.

Ben took out a light and shook it. The bug inside gave off a faint green glow, just enough light to see what they were after. Not far off, resting in the middle of the room, was a small glass dome sitting on a pedestal. Inside it was something that William had never seen before. It looked like a small box with an arrow attached to the front of it that moved back and forth erratically. He held up his bug light, but it didn't help him see much. "Is that the second key?" he asked, even though he was almost certain that it was.

"Well done, William," Ben replied with an arrogance about his voice. "You may prove yourself yet. Your father may have found this one, but it was I who discovered what it was used for." Ben pushed his chest out proudly.

"It looks like a clock," Charley said, holding his light out as far as he could.

Ben shook his head. "It's a metronome."

"A what?" Charley said making his dumb-face. "Met-tra-nom," he repeated slowly. Suddenly, he opened his eyes widely like he'd had an epiphany. "Oh yeah, my girlfriend had one of those. They really hurt to get your finger stuck in," he said, nodding his head confidently.

"No!" Ben snarled. "Every good instrument has a metronome to let you know when to play notes. However, the one for the puzzle organ happens to be unpredictable."

William could hear a tick-tock in the distance. It was certainly off beat. The rhythm would go by without a tick, followed by five in a row, yet somehow it had a rhythm that made him want to dance. Worried about their last experience, he asked, "How are we supposed to get it?"

"I think I learned my lesson," Charley said. "Maybe someone else wants to try first?"

Ben strode up to the pedestal with his light and shined it on the metronome. The light reflected off the glass container that covered it. He pushed the glass container trying to lift it, but it wouldn't budge.

Something told William that the glass was just as stuck as Excalibur in stone; it wasn't going to budge.

"I'll just stand back here," Charley said, unknowingly backing into a button against the wall. The button gave way behind him and a loud rushing sound, like a waterfall, rang through the room. A panel at the far end of the chamber opened halfway.

Startled, Charley pushed himself off the button and, as quickly as it had come, the sound was gone and the panel closed.

"What was that?" William asked looking around.

Charley nervously locked his knees, making him move like a robot. "It sounded like water." He didn't have a fear of water; he just didn't like getting his hair wet.

Ben's face became rather serious with his eyebrows drawn downward. "Water," he mumbled. "Why does there have to be water?"

William could see how Ben might not be a fan of water. His short arms and legs probably meant he wasn't much of an athlete in a pool.

"It would seem that Charley finds trouble wherever he is. However, this trouble was undoubtedly part of your father's doing." Ben glared at William with narrowed eyes.

"What happened when I pushed the button?" Charley asked sheepishly, looking over his shoulder at the round button protruding on the wall.

Ben pointed to a wall at the far side of the room where the panel had partially opened. "It opens the panel at the far side of the room all the way if you push both buttons together." He held up one finger and pointed at another button against a wall adjacent to Charley.

William was starting to understand why three people would be needed. There was no way to push all the buttons at the same time without help.

"What if there's another antigravity thing?" Charley shuttered.

Ben looked at William. "I can assure you that there isn't. It was never in Arthur's nature to repeat things." He grabbed his chin, thinking. "And I am almost certain that you, William, have all the answers that we need." The corners of his lips raised with delight.

The combination of a drawn brow and vicious smile projecting from Ben's face made William's stomach turn. He wasn't sure what was behind the panel, but regardless of what it was, he was determined to get through it. That was more than he could say about Ben; William was sure that Ben wouldn't risk his life for his father's like he would.

After discussing the only logical plan, they got into position. Ben and Charley stationed themselves against the wall, each in front of a button, while William waited anxiously at the far end of the room where the panel was going to open. Ben was absolutely convinced that whatever was behind the panel, William was going to be able to figure it out. William wasn't quite as confident. His father had taught him how to make boomerangs, but he couldn't figure out how he could have prepared him for this.

Ben counted aloud. On three, Ben and Charley pushed the buttons and the thunderous boom of rushing water returned. At the far end of the room, the panel, which had only opened partially before, now released a picture puzzle. Ben had been right to some degree. Solving a picture puzzle was right up William's alley.

"Hurry," Ben shouted over the booming water.

William sized up the picture puzzle confidently. It was no bigger than one that would have been on his father's desk, but it was woefully undetailed. It made it much more difficult than the average picture puzzle. It had to be something amorphous, like a cloud. There were no edges, no lines to put together, nothing but shades of blue. It was like trying to solve a puzzle of ten thousand pieces that were all white; this was going to take some time.

"Are you all right?" Charley called out.

William turned around. "I'm fine," he called back. "I just need a minute." He let his mind go blank. He waited for something to come, an idea, anything, but there was nothing that arose. Stumped, he felt his feet turn frigid. Looking down, he found his shoes soaking wet in a pool of water that was rising. It became clear why he heard rushing water. Seemingly out of nowhere, it was gushing in from the walls on every side of him.

"Right now, you don't have a minute!" Ben shouted impatiently over the sound of rushing water. "Hurry!" He was straining, pushing backward against the button. For him, the water was nearly to his knees.

Charley, wide-eyed, looked toward William. It was Charley's panicked expression. William had seen it once before but never in a room filling with water.

William cleared his head and looked at the puzzle again. *What would my father do?* The thunderous sound of water clapping against the walls didn't help his concentration. In the short time that his attention had been off the panel, the water had risen. Up to his midcalf was covered in a frigid pool of turbid water.

Again, William looked at the puzzle, and he realized—he had seen this picture before. He could see it now. It had to have been the picture from his father's desk. He remembered seeing it just before leaving Mrs. Burbank. All the shades of blue were there, just jumbled. It rushed from his thoughts and trickled to his hands. His fingers twirled like synchronized dancers, manipulating the pieces into their spots until it looked just right: a nebulous shape of blue. A sense of gratification swept over William as he heard a click. Turning, he could see the glass container over the metronome open.

Ben couldn't contain himself. The minute the glass lifted, he let go of the button and rushed to the metronome. His short legs sloshed through the water that was now waist-deep. Looking rather satisfied, he took the metronome from the pedestal and ran to escape.

Charley let go of his button too.

On the other side of the room, William half expected the water to stop gushing once the buttons were released, but there was no such relief. The water poured in just the same, filling the room quickly. His heart raced as he looked at each of the doors they had passed. They were closing. Panicked, he pushed one foot in front of the other to chase after Ben. The water splashed up his waist. When he reached the other side of the room, he grabbed Charley by the hand and felt Charley tug him past the first door.

The tide was rising faster than he could move. It was deep enough to swim now, but he needed both hands. Reluctantly, he let go of Charley and dove forward. He could see Ben, not more than ten feet in front of him, doing the same. Following closely on Charley's heels, William's arms flailed in an uncoordinated freestyle swim. It was less than graceful, but it got him past the second door.

Only one more door to safety. William could see Charley almost there, but the door was nearly closed. He tried to push off the ground more than once, but he lost his balance and slipped under the water. He gasped for air at the surface as the current sloshed him against the walls. He could see the window on the door that he had seen before entering and wished he was on the other side of it. Light shimmered through it and gave a moonlight glow to the dark pool. He suddenly realized that if he ran out of air, it would be the last thing he would see.

Through the water spilling out into the hallway, a hand reached from beyond the open edge of the door. It was Jay's hand. It cut through the water like the hull of a ship and latched on to Ben.

"Come on," Ben shouted.

Turning over in the water, William couldn't keep his head up. Out of control, he reached outward. Luckily, he found Charley's arm.

Charley reached outward, grabbing Ben's foot just as Jay pulled him through the water. In a long chain, they held on to one another. Ben and Charley slipped past the door with inches to spare, but inches weren't enough for William.

Faced with the prospect of being crushed by a steel door, William made a split-second decision: he let go. The door pinched against his hand just as he moved and clenched closed tightly. Panicking, he dove into the water and looked through the hazy oval window to safety. Charley was pounding on the glass.

Surfacing for air, he found there wasn't much room to breathe. A few more seconds and the room would be filled to the brim. He took a deep breath and dove. There must be some way out. His hands searched the door for something. There must be a handle. His hands found none. How do you open a door if it has no handle? It quickly dawned on him. This whole place had doors without handles. They had door puzzles.

Blue in the face, William surfaced. He spat water out of his mouth. The remaining air shrank from a bubble to nothing as he breathed, filling his lungs one last time before he plunged. As plain as day, a door puzzle was right where a handle should have been. He moved the pieces, straining for oxygen. Spots danced in front of his eyes from the lack of air. How do I solve this? How!? Piecing the puzzle together in his mind, he calculated each move. Like a processer, his brain computed a hundred moves before he even touched a piece. Exhausted, he turned the pieces under his fingers. Click by click they slid into place until it was complete, but the door didn't open. Instead, the rapid current shifted to a swirl, pulling his lifeless body like driftwood. Spinning down toward a drain, he was losing consciousness. The sweet blackness wanted to consume him, warm and comforting. The only thing that disrupted it was Charley's pounding on the glass. Softly, he closed his eyes.

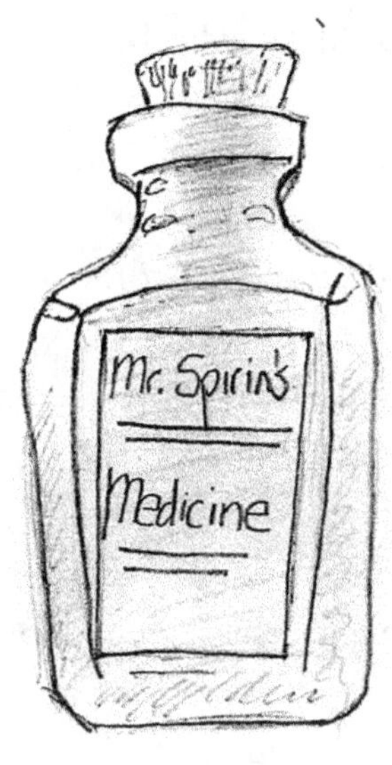

Chapter 20

DROWNED BUT NOT DEAD

William awoke wondering if he was dead or not. He was lying on his side, wrapped in a soft blanket. His clothes were dry, and he was comfortably warm. Next to his bed, he saw a bottle. Its red-and-green label read Mr. Spirin's Miracle Medicine. His dry lips smacked together with the faint taste of medicine on his breath. He sat up expecting his body to ache, but there wasn't much pain. Instead, he coughed. Water rushed from his mouth as it was replaced by air in his lungs. He choked and spat until it was gone.

Wondering if he was alone, he looked around. There were curtains hanging decoratively in all directions. This place didn't look familiar. Off to the side, he heard a chime. The sweet scent of incense was floating in the air.

"I see you woke up. I was worried you might not. Even Mr. Spirin's medicine has its limits," said Miss Lockit. She was resting on a pillow with her legs crossed underneath her. She swayed from side to side, letting her keys chime together.

"What happened?" William asked. Truthfully, he didn't remember much. There was the door puzzle and then blackness: cold, wet blackness.

"You drowned," Miss Lockit answered frankly.

William waited for the details, but Miss Lockit said nothing. She continued her deep meditation. "Oh, I see. Good to know," William said.

"Ohm . . .ohm," Miss Lockit said, swaying from side to side. "It's a good thing you are good at puzzles. Just like your father."

"He's the one who taught me. He never told me why, but I guess there are a lot of things he didn't tell me."

"You worry a lot about things that happened in the past," Miss Lockit said.

William wasn't sure what to think. So I shouldn't worry about them? "I nearly drowned," he pointed out.

"No, dear. You did drown." Miss Lockit hummed and closed her eyes. She took a deep whiff of the incense with her nose in the air.

The past was all William cared about lately. There was his father, Uncle Ben, and the puzzle organ. A lot of the story was missing. "I can't help thinking about the past. It doesn't make sense," he responded.

"I know," Miss Lockit said. "But there's nothing like a good drowning to make you think about the future. Wouldn't you agree?"

William begged to differ. There were a thousand other things he could do to focus on the future. "I take it I'm not the first to drown here?"

"Heavens, no. Did you think you were the only one?" Miss Lockit chuckled.

"I guess so."

"You should talk to Mr. Millner. He nearly got himself killed when he tried to get the metronome with Ben. He used to be so adventurous."

William couldn't picture Mr. Millner being adventurous. The only thing he could think of was an unbalanced, hygienically-challenged person. It made him wonder what else he didn't know about the past. "It's hard to imagine him that way."

"I know," she said. "I imagine it's probably just as hard to imagine Ben as a close friend of your father." She flung her head and her long hair fell in front of her face, covering her eyes.

"My dad never mentioned him."

"I know."

William frowned. It was a sore spot for him. Why would my father never mention it to me? "I wish he would have said something."

Miss Lockit stopped swaying. She looked at William like she was seeing into his tender heart. "I know," she replied. "But don't feel so bad. It was better this way."

William hardly agreed. "What do you mean?"

"What would you have done even if he had told you?"

"I'm not sure," William managed to stutter. His voice was filled with uncertainty.

"Would you have believed him?"

"Maybe," he said, shrugging his shoulders.

"Did you know Ben, Mr. Millner, and your father were close friends?"

William had figured as much from the picture on his father's desk. He nodded.

Miss Lockit uncrossed her legs and rested them in front of her. "It seems odd that friends could end up like this. I've wondered about it for a long time, but Ben was angry."

Why?" William asked. He scratched the top of his head. He hoped this would give some insight into why Ben was so curt with him.

Miss Lockit stood and walked across the floor agilely. Her footsteps were lighter than a gazelle. She sat next to William just like she'd sat next to Mr. Millner to calm him down. "Knowledge is a powerful thing. Knowing too much is just as bad as knowing too little."

William was confused. "How can knowing too much be a bad thing?"

"You might stumble onto something that you didn't want to know. What would you do then?" Miss Lockit asked.

Miss Lockit's gaze was intoxicating. William felt like it drilled into his soul. "I . . . I don't know. I guess I would keep it a secret," he guessed.

"Isn't it surprising how much you think like your father? Because that's exactly what he did. Great minds think alike, I suppose. When your father found out how to open the last part of the puzzle organ, it endangered him. Worst of all, it endangered you, so he left. He left behind a confused Mr. Millner, a re-locked puzzle organ, and a bitter Ben to manage it all."

"So, Ben is mad that he left?"

"That's a good way of looking at it."

"He wants revenge?"

"He's always been bitter, but he's not vengeful."

"Then why would he take my dad and lock him in a coffin?"

"Ah, a good question. Not one I can answer though. Maybe I need a good drowning to clear my head so I can figure it out." She put her hand against her chin like she was thinking.

William shook his head back and forth. "Be my guest, but you should keep that medicine close by."

Mr. Wyatt came bursting through the curtains. He threw them to the side like they were an annoyance. "What is with all the curtains?" he asked angrily.

"They help focus your inner energy," Miss Lockit replied. She gracefully tiptoed back to her pillow and sat down.

"That is the last blooming thing I need," Mr. Wyatt replied. "If I need focus, I'll shoot at stuff." He held his finger up like it was a gun and let off a round. Pretending to shoot around the room, he noticed

William. "Glad to see you awake, mate. Gave us a good scare."

"I'm a bit foggy on the details," William said. He rubbed his head, trying to remember.

"As we say in the outback, you got flushed down the pit like a big old . . ."

"Don't say it!" Miss Lockit cut him off.

"Right, you drowned," Mr. Wyatt said, correcting himself. "If it hadn't been for Mr. Millner, you might have died. He knew right where to find you. It's a good thing too. A few more minutes and you would have sunk to the bottom."

Thinking of the water made William shiver. He coughed again to make sure his lungs were clear.

"I've been thinking," Mr. Wyatt said. "Now might be a good time to give you these." He reached into his pocket and took out three white balls.

William knew what they were. How could he forget the paralytic powder that had frozen him into a statue? "What do I do with these?"

"They're for you, mate. These little puppies saved my life once." Mr. Wyatt looked like he was going into another sales pitch. "There I was, running in my skivvies through the jungle about to be eaten by a pack of wild Tasmanian devils, with only my wits about me and one of these." He puffed his chest out proudly.

"And? What happened?" William persuaded him to continue.

Mr. Wyatt looked at Miss Lockit's uneasily and seemed to revise his story. "Well, I'm still alive, as you can see. I'll let you fill in the details."

William did his best to block out the image of Mr. Wyatt in his "skivvies."

"The point is, the minute you get the thinking cap, you use these, and BAM, Ben is frozen stiff. You walk away with the thinking cap, free as a jaybird."

William took the pellets from Mr. Wyatt and tucked them into his pocket. "About Ben…he seems a little edgy lately." He cringed at the thought of returning.

"That's because he's worried," Vanessa said from the shadows. She stepped out from behind the curtains.

William was surprised to see Vanessa. How long has she been listening? He hadn't heard her come in.

"Give him a moment, love. He's had a tough day," Mr. Wyatt warned.

"Worried?" William asked Vanessa. "About what?" He got unsteadily to his feet, trying to prove that he had recovered enough.

Vanessa looked concerned. The atmosphere turned serious, and the room went still. The smoke from the incense floated through the air in slow motion as the moment was absorbed. "Last time he opened the puzzle organ, your father eventually locked the thinking cap back inside. I'm sure he's worried that you will do the same. Like father like son, I suppose."

William could sense the tension around Ben. Ben was getting more irritable the closer they came to opening the puzzle organ. "What do I do?"

Vanessa walked past a curtain. It dragged over her shoulder as she went by. "He is going to betray you, just like he betrayed your father. I guess the only thing you can do is act first. You don't want to end up in a coffin."

William could hardly fathom the idea of being locked up for months at a time. He agreed with Vanessa. He couldn't let Ben have the upper hand. He squeezed the pellets that Mr. Wyatt had given him. It wasn't the plan that he wanted, but it was all that he had. He just needed to look for just the right moment to strike.

Chapter 21

THE ICY BAT CAVE

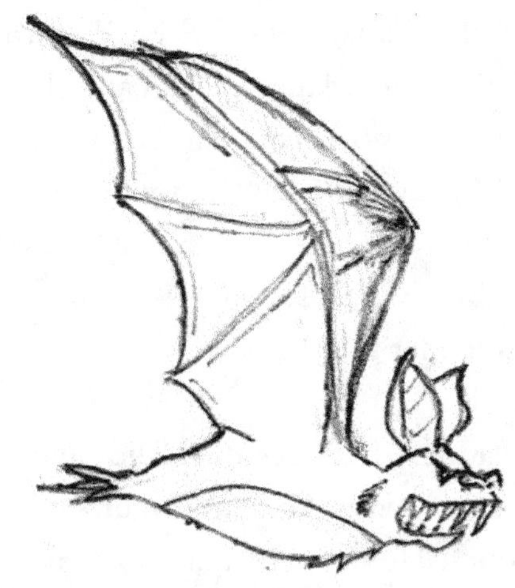

"I don't wanna get up," Charley moaned.

William was tapping him on the shoulder. He couldn't sleep, not after everything that had happened. "Breakfast is ready," William lied.

"Coming," Charley said, instantly awake. When he found out there wasn't any food ready, he plopped back in bed. "I'm glad you're safe and all, but do we really need to get up?"

Last night, William had been escorted back. When he returned safe, Ben seemed relieved to some degree. It wasn't a loving relief, however. His cold greetings were more like he was giving him his thirty-day notice and a severance package; it wouldn't be long before he

189

wasn't needed any longer. However, for now, Ben needed to assure himself that William didn't get lost and die. Ben had reluctantly given back the Never-Lost Watch as insurance. It put William's emotions back on edge. Emotionally spent, they had decided it would be best to start again in the morning.

"How much more sleep do you need? Like an hour?" William asked Charley.

Charley pulled the blanket over his head. "More like a day."

"A day!" William almost laughed. "I can't sleep another minute."

"Too excited over almost dying again?"

William rolled his eyes. "I have something for you. It's from Mr. Wyatt," he said, trying to entice Charley out of bed.

Charley licked his Disguise Dentures. "Oh yeah? What is it?"

"He called it a ladder in a pocket."

"What does it do?"

"I guess it's a ladder? Let's see, how did he put it?" Mr. Wyatt had given it to William last night. William assumed it was another Wyatt Incorporated product. He thought hard to remember the sales pitch. "What would you say is a practical item that you always wish you had but never carry with you?"

"A girlfriend?" Charley replied sarcastically.

William chuckled and did his best Mr. Wyatt accent. "NO, a ladder! As we all know, big things come in small packages, and thanks to patented technology, you can have a compact ladder that fits right in your pocket. That is a Mr. Wyatt guarantee."

"That is ludicrous. Why would anyone want a ladder in their pocket? It has to be ginormous."

"He said he once used it to climb three stories to a balcony window and sing like Romeo to Juliet." William chuckled.

"Did it work?" Charley asked. He was sitting up in bed, intently leaning forward.

"He said it did."

"Give it to me!" Charley demanded.

William was surprised. He handed over the small package to Charley, who popped it open. It resembled something of a twisted ball of wire. Bending and pulling, Charley tried to open the ladder, but nothing worked. Giving up, he put it into his pocket, determined that he would figure out how it worked after he had a full stomach. "Fits pretty good. Now I need to find a balcony."

"And a girl."

Breakfast was quick. Mr. Millner joined them, sitting quietly across from William and muttering to himself. Even when William tried to ask him questions, Mr. Millner wouldn't respond.

Mr. Millner pulled his patch up off his eye while he ate. His green and blue eyes rolled around the room but never once stopped on William.

William wanted to thank Mr. Millner. He even tried to get his attention by standing in front of him, but Mr. Millner quickly looked away and moved around him. Ben said it was because Mr. Millner was nervous about today, but he didn't seem nervous. He had no trouble leading the way to the next key to the puzzle organ.

Once again, they stopped at a door. This one looked like a freezer covered in frost. A cracked thermometer on the outside had a needle dipping below zero.

"The last piece lies beyond," Ben said. He seemed anxious with small beads of sweat across his forehead.

William put his hand to the door. The frost melted below his fingertips. "What's in there?"

"It better be filled with ice cream," Charley said.

"Polar bats," Ben responded. He wiped the sweat from his brow.

Charley made his dumb-face. "I'm no English professor, but don't you mean polar bears?"

"No, bats," Ben asserted. "Sensitive little creatures and unfortunately as aggressive as hornets if disturbed."

William's stomach had a sinking feeling. It sounded like another near-death experience. "How do you want to get around them?"

"I suggest you remain as quiet as possible," Ben stated with one eye squinting toward Charley.

"Okay," Charley barely whispered. "I'm pretty good at the quiet game. Especially when Mrs. Burbank makes me play."

Ben stopped and looked at Charley. "Well then, she was a smart woman to make you play. I have something that might help us, too."

Jay opened a bag and dumped its contents onto the floor. Household items rolled across the ground: dish soap, gasoline, fertilizer, epoxy resin, and gravy mixtures were just a few of them. The last item to fall from the sack was a bucket.

William's eyes widened. He knew exactly what these were for: his father's glue. The last time he mixed it, he had carelessly gotten it on Mrs. Burbank's toilet seat. He couldn't think of anything else such a curious collection of items would make.

Ben started to measure out ingredients.

"What are we supposed to do with it?" William asked.

"Believe it or not, these bats are your father's creation," Ben angrily stated through clenched teeth. "And I am fairly certain that he engineered a way to get around them: they love this glue."

Charley watched as the items were mixed together. "So, do girls love it too? I mean, not that it attracts girls. I mean, that would be crazy because there is no such thing. That would be almost like a love potion turned into a love glue, which isn't real, right?"

"No, I'm afraid not." Ben smiled and looked up at Charley. "Not to worry, you have your witty brain to attract women." His voice was filled with sarcasm.

Charley didn't notice the sarcasm. He squinted one eye and pointed at Ben. "Right you are, and I have a van."

When the glue was ready, Jay yanked open the metal door. Frost sputtered from its hinges and melted on William's face.

Quietly, William held the bucket of glue and followed Jay's heels as he made his way inside. The ice-chilled air hit him, causing his breath to turn to a cool mist. The air froze the slippery ground. The ceiling had icicles as big as stalactites that hung downward, making it look like they were in a cave. Just in front of him, William could make out a narrow path that dropped off on either side to a deep, dark pit of blackness. He leaned to one edge to look down. A slope ran outward, away from the path, for a short distance until it completely dropped off. For all he knew, the drop-off could have been as big as a mountain. His feet quivered at the thought of falling. His feet shook uneasily as he backed away from the edge. He could tell that Charley was equally as nervous about falling. William would have liked to walk next to Charley, but it wasn't worth the risk. The path was far too narrow, and one misstep would send him sliding to the bottom of nowhere. He gripped the bucket of glue with both hands, trying to hold it steady while he slid across the icy footpath.

Jay found it difficult to get his balance; the path didn't accommodate his big feet. He was probably regretting his choice to accompany them.

Not far from the door, the path widened to a landing large enough for some elbow room. William let out a sigh of relief as he stepped next to Charley. He looked for the continuation of the path but couldn't find one. It seemed to have come to an abrupt halt. Had they continued straight, they would have walked off an edge into a deep crevasse. This was more than just a drop-off like before. It seemed to be a large pit that was blocking their way. He leaned to look over the edge once again to see nothing but a slope that went off into darkness. The visible edges circled around on either side. Squinting his eyes into the dim light, he could just barely make out another path on the far side. It was more than out of reach. Not even with his best jump could he make it that far. In fact, he even doubted Jay could step over the pit. There must be another way. Was this the end? Ben was whispering to Jay. It didn't seem like the right time to ask questions. Instead, he held his tongue and turned his eyes in either direction, looking for answers. To his surprise, he saw a footpath that skirted the edges of the crevasse. He hadn't seen it before because it was far too small for any normal foot. William thought that his own shoes were even too large to maintain balance on it. He certainly wasn't about to try it with a vat of glue in his hands. This certainly meant that Charley and Jay's foot size was out of the question. Even with small feet, the added danger of ice made it look more than precarious. It was a sure way to die.

William's nerves were starting to grow uneasy when he saw Ben point to the small footpath as he whispered to Jay. He hoped it was the only obstacle they would face. Then he heard it: loud screeches echoed off the walls high above them.

"What's that?" Charley asked. He ducked and looked up.

Ben snapped at Charley to be quiet as he pointed one finger at the ceiling. Even in the chilled air, sweat was beading across his forehead. The icicles were crawling with bats. Small wings fluttered outward, showing a white tuft of hair on their bellies. Razor-sharp fangs flashed into view. The only bat-free area was an icicle hanging over the crevasse in front of them. Stuck at the tip was a small object imbedded in ice.

William gauged the distance to the icicle over the crevasse. He wasn't sure how long Jay's arm was, but if he were to guess, he'd say it was more than a couple of feet out of his grasp.

"Is that it?" William whispered, but he was immediately hushed by Ben, who held up his hands and frantically waved at him to be quiet. Startled, William fumbled the glue in his hands. He felt lucky he didn't tumble off the edge. He balanced himself and looked toward the object suspended over the pit in ice and wondered how anyone could get it. Hypothetically, he thought about rock climbing equipment being used to suspend oneself from the ceiling. It might have worked, but he surely wasn't going to do it. Likewise, he was sure that his father hadn't taught him any skills to accomplish something like that.

Ben looked infuriated and pointed firmly to the ceiling. When his finger was done shaking in anger, he turned and quietly talked with Jay again.

William was irritated at Ben's behavior. He put the heavy bucket down. His arms were exhausted from straining to hold it. He put his hand over his pocket, feeling the paralytic pellets that Mr. Wyatt had given him. He halfway wondered if this was the right time to stop Ben in his tracks. He had enough pellets to stop Jay and Ben, but what about Mr. Millner? He moved his hand from his pocket, convinced that now wasn't the right time. Besides, any false step now might bring a parade of bats swooping down. He didn't have enough pellets for them too. He felt a poke from Charley and gently turned.

Charley dug through his pocket and whispered, "Romeo up a balcony. I guess Mr. Wyatt was right: you never know when you might need a ladder." He removed Mr. Wyatt's Pocket Ladder. If it could reach up a three-story balcony, it could be used to lean against the icicle from where they were standing.

William held the metal ladder in his hand. It coiled like a ball of wire. "How does it work?" He gauged the distance to the icicle again, wondering if the wire could really make it. He twisted it firmly in his hands. Regardless of how he turned or pulled, it remained a loop of wire.

"I think you push that thing," Charley replied, pointing at a wire poking out. "Let me see it. If I can duct tape a van engine, I can get this ladder to work." He took the Pocket Ladder from William. Like he was pulling the string on a firework, he tugged. Without warning, the coil quickly burst to life, uncoiling end over end with rungs coming outward at lightning pace. Spinning outward, one of the rungs caught Charley by his shirt. He jerked forward and went flying, scraping across the ground toward the edge of the crevasse. When the last coil had unwound, the ladder came crashing down. It landed with one end near William's feet and the other on the far side of the crevasse. Its rungs were like a bridge that went directly under the icicle.

Charley grasped at the ladder, which came unhitched from his clothing. The momentum from the ladder uncoiling had pushed him over the ledge and partway down the slippery slope leading to the edge of blackness. He reached to grab a rung with no luck. The ladder was out of reach, leaving Charley precariously clutching for dear life on a steep incline.

"Charley!" William yelled.

The room erupted in screeching from above. Wings opened and the ceiling became a blanket of white tufts of fur with protruding teeth.

William looked on helplessly. All he had was a bucket of glue. "Charley, hold on," he yelled.

Charley flailed with his hands, trying to grab on. His palms scraped against the ice. His fingernails carved grooves trying to slow himself down, but it was in vain. He slipped downward until he vanished over the edge.

Stunned, William stared in disbelief. *This can't be the end. It can't!*

"Quick, now is our chance!" Ben yelled. He climbed aboard Jay's foot, determined to get the item while the bats were distracted.

"But Charley," William yelled. "We must save Charley!" Tears welled in his eyes.

"There's no time," Ben said intently. "He is gone."

As their eyes met, William could see the evil in Ben. Ben wasn't going to help Charley. All he cared about was the thinking cap. Ben would use William just as he'd used his father, Mr. Millner, and Vanessa. Today, it was Charley. Ben wasn't going to help. This was a wild goose chase to get what Ben wanted.

"If you want to open the puzzle organ, this is your chance," Ben said. His brow was drawn intently as he reached one hand toward William. "Don't waste your chances like your father did."

"I . . . I . . . can't," William said. He could never forgive himself if he took Ben's hand. Leaving Ben's hand hanging, he charged toward the edge of the crevasse. From the corner of his eye, he could see Ben and Jay running along the rungs of the ladder toward the icicle.

At the edge, he looked over, preparing for the worst. His heart lifted as he saw Charley hanging on for dear life. Charley had managed to grab a protruding icicle. "Hang on!" William yelled in desperation.

"I don't think this is exactly how Romeo did it," Charley called back. "Remind me to give that ladder a one-star review."

William raced for the bucket of glue. He stumbled forward, carrying it between his legs, and threw it down the slope moments before Charley lost his grip.

The blob of glue came crashing down on top of Charley, who became tangled in a gooey mess. It didn't matter if he wasn't holding on anymore; he wasn't going anywhere.

"Are you all right?" William yelled, but his voice was drowned out in the screeching from above. Like kamikazes, the bats came streaking through the air at Charley. They landed on him left and right, becoming tangled in the glue too.

Charley rolled and turned, but he was stuck like a fly on paper. Razor-sharp teeth surrounded him on every side.

William looked upward as another wave of bats was coming. There wasn't enough glue in the world to stop that many bats. He reached into his pocket, desperately looking for something. Anything. Panicked, he knew Charley was moments from his doom. He could see the black cloud of wings plunging upon him. To his surprise, he pulled the three balls of paralyzing powder from his pocket that Mr. Wyatt had given him. He didn't have time to think. His arm flung everything he had at the bats.

The white powder erupted and engulfed Charley as the bats descended upon him. The horde dropped from the white dust as hard as stone. Charley was like a statue in the midst of them, a stunned look on his face.

Running over the ladder, coming back from the icicle over the crevasse, Jay suddenly leaned forward and grabbed William on his way out of the icy cave. A fresh batch of polar bats was screeching down upon him. His long arm reached down to grab Charley too. The glue was no match for Jay. With Charley—a paralyzed glue mess—in one hand, Ben riding his shoulders, and William aboard one foot, he bolted for the door.

Chapter 22

THE OFFICE

The clock on the wall ticked as Ben sat quietly at his desk in a green chair. His lively green suit match it perfectly making it act like camouflage. With a desk in front of him, most of him was hidden from sight anyway. He held a magnifying glass over the desk examining the last key to the puzzle organ. Ben's lips reflected through the lens, making them look grossly out of pro-portion.

Across the desk, William sat in an armchair next to Charley. Charley's skin was coarse and red, having had glue picked from it the last few hours.

William thought Ben's office was somewhat eclectic. Stacks of papers scattered about the room rose from the floor to the ceiling. There wasn't a single edge of paper out of place. Each stack was spaced at just the right interval to allow for walking paths. There were rows of bookshelves lined with volumes of all sizes, from extraordinarily large to no bigger than a penny. Some were old, others new, but all of them had a healthy pile of dust.

Jay had made it into the room too, by some miracle. It had been an acrobatic act, twisting to avoid the tall stacks of paper. His arms bent and his knees buckled around the paper towers, but he hadn't knocked a single sheet out of place. When all was said and done, he came to rest sitting with a paper stack between his legs.

Ben was intently holding the third key to the puzzle organ under the magnifying glass. Unlike the metronome and the tuner sitting on the desk next to him, this was nothing more than a piece of paper. However, something about the way he muttered under his breath and turned the paper over in his hands made it seem like he was out of his element. He hadn't said more than two words about the key since leaving the ice cave.

Ben held the piece of paper. His head didn't move as his glance bounced from William and back to the paper to continue investigating. "No," he said with a half-cocked smile that reeked of frustration. "I just need a moment."

"Didn't you open that organ already?" Charley asked. He was leaning comfortably back in his chair, blowing air through his fingertips held over his mouth. He was bored.

Ben breathed a sigh from his nostrils with his eyes closed. His tone turned sharp with irritation. "Yes, I have opened it before." It came across as a sore point.

"So, what's the problem?" Charley asked. The air passing through his fingers whistled.

Ben cleared his throat and cocked his head like Charley had just insulted him. "Just because I've done it once, doesn't mean I can do it again."

"You mean it's not like riding a bike?" Charley asked. He wiggled his fingers over his mouth, feeling the air pass through. "Because, I don't think I could ever forget how to ride a bike. A unicycle perhaps, but it only has one wheel. You know what I mean?" He sat up in his chair in anticipation of an answer. When no answer came, he continued to talk. "I mean, there are other things. Not just a unicycle. I bet walking on a tightrope is something you could easily forget too. Is it like a tightrope?"

Ben was shaking his head. When Charley finally stopped talking nonsense, he spoke. "No, it's nothing like that." Another sigh came from his lips. "If you must know, the puzzle organ is a complex lock."

"Like a tightrope," Charley whispered while nodding his head and squinting his eyes like he understood.

Ben's fingers turned a blanched white around the paper. "Again, no." His voice was calm with flagrant annoyance. He put the paper down on the desk in front of him and pushed the magnifying glass out of the way. "Whoever opens the puzzle organ has the ability to change the combination, in a sense." He cleared his throat and stared at William almost as though he blamed him. "The last person to do so was William's father." His eyes stayed locked on William for some time until they unforgivingly looked away.

William couldn't see why Ben would have blamed him. He scrunched back into his chair and tried to ignore Ben's accusation.

Charley nodded and squinted his eyes again. "Like a unicycle," he whispered.

"NO, you imbecile," Ben nearly burst aloud. He leaned forward over the piece of paper until he regained his composure. Moments passed, but he didn't say another word for some time. It was as if speaking to Charley was pointless to Ben. Eventually, the cross expression faded from his forehead, and he went about his intense study of the paper again.

William wanted answers too, but he didn't want to face Ben's fiery gaze again. For all the unanswered questions that he had, he could have interrogated Ben for hours. At least, that was how he felt. Yet, despite his longing to get answers, there was one thing that bothered him more than anything right now. It was a question that seemed to sit under his skin. No matter how hard he tried to suppress it, it floated to the top again, bringing not only anger but frustration. How could Ben leave Charley behind? William sat on the question, trying to bury the anger so deep that it would hide under the seat that he was resting on. For a moment he thought he had suppressed it—until it came springing back like a song lyric that he couldn't forget. It infuriated him. He tried to think of a reasonable explanation for what Ben had done, but there just wasn't one. He finally concluded that Vanessa had been right. The betrayal had already begun. If William hadn't helped Charley, he might have lost him forever. No matter how many times he diverted his thoughts, they ended back at the same spot. What happens if Ben does the same to me? He feared the worst. He might even end up being locked in a coffin.

Charley leaned forward in his chair, staring at the paper in Ben's hands. "It's another musical instrument thing, isn't it?" He whistled a tune into the air. "If it helps, I have some sweet musical skills." He raised his hands to play his air-guitar and thumbed his imaginary strings while rolling heavy metal tunes off his tongue. "I can even do bass," he said, lowering his voice an octave. Headbanging, Charley stood and wailed his pretend instrument. "Any requests?" he asked as his foot twirled in the air. Coming down, his shoe caught the edge of a paper stack, nearly knocking it over.

"Enough!" Ben shouted; his voice staggeringly loud. He stood from his chair. "I have had enough of this."

Charley froze in place. His fingers plucked their last string and his mouth hummed its final tune as it died out over four beats. "Would you prefer country?"

"Sit down!" Ben commanded.

Charley slowly returned to his seat with a surprised look on his face. "No worries. Metal isn't for everyone. In fact, I knew this girl that liked wind instruments. I tried playing an air-kazoo, but there was way too much spit that comes out when you vibrate your lips. That ended our relationship really quick."

Ben was fuming. His face was purple and knotted in anger.

Charley put his fingers over his mouth and pretended to zip his lips closed. It lasted for a moment. "You know, you look a lot like Mrs. Burbank when you do that," he muttered.

Ben's temper finally boiled over. He slammed the paper on the desk and stood up. "Of course I do, you imbecile! And if I hadn't sent her to watch over William, he would be nothing more than a lifeless corpse like his father by now! But for the life of me, I can't figure out why William is so important. Why am I even helping? I can't even be sure William won't abandon me like his father did all those years ago. Time is running out if we are going to open the puzzle organ, and all I have is a bunch of blithering idiots to help me." Sweat was running down Ben's face. Suddenly he seemed to realize how angry he had become and patted himself on the chest. "I'm sorry," he civilly apologized.

William dropped his jaw in amazement. "It was you? You sent Mrs. Burbank?" It was more than shock. He was horrified.

Ben shook his head back and forth but didn't say a word.

William knew what he needed to do. "Why did you lock my father up?" he calmly asked.

Jay poked his head out from around a stack of papers to stare at the commotion.

Ben sat down in his chair and rested his arms on the sides. "It's not like that, William. I had no choice." He covered his face with his palm.

Chills ran up and down William's spine. "My father used to say that choice was all that we have." He leaned forward in his chair. "It was your choice to lock him in that coffin." He bent his arms, preparing. "But, if you had no choice, then you'll understand that I don't have one either." He jumped from his chair and snatched the three keys to the puzzle organ. Springing backward, he locked eyes with Ben as he pushed stacks of paper to the ground. They tumbled into one another like dominos, casting the room into utter chaos. Papers went crashing to the floor in every direction, making a virtual storm of white office stationery. William grabbed Charley by the arm and raced for the door.

Ben screamed from under a pile of documents. "Don't do this. You don't know what you're doing!" His tiny arms flailed, trying to uncover himself from the avalanche.

Jay rose out of a pile of papers that drifted off his shoulders like snow falling. At full height, he was hunched horribly against the ceiling and couldn't move fast in such an awkwardly scrunched position.

William didn't listen. He was convinced that everything behind him was a pack of lies. There was only one place he could think to go. He looked at the Never-Lost Watch around his wrist and said, "Take me to Mr. Wyatt's shop." Running through the halls, he repeated a quote from his father: "'How easy it is to make people believe a lie, and [how] hard it is to undo that work again!' Mark Twain."

Chapter 23

FUGITIVES ON THE RUN

Off in the distance, down the road, they could see it: Mr. Wyatt's store. There had been no sign of Jay or Ben. William didn't think they could outrun Jay even at their best. He figured Ben must still be figuring out where they'd gone. Out of fear, he and Charley hadn't stopped once.

Not more than a hundred yards from Mr. Wyatt's store, William ran into a crowd walking in orderly lines. William ran through them, dodging dresses and cutting between fine suits. He knew he would be safe in Mr. Wyatt's shop.

One hundred yards became fifty and fifty yards became twenty-five. A couple more steps was all he needed.

William put one foot on the stairs. We made it! His heart swelled with pride thinking that he had outsmarted Ben—until a hand caught him on the shoulder. He went pale.

"William? What are you doing here?" Vanessa said. She was breathing heavily.

"Yes, yes, what's the hurry?" Mr. Millner said, panting next to her.

William let out a sigh of relief. "The pieces to the puzzle organ. . . I had to run."

Charley looked at Vanessa. "It's no big deal. No need to congratulate us or anything," he said with an elevated tone, his chest puffed out proudly. "Looks like you have been running too," he said, noticing Vanessa panting.

"Ah, yeah, the crowds," Vanessa explained. "Can you believe them? I saw you running and came over as quick as I could." Her voice quivered.

"You saw us running?" William asked. In a crowd like this it would be easier to spot a needle in a haystack.

"Yes, got here fast, fast, fast," Mr. Millner added. He shook his head back and forth like he had a tremor.

Something didn't feel right. William knew that Mr. Millner was always off, but Venessa wasn't herself. "Let's get inside quick," he said, rising to the next stair.

Vanessa pulled at William's arm and stood in front of him. "I have a better idea."

"Hehehehe," Mr. Millner snickered gleefully. He eagerly grabbed the keys to the puzzle organ from William's hands. "Now we can do it! Open the puzzle organ. Yes, yes, yes."

Startled, William reached for the keys to get them back, but Vanessa stopped him. "Don't worry, Mr. Millner can keep them safe."

"Ben can't be far behind. He'll be looking for us," William warned.

"This way," Mr. Millner replied. "Me's knows the way,"

"You're right," Vanessa replied. She looked out over the crowd. "We need to get somewhere safe."

"Back to your place?" Charley asked, winking one eye.

"Let's go." She dragged William firmly by the shoulder.

Wherever they were going, William didn't recognize it. The crowd thinned and the streets became dark, overshadowed by high-rising buildings. The brick was covered in soot, and so were the people that were loitering around them. More than once, a cup begging for money was shoved into his chest. It was safe to say they were off the beaten path.

"A safe place," Mr. Millner vaguely repeated. He gripped the pieces to the puzzle organ like he was cradling a baby. The smile across his face was sheer joy. He skipped with delight. "Now we open it. I will be all better. It will all go away."

William had an unsteady feeling that was growing with each step. He looked back over his shoulder. He couldn't turn back. What if Ben or Jay was close on their heels?

At the edge of town, they found a canal that ran underground. They had to pull blackened roots from the opening to enter. Inside, road signs lined the walls, pointing in all directions. Mr. Millner turned whimsically, sputtering nonsensical sounds at every one. The air grew thicker and the light faded. William tripped along rocks in the dark. He could no longer see Vanessa, a few yards in front of him.

It didn't make any sense. *Why would we run away from Mr. Wyatt?* "Where are we going?" William asked. No reply came. Mr. Millner's joyful chuckling echoed off the walls as he cackled with delight.

Charley grabbed William by the shoulder. "I don't know about you," he whispered, "but my antenna is sending me warning signals that travel farther than AM radio."

William agreed. He stared at Mr. Millner's silhouette in the dark. There was no motion, no sound. He could have passed as a shadow in the night.

"Vanessa," William cried. *Where did she go?*

"Darling?" Charley called out. It was answered by silence.

William was in disbelief. *What is going on?* "Mr. Millner," he called again.

"It's a safe place," Mr. Millner's voice said, distant and soft. "Shhh, the coffins don't like to be woken."

William saw the hazy outline of coffins against the wall. He backed away, looking to turn around, when he stumbled across two coffins on the ground with their lids open.

"Coffins! I hate coffins," Charley stated. He shivered at the sight.

A light flickered on, drawing William's eyes. Sitting below the light was a short man in a green suit.

William staggered backward in terror. His legs wanted to escape, but they were frozen with fear. He tugged at them to make them work, but his horror cemented him in place. Before his legs moved, a sack fell over his head. He felt Jay lift him into the air. He could hear muffled kicking and screaming from Charley. His mouth opened to scream, but a loud thump came across his head. Dizzy, he swayed from side to side until his eyes closed.

Chapter 24

LOCKED IN A BOX

William had a throbbing headache as his eyes opened. He was lying on his back with a lump on his skull. Confused, all he could see was a light hanging from the ceiling overhead. He reached to rub his aching bump, but his arms wouldn't move. He tried his legs, but he couldn't move them much either. *What is going on?* He felt a panic build as he looked down and saw a silky lining around him and a lid restricting his movement; he was trapped in a coffin. His thoughts raced as he thought back to the moments before he'd passed out, but it was hazy. *Did Jay hit me?* "Psst, psst," came a noise next to him. He lifted his head to catch a glimpse of Charley lying inside a coffin next to him.

"I hate coffins!" Charley shouted in an irritated voice. "What happened?"

William strained his thoughts. What he could barely remember was a misrepresented glob of memories, but one thing was for sure: Mr. Millner had led them right back to Ben. "Did Mr. Millner betray us? We never should have trusted him," he said under his breath. He had so many questions.

"Where is Vanessa?" Charley asked, looking around the room.

"I'm not sure," William replied. There was no sign of her that he could tell, but being trapped in a coffin, he couldn't see much.

Charley struggled from side to side. It caused his coffin to rattle on the floor, but it didn't bring him any closer to being free. "What should we do now?" he asked, panting.

"There's not much you can do," Ben interjected. His face appeared over the edge of the coffin, standing directly over William. His eyes narrowed as he looked up and down the length of him. "I didn't want it to be like this. It didn't have to be like this." He shook his head.

"Is that what you told my father?!" William shouted back.

Ben rolled his eyes. "I cared for your father more than you know. He was an unfortunate casualty. I had no choice, just like you are giving me no choice now."

"I'll give you a choice. Let us go or—" Charley paused to think. "Or, I will never talk to you again."

Ben smiled back at Charley's laughable threat. "I think I can live with that," he snickered.

"Charley rocked his shoulders from side to side trying to escape. It rattled his coffin against the ground again.

Ben looked down on William again with a serious expression on his face. "The minute you spoke with Vanessa—a burglar, mind you— you turned down the wrong path. For what it's worth, I never lied to you. I admit, there are details about your father that I excluded. I am guilty of omitting truth, but not distorting it. There is a big difference."

William couldn't swallow what Ben was saying. The words felt like poison in his ears. It didn't matter how Ben tried to twist his words; it all amounted to one thing: lying. "Did you forget to tell me about Mrs. Burbank too? How can I trust you?"

"If it weren't for Mrs. Burbank, you would have found yourself much worse off than being trapped in a coffin. I know it's hard to accept, but I locked your father up for his own good," Ben said casually flipping his hand in the air. "It's for your own good that I locked you in this coffin too. Everything was for your own good." His voice sounded like a parent disciplining their child and at the same time unusually convincing. "There are forces at work you couldn't possibly comprehend."

William turned his head and snorted defiantly. There was nothing that Ben could say that would turn the tide on the situation. He was never going to help him open the puzzle organ.

Ben hung his head. "There's no way out of this one, I can see." He took a long look at William. "I had to lock up your father. I promised him I would," he said, still trying to engage William, but his words fell on deaf ears. "It was a long time ago when we opened the puzzle organ. Everything might have worked out, but your father left. He left me alone to defend it, even though he knew it needed to be done. I was bitter that he abandoned me and bitter about . . . you. You were all he cared about in this world. He knew you couldn't be raised here. Not in this place. Not now, not then. He wanted something different for you, and responsibility got in his way. So, it became my duty. I had to stop the thinking cap from falling into the wrong hands even if it meant stopping your father." Ben paused and sighed. "Please! Don't make me lock you away too."

"My father never would have betrayed you!" William forcefully replied. "Why would he take me away and not tell me anything? Why would he abandon you?" A tear rolled off his cheek as words came out through a tightened esophagus filled with emotion. He clenched down, trying to control his reactions.

Ben sighed. "Your father knew too much. They manipulated him just like they are manipulating you. I couldn't allow that to happen then, nor can I allow it to happen now!" He held one fist in the air and squeezed tightly.

"Look, I can see there are some issues here," Charley said. "If I could just get my van and fix it up, we could get out of everyone's hair. Wouldn't want to wear out our welcome."

William was beyond hearing reason. He didn't want to hear Ben any longer. He couldn't consider a shred of it true, not after what Ben had done. "Open the puzzle organ by yourself!"

Ben sighed in disappointment. Pushing off the edge of the coffin, he disappeared. When he reappeared, his eyebrows were drawn downward angrily, and his forehead was furrowed. He sniveled, "You are a fool. You're just as stubborn as your father. I have a duty, and I intend to keep it. If I must lock you away, so be it." Over the edge of the coffin, Ben held a cup full of black, boiling liquid. It turned and hissed as bubbles rose from it. "Do you recognize this?" he asked.

William's thoughts turned back to the town. He had seen that black liquid before. Everyone had been terrified of it when he threw it into a crowd. After seeing what horrible things had happened to the fools who drank it, he had no intention of ever touching the stuff. It was a curse in liquid form. He shriveled at the thought of the cup tipping into his coffin.

Ben smiled at the disturbed look on William's face. "It won't kill you. It is only used to maim…unless you use too much. You leave me little choice. Help me or else."

"Go ahead. I can take it," William said, quivering.

"Oh no, this one's not for you," Ben said, glancing at Charley's coffin. "I made sure this batch would take all his hair off."

Charley shrieked. "My hair! Come on now. I'll be an attractive bald guy, but still. It'll ruin my Elvis impersonation."

"Leave him alone. He has nothing to do with this," William argued.

Ben shook his head. "You don't understand, do you? He has everything to do with it. Help me or your friends will suffer. We'll start with Charley and then move on. I'm sure Mr. Wyatt and Miss Lockit wouldn't mind a visit too. When all is said and done, we will start working on your sleeping father."

William choked at the thought. What choice do I have? It wasn't his own safety he was playing with anymore, and he couldn't ask everyone to suffer for him. He felt like a fish on a hook. The barb was in too deep to get out. He could only hope to break the line and wiggle back into the water. Every bit of him wanted to swim away, but he couldn't. Reluctantly, he nodded.

Ben smiled, "Splendid! I suggest you and I head to the puzzle organ." Walking around the room, he placed the black cup on the edge of Charley's coffin to free his hands. Pulling the key from around his neck, he put it in William's coffin.

Chapter 25

CHARLEY AND JAY

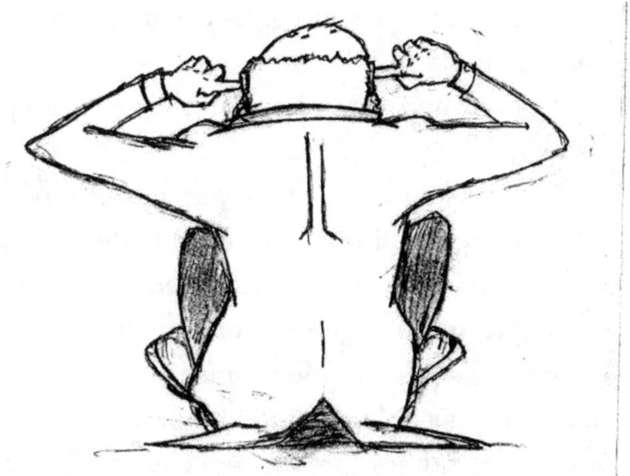

Ben dragged William away and the room went silent. The bubbling of the black fluid resting on the side of Charley's coffin was all that could be heard. It popped and fizzed into the air, on the brink of boiling over the rim of the cup.

"You know, Ben is a real bully," Charley said, finally breaking the stillness. "Does he really have to lock people in coffins? It's barbaric!"

Jay didn't seem amused. He grumbled under his breath and ignored Charley. He had come into the room the minute Ben left with William.

"I know why you work for Ben: the perks. I had a job like that once. It was at a gas station, and we got to eat all the leftover hot dogs and churros at the end of my shift." Charley grinned and licked his lips. "Man, do I miss that job."

Jay turned his back on Charley and hung his head.

"I bet you could get a better job. Did you ever consider pro wrestling? You would be amazing. They could call you Jay the Giant." Charley curled his lower lip and nodded in satisfaction. "That has a sweet ring to it. Tell you what, you let me out, and I'll help you with your pro wrestling career. We can make you a great costume too, because I know what good spandex looks like."

Jay sat on the ground, completely ignoring Charley's ramblings, and the room fell eerily quiet again.

"Say, are these real coffins?" Charley asked. "I hope they've never been used" He shuddered. "I don't like dead bodies. No, sir."

Jay's forehead wrinkled downward, filled with irritated grooves. He raised his fingers and plugged off his ears. His head turned away from Charley trying his best to ignore him.

"You know, it's quiet in here. No radio or anything? Not to worry, bro; I have some sweet tunes that can serenade us if you would like." Charley pursed his lips and whistled. A half-cocked melody of a well-known rock song came out of his lips until he paused to perform the lyrics, "du dunanan danana nenenenene." Before he could finish his musical masterpiece, a hand slipped over his mouth. His lips vibrated and spat against them.

"Shhhh," Vanessa whispered. She gently moved her hand. "Where is William?" Her voice sounded high-strung and concerned.

Charley smiled. "Your skin is so soft. Do you use lotion?" he replied. He shut his eyes and rolled his cheek, pretending to brush up against her hand.

Vanessa shook her head. "We need to find William right now!" she urged. The tension in her voice raised three notches as she glanced at Jay. If Charley didn't say something useful, she might strangle him.

"As you can see, he is not here, but I am having a heck of a time with Jay and this blasted coffin," Charley said, wiggling from side to side. "Ben said something about going to open the puzzle organ."

Vanessa's face flushed white and her eyes dilated like they'd had belladonna poured in them. A bead of nervous sweat appeared on her forehead. "I need to get to him. I have to get the–er, help William," she stuttered.

"What about me?" Charley asked, shifting again.

Vanessa shrugged her shoulders. "I'm sorry, but there's no time. You're smart; figure it—" She paused mid-sentence. "Actually, no offense, you're not that smart."

"None taken. Besides, I know you're clever, and opposites attract," Charley said, winking.

Vanessa shook her head again. It was obvious that Charley only had one thing on his mind. She turned to leave.

"Wait, don't just leave me here." Charley violently shook the coffin, rocking from side to side.

Vanessa turned with one finger over her mouth, trying to shush Charley. Instead, her already pale face blanched white. She suddenly pounced forward headed for the coffin with one arm stretched outward—toward the glass of black liquid that Charley had knocked from the rim of his coffin. It was falling downward, about to shatter on the ground. Sprawling forward on her belly, her hand cradled the cup the instant before it shattered. Bubbles frothed off the surface, making a fizzing noise. She slowly stood up. For the moment, it appeared they had missed detection from Jay.

"Did you catch it?" Charley burst aloud.

Jay pulled his fingers from his ears, turned, and got to his feet. If his face had been irritated before, now it was lit with a fiery furnace. His tolerance had been worn thin, to the point of breaking, and the sight of Vanessa caused him to holler loud enough to blow his mustache off. Instantly, his hand swiped downward, ready to strike.

Still holding the cup, Vanessa leaped from the ground, turned upside down, and landed on her feet, narrowly avoiding the hand pummeling toward her.

Jay swiped again, quicker than the first. It was like he was swatting a fly. His hand made a swooshing noise through the air.

Vanessa pushed off the coffin with one leg and spun in the air. She landed like a cat, just beyond the reach of Jay's hand. Her hand was grasping hard around the black liquid.

Jay clenched his teeth and raised his arms, determined. He brought his hands together to crush her between them.

Vanessa once again jumped into the air in a cartwheel, letting Jay's hands sail beneath her. His fingernails brushed against her hair. The cup twirled in her hands while she let one leg stretch outward toward Jay's face. A loud crack sounded as Vanessa's heel landed hard across Jay's jaw.

Spit flew from Jay's lips, and his eyes rolled to the back of his head. Dazed, his body went lifeless, and he tumbled to the floor. Instinctively his arms stretched forward.

Vanessa looked at the cup. She nodded, satisfied; she hadn't spilled a drop.

As Vanessa looked at the cup triumphantly, Jay lumbered forward, and his finger clipped the cup out of her hand. Vanessa jerked away, but it was too late. The cup shattered and the dark liquid spattered across the room like rain.

As it came downward, Charley held his lips, trying to keep it out of his mouth. He struggled from side to side as the black liquid ran down his arms and legs. It was no use. It pooled across his skin, burning.

Vanessa yelled angrily at the calamity. She rubbed her hands against her black shirt, squeegeeing droplets of black that were soaking into the leather.

"What? I've had Grandma's caliente salsa. This isn't as bad as that," Charley said, holding his breath. His face winced in a bright shade of red.

Vanessa shook her head, jumping up and down. "You don't understand." She grimaced in pain. "If only we had some of Mr. Spirin's Miracle Medicine."

Charley's eyes widened. "I need a kiss!" he declared.

"Are you insane? This is hardly the time," Vanessa gruffly replied, rolling her eyes in disgust.

Jay, still dazed, lifted his head and mumbled as he tried to get to his hands and knees.

"You don't understand. Kiss me right now!" Charley demanded. A large, painful boil burst onto his cheek, causing him to flinch in pain as he pursed his lips, ready to kiss.

"Not in this lifetime," Vanessa replied. A blister popped up on her lips.

Jay managed to keep himself propped upward. It would be moments before he was on his feet.

Another boil, red and hot, burst onto Charley's forehead. It was covering his eye, making it hard for him to see outward. He turned his head to the side trying to see past it. "I have Mr. Wyatt's Disguise Dentures," he declared.

Vanessa, bouncing on one foot to avoid a painful blister on the bottom of the other, stopped jumping and looked down at Charley in his coffin. There was no time to argue. She bent down and pecked Charley on the lips.

A click sounded as a tooth fell from Charley's Disguise Dentures, and a pill rolled onto his tongue. His neck jolted as he swallowed the tooth and tablet together. He made a gulping noise as the medication tracked its way down his esophagus. Once it was down the hatch, he looked at Vanessa, whose face was twisted in disgust.

"Don't worry, I swallowed a quarter once. Popped it right out in a day or two. I'll get the tooth later," Charley said with a satisfied grin.

Another blister appeared on Vanessa's face. "Is that all you have?"

Her eye swelled to the tip of her nose.

"Kiss me again and find out," Charley replied, as giddy as a clam.

"Kiss me, you fool," Vanessa said. Pushing the boil out of the way so she could get to his lips, she leaned forward and kissed Charley on the mouth again. Another tooth came loose, and she snatched the pill that rolled out.

"I love these dentures," Charley said, smiling. Air rushed through gaps in his front teeth, giving him a lisp.

Suddenly, the door opened. In came Mr. Wyatt and Miss Lockit. They stopped dead in their tracks, seeing Vanessa holding her lips close to Charley's.

"Are we interrupting?" asked Miss Lockit.

"Um, no . . ." Vanessa said. She scooted away, embarrassed. One gulp later, the capsule was down her throat.

Mr. Wyatt had a big grin as he looked at the empty slots in Charley's dentures. "'Atta boy!"

Charley proudly nodded. He squinted his eyes with excitement to accentuate how much he loved the dentures.

All eyes turned to Jay, who rose to his feet one foot at a time.

Miss Lockit sat on the ground and crossed her legs in a meditation pose. "I do not condone violence," she said, swaying back and forth, chiming her keys together.

Mr. Wyatt reached into his pocket and took out a coil of wire. With one shake, a ladder came bursting out to full length, knocking Jay square in the jaw.

Stunned, Jay turned around and fell lifelessly to the ground. A cloud of dust rolled upward around him when he landed. It was a knockout.

Mr. Wyatt sheepishly shrugged his shoulders. He looked down at his ladder. "I love this thing," he remarked. "And, if you didn't notice, it is also a great self-defense tool." He started into one of his sales pitches. "There I was, stark naked, two broken ankles with a pack of dingo's. . ."

Miss Lockit broke her medication, "Thank you. I think we can do without another story at the moment."

Chapter 26

SOLVING THE PUZZLE

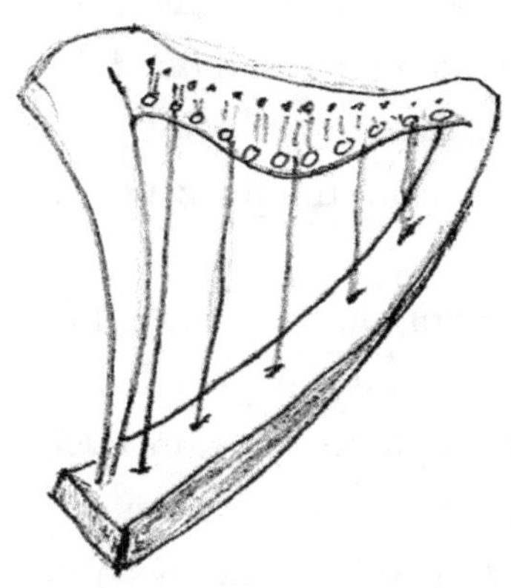

William sat in front of the puzzle organ. There were a dizzying number of handles in front of him. Ben stood overbearingly over his shoulder. He expected results, and William had no idea how to produce them.

"I don't know what I'm doing," William protested. It wasn't a lie. There was no trick his father had left for him.

Ben leaned closer. "You know exactly what to do. You just need a little help," he said with utter confidence. "May I remind you of one of your father's quotes he gave me? 'A man is but the product of his thoughts. What he thinks, he becomes.' Mahatma Gandhi."

William knew the quote, but it didn't matter that much. Just thinking about opening the puzzle organ wasn't going to open it for him. He was going to have to pull the handles, and that made him nervous. The brief memories he had of the puzzle organ were terrifying. It was always associated with his life flashing before his eyes.

Ben started to remove the items for the puzzle organ from his pocket. The first one out was the tuner. Its strings were like a harp, and Ben played them as such. His fingers stroked across the small cords, and a harmonious sound reverberated off the tiny instrument. While it was still humming its tune, he grabbed a handle on the puzzle organ.

William ducked, expecting a boom to knock him through the air, but it never came. Instead, the puzzle organ tooted a musical note in return.

Pulling and twisting on the handle, Ben forced the organ to hum up and down in pitch until it matched the tuner. When the noise was calibrated to the perfect tone, he grinned with delight. "You'll never be able to open the puzzle organ if it's out of tune," he stated.

William was just glad he hadn't been thrown across the floor.

Ben rested the tuner atop the puzzle organ and removed the metronome from his pocket. His fingers twisted a knob on it like winding a toy car.

A pendulum rocked back and forth, and William could hear a quiet tick-tock.

Ben smiled as he placed the metronome next to the tuner atop the puzzle organ.

William eyed the pendulum, swinging back and forth. Its ticking blended a harmonious melody with the tuner, serenading the room with a peculiar, ominous sound of beauty. He shrugged, not appreciating its full significance, hoping Ben didn't pull any more handles.

"Like any musical instrument, you must play the handles in the correct timing," Ben said. He pointed to the pendulum rocking back and forth. "One, two, three. One, two three. One, two, three." He tapped his foot against the ground and spun his finger in the air in time with the ticking. "The timing changes periodically, and this little device tells us which one to use."

It was more like a musical instrument than William had thought. This entire time, he hadn't seen the puzzle organ for much more than a destructive device, yet they were having a conversation about tones and timing. He suddenly wished he had paid more attention in piano lessons.

Ben took the third item from his pocket, which was nothing but a small piece of paper. He spread it open with his hands and rested it against the puzzle organ in front of William's eyes.

William glanced at the paper. He half expected to see a sheet of music that he wouldn't be able to play. After all, not only could he not hum a note if he tried; he couldn't read bar music at all. Fortunately, it was nothing of the sort. Before his eyes was a list of quotes numbered from one to ten. They weren't just any quotes, either. These had been on his father's wall of inspiration.

"The last clue to the puzzle organ is somewhat of a mystery. Your father always had a way of keeping secrets from me," Ben said gruffly, his voice full of resentment. "We always knew that someday, we might have to get the thinking cap again. It's too powerful of an instrument to be locked away forever. At least, your father had the foresight to recognize that, but he didn't think it was necessary to keep me apprised of the fact that he recoded the last piece to the puzzle organ. We should have a guide, or something, on which handles to pull." He pointed at the piece of paper; his finger shaking with bitterness. Then he dropped his finger down at his side and looked at William.

With William sitting and Ben standing, they were about eye level with one another. William squirmed uncomfortably in his seat, trying to avoid direct eye contact.

Ben pursed his lips and put his hand against his chin like he was thinking. "It's clear that your father didn't leave us directionless. No, that's not like your father," Ben said, shaking his head. "But using you?

It's clever, really, if you think about it. Give the last clue to someone who didn't even know what to use it for. It separates the key from the lock, in a sense." He looked down at William, satisfied that he had everything that he needed. "And, who would have known that you were the last key?"

William didn't want to answer. He let the question float into silence. He diverted his eyes again, away from Ben, trying to pretend that he wasn't there, and his gaze found its way to the piece of paper. They were just words. He quietly began reading them to himself, and he knew every quote by heart. It excited him to see something that he understood rather than a whimsical item that tried to tap into his lacking musical talent. It just didn't make sense yet. How do quotes have anything to do with music? He needed time to think about it, but opening the organ under duress from Ben was not what he wanted to do today. "I have no idea," he said, casually turning his head.

"You know, your father was no good at lying either, so I'll ask again. What does it mean?" His tone was more serious. His face showed that he wasn't in the mood for games.

"Maybe you should ask him," William replied flippantly.

Ben didn't look pleased. He gritted his teeth. "One day, you will understand that I am doing this for your own good. Now, don't make this harder than it has to be."

William knew a threat when he heard one. Ben's tone said as much. He looked at the paper again. Why are the quotes numbered? He went up and down the list and turned his thoughts to his father's wall. He closed his eyes and imagined picking each quote. They were scattered in different directions, but never more than an arm's reach away. He turned the quotes over in his mind's eye. When he picked the last quote, he opened his eyes to look at the puzzle organ again.

A veil dropped. What had looked like utter chaos before suddenly had shape and meaning. It was like abstract art taking structure and form. The exact pattern of his father's wall of inspiration lay before him. Instead of quotes, it was the handles of the puzzle organ. He was astounded. He hadn't seen it before. *How could I have missed it?* It had been there the whole time. He could easily pick out handles corresponding to quotes. From one to ten, he could see them all. He could open the puzzle organ.

Ben tapped his foot on the ground impatiently. "Why don't you make it easier on both of us and just get on with it?"

What am I supposed to do? William's eyes darted between the handles that would open the puzzle organ. What choice do I have? He was backed into a corner.

Closing his eyes, William touched the first handle. He imagined himself in his father's office. He didn't need to look to make sure he had his hand in the right place; there was no doubt. He took a deep breath to steady himself.

In time with the metronome, he pulled a handle. Instead of a destructive boom, the puzzle organ bellowed a dark melody. Adding the second handle let it increase. It sent chills running down his spine that made him shiver. Tumblers rolled into alignment with the sound of a thousand gear boxes. The organ was unlocking.

"One, two, three . . ." He counted aloud the handles, going down the list of quotes. His thoughts raced. Am I making the right choice? "Four, five, six . . ." Somewhere deep down, he understood why his father was gone. This moment oddly provided clarity. He felt like this exact same thing could have happened to his father, being exploited, and now he was a victim for knowing too much just the same. "Eight . . ." Even without all the answers, his father's disappearance made sense. Rather than be manipulated, his father had made a hard choice. He'd left this place even though it meant abandoning Ben and the organ. "Nine . . ." His clammy, nervous palm held the last handle, trembling. My father wouldn't do this, and neither can I! He moved his hand to a different handle and pulled.

The melody abruptly stopped and a vicious boom came bursting forward with a giant gust of wind. It threw William backwards, tipping his seat over. He rolled on the ground like a tumbleweed. The walls shook like an earthquake. Loose floorboards uprooted into the air, dashing across the room. Windows half boarded up didn't have a chance. Splintered shutters ripped from their hinges, bursting outward. Broken glass shattered through cracked windows. The large curtain that hung nearby tore from its clasps, ripped to shreds.

When the noise stopped, the room was still. Ears ringing loudly from the blast, William pushed debris off him. He couldn't hear a thing, like cotton had been stuffed in his ears. Dust filled his lungs as he caught a breath. He surveyed his arms and legs, which luckily only revealed scratches. The room, however, was a chaotic mess.

Ben stood up and brushed himself off. He took off his green suit jacket, which had been torn to bits, and threw it to the ground angrily.

William could see Ben's lips move. It looked like he was yelling at him from afar, but he couldn't hear the words. To his horror, Ben made his way to the puzzle organ.

William tried unsteadily to get to his feet. The puzzle organ had delivered a heavy blow. He tried to keep his balance by focusing on Ben off in the distance as a single point. It was no good. Like he had been spun in a circle, he dizzily stumbled through broken glass and holes in the floorboards. Falling to his knees, he saw Ben start to pull levers. There was no sound that he could hear. He was deaf. Still, he knew what was happening. *Ben remembers the handles I pulled!* He flinched in terror and yelled. The air passed through his mouth, but he could hear nothing. He doubted Ben could hear him either. All he could do was watch.

Ben pulled the final lever, and a cabinet on the puzzle organ flung open. It had been unlocked. Ben reached inside to produce a hat. It was tall with a pointy tip that bent. It was a brilliant bright purple with a piece of yellow ribbon laced around the bottom. Quilting patches were sewn along its length. It was the thinking cap.

Ben smiled like never before. He brushed dust off the hat proudly. His eyes were gleaming with excitement as he held it in the air, savoring the moment.

William's stomach sank. I've got to stop him! He frantically fumbled through his pockets, grabbing ahold of the first thing that he could wrap his fingers around. Out he pulled Mr. Wyatt's Animal Whistle. He brought the whistle to his lips and gave the loudest moo that he could muster. It was practically the only sound that he could make. He hoped it sounded reasonable, since he couldn't hear it.

Within seconds, a charging bull rampaged into the room, blowing through debris. William couldn't believe his eyes. It was hurtling toward him and Ben. He jumped to the side and dropped his whistle in a panic, trying to avoid the raging bull. As the beast rushed by with a gust of wind, his hooves passed inches from William's head. His whistle wasn't so lucky; it splintered under the bull's hooves. Horns pointed at Ben, the bull raced onward.

Ben frantically jumped out of the way. It wasn't enough. His shirt caught the tip of the horn, sending him spinning to the side. The thinking cap tumbled from his grasp and flew end over end in the air.

William looked upward just as the thinking cap landed atop his head.

Chapter 27

THE THINKING CAP

William's mind was transported to another time and place. Memories shot past him like a kite riding the wind. They shouted remembrances from the past. His childhood, his friendships, and his father went zipping by in vivid recollections. Like a thousand movies playing at once, the images floated by. It was inspiring. More and more, he wanted to see and touch the unimaginable. Answers to questions that hadn't been asked were at his fingertips. It was a chaos of knowledge. Things he knew, things he didn't know, untold stories all bundled together like it would rip his mind in two. If he wasn't careful, he would become lost in the pleasure of knowing everything.

He had to focus. The knowledge came streaming in, like an elephant on his shoulders that would crush him. Straining, he bit down and bridled his thoughts. The images settled and instead of spinning wildly, they turned in a whirlwind under his control. They followed his thoughts like water follows a river.

My father. What happened to my father? An image plucked loose from the hurricane and twisted down on top of him. It swallowed him whole.

William saw his father sitting across from Ben, arguing. He shouted at them but nothing happened. They were nothing more than images of a time in the past. He couldn't change it, but he could see it.

"You must come back! I can't do it alone!" Ben shouted angrily. "This new burglar is coming for the thinking cap!"

"The puzzle organ has always kept the thinking cap safe," Arthur replied in disagreement. "You're overreacting." He relaxed backward into his chair.

Ben leaned forward. "No! you don't understand. This one is different," he spat, angrily throwing his hands outward. "There is something about her. She came too close to opening the puzzle organ! I don't know how, but she knows things. It's like she has opened it before," Ben said. He stood up, wiping sweat from his brow. The air was thick with tension. "The institute is in pieces and she isn't going to stop."

Arthur shook his head from side to side nervously. "I can't return! I left that behind."

Ben gritted his teeth in frustration. "You always knew we might have to open it again. If the thinking cap falls into the wrong hands, this whole world ends too. You know that better than anyone." He paced the ground.

Arthur shook his head. "I have—my son—" He turned and

looked at a picture on the wall.

Ben interrupted. "He isn't safe! No one is safe! Can't you see that? If you don't come with me and help secure the thinking cap, she will come for you. I promise you that!" He looked at the same picture on the wall that Arthur was viewing. Younger, hair combed to the side, and disgruntled from having to sit for the picture, it was William. Ben shook his finger in the air at the depiction. "I guarantee she will come for him next. You must agree. Now it is time to open the puzzle organ again."

Arthur shook his head. The weight of the decision was obvious in his expression.

"If you really love him. If you truly care, you must come," Ben said somberly.

Arthur depressed his shoulders, almost beaten into submission.

Ben pushed harder, trying to tip Arthur over the line. His voice lowered and he drew closer. "Once you cared for the institute more than anything. If any of those feelings remain, you must come. At the very least, to save your son. I can't open the puzzle organ alone. Not after what you did." There was a sense of bitterness that clung to his words.

Arthur dropped his head. Broken, he nodded in agreement.

The image brushed apart like the wind blowing sand off a stone. A new image painted itself before William. It was a dark place, nothing like the first.

William's father struggled from side to side, bound in a coffin. "I'll never tell you anything!" Arthur shouted.

From out of the shadows, Vanessa came into the light. Her dark hair swooped across her face, giving her a sinister look. "You never should have come back."

"Why are you doing this?" Arthur cried.

Mr. Millner was shriveling next to the coffin. He hunched forward, embarrassed to hear Arthur protesting. He curved his back to hide his humiliation.

Vanessa looked down on Arthur and grinned. "You really don't know, do you?" She paced back and forth. "DO YOU!?" Her anger burst out as she overturned a nearby chair and desk. They crashed against the ground. She looked at Mr. Millner and then commandingly stood over Arthur while gripping the edge of the coffin. "You did this to him. You and Ben did this to him and then left him for dead. He doesn't even exist without the thinking cap, and you ask me why I'm doing this?"

Arthur twisted in his coffin, trying to escape. "This is madness," he cried.

Vanessa laughed and pointed to her hearing aids. "Do you see this? This is your fault. I trusted you once. I trusted Ben!" Her hair fell in front of her eyes, masking her face. "What a fool I was. Opening the puzzle organ was your idea, but who paid the price?" She raised one finger and pointed toward Mr. Millner. "Do you see what you did to him? It's about time the tables were turned."

"You can't control the thinking cap. No one can. Don't you understand? Look what happened to Mr. Millner. Giving him the thinking cap won't help you. It'll unleash the greatest power you know. That's why we had to put it back!"

"Mr. Millner! Mr. Millner! I lost everything because you opened the puzzle organ. You don't think I see what happened to him every day? I lost my hearing trying to undo what you did. Everyone I care about is gone because of what you've done."

"You must trust me. The thinking cap needs to stay where it is or more people will get hurt."

"I'm counting on it," Vanessa said, wickedly curling her lips. "It will be unleashed!"

Arthur fought with his might to escape. His coffin rattled against the ground but moved nowhere. "Fine, go ahead and try to open the puzzle organ. You will be doing it without my help," he said firmly.

"I thought you might say something like that. I came prepared," Vanessa said. She produced a Truth Hat.

Mr. Millner groaned. "Wait, wait, is it too much? Mr. Millner is fine. I'm fine," he nervously whined.

"It has to be done," Vanessa said. She pushed Mr. Millner to the ground.

"Don't do this! Please!" Arthur said. He rocked to either side as the hat came down on his brow. When it touched his skin, the rocking stopped.

Vanessa leaned in so close her hair fell across Arthur's face. "How do I open the puzzle organ?" she whispered.

Arthur struggled to keep the words inside. His lips bit together until they were white. It was no use. He would tell her everything. "Once you have the three items to open the puzzle organ, there is one last thing." He smashed his jaws together, fighting back, but it was hopeless. "My son—" The words escaped through clenched teeth.

Vanessa smiled. "Thank you."

Ben and Jay suddenly came bursting into the room.

"Get away from him!" Ben shouted.

Vanessa chuckled.

Ben flung white pellets across the room.

Mr. Millner dove to the ground, tears falling from his eyes. "No, no, stop!" he screamed as white powder enveloped him.

An agile Vanessa jumped aside and plucked a pellet from the air. She twisted her arm, sending it in a new course toward Jay. White smoke puffed as it struck its target.

Desperately, Ben raced toward Arthur's coffin, but he was no match for Vanessa's longer legs.

"I'm not done with him yet," Vanessa shouted. She grabbed Ben by the back of his green suit jacket and hoisted him into the air.

Ben dangled, his feet off the ground.

"If you have a question for him, you'll have to wait your turn!" Vanessa said. "I have a few more to ask."

Ben looked down at Arthur. Their eyes met for only a moment, but the exchange said everything. This wasn't the ending they had hoped for.

Ben slipped out of his jacket and dropped to the floor, escaping Vanessa's grasp. He raced to the coffin and dropped a pellet in that erupted in a purple haze.

Like he was entering a deep sleep, Arthur's eyes rolled closed and the purple vanished.

Vanessa pulled Ben away. "No! What have you done!?" She grabbed Arthur by the shoulders and shook him.

"You can't use him anymore," Ben said. He looked longingly at the coffin and held one hand against it. "I'm sorry, old friend. I hope you can forgive me when you wake. . . someday."

Vanessa appeared frantic. She reached into the coffin and violently shook Arthur's shoulders. Then, all of the sudden, she stopped. Her desperate outburst vanished. "You haven't stopped me. I know what I need." She turned and stared back at Ben.

Jay wrenched his fingers as they began to thaw from the paralysis.

"Leave his son out of this," Ben cried.

Vanessa didn't say a word in return.

"I will stop you!" Ben said.

Vanessa threw a dark cloak around herself. A large hood fell forward and masked her eyes. "You may try," she said as she vanished into the shadows.

Ben darted toward her but found nothing. He returned to the coffin and leaned over to see Arthur sleeping. "I'm sorry. This is my fault. I know you can wake up." He looked out at Jay, who was finally moving his legs and arms. "Quickly, we have to help Arthur's son before Vanessa can get to him." He looked longingly back at the coffin once again. "If William ever finds out, he may never forgive me. We need his help getting the thinking cap. There is no time to lose," Ben said as he climbed aboard Jay's foot.

The images stopped and once again, like colored sand in the wind, fluttered into the air.

William's heart was racing like it would jump out of his chest. It wasn't just anxiety. He felt blind that he hadn't understood before, but Ben was right. Without clear hindsight, he would have put the blame on Ben for trapping his father in a coffin. William still did, but now it was with clarity. He was angry at himself for not seeing, angry at Ben for allowing his guilt to keep the truth from him, but most of all, he was angry at Vanessa. It curdled his pride to a sheepish speck. How could Vanessa do this?

Before William could think or feel more, a new image appeared. He was back home. Around him, friends played outside, but something wasn't right. A figure dressed in a dark cloak roamed the streets.

Vanessa pulled her cloak tighter as she quietly walked along the sidewalk toward William's house. Neighborhood children darted in either direction to clear the way. In front of the mansion gate, she glanced toward William's room. "I will get you," she whispered with a beautiful, stone-cold face.

The image broke away. It fluttered into pieces, leaving William amid a swirling hurricane of information. It was too much to handle. Collapsing to his knees, he restrained his thoughts for peace. The truth ate at him like a parasite. He could feel the desire of the thinking cap waiting on edge to fill him with whatever he wanted. The truth stung his mind, fracturing it. If he stayed much longer, it would take him over.

William felt the thinking cap being lifted off his head. It was a relief. The information faded off into the distance, and he was sent careening back to reality.

Chapter 28

TRUE BETRAYAL

Dazed and confused, William was lying on his back, looking up at Vanessa. She pursed her lips and smiled down at him.

Vanessa twirled the thinking cap in her fingers, admiring it. She had a gleeful smile of victory, but her eyes told a different story. They were filled with the sweet taste of revenge. She wasn't the same anymore.

"Where's Charley?" William asked. He rubbed his ears. He was surprised he could hear at all after the recent blast from the puzzle organ.

"You were lucky," Vanessa said. "If you get to it in time, the thinking cap can do some extraordinary things. Sadly, for me, it's too late." She rubbed her hearing aids. "Don't worry, I sent Charley on a task with Mr. Wyatt and Miss Lockit."

"Don't hurt him," William stammered. It was hard to think straight. His mind felt like it had been through a meat grinder. It was exhausted, straining to stay active.

"He's safe," Vanessa replied.

"Why did you do this? I don't understand." William struggled to clear his mind.

Vanessa frowned and shook her head. The act was up. "I never had any intention of hurting your father or you—unless I had to, of course. I even tried to keep Charley safe. Don't worry, I convinced him he needed to get your father."

"My father. I need to help him," William said. He was starting to feel his wits come back to him.

"Did you find out how to wake him? Oh, Ben didn't tell you? There isn't a way. All you can do is wait and hope for the best. Unfortunately, Ben put him under so deep that he could sleep forever. I hate to be the one to inform you, but no one seems to want to tell you the truth," Vanessa replied with delight, finally able to heave the truth at William.

William didn't believe her. He couldn't. The thinking cap hadn't told him how to free his father, but it had given him something different. It had left him with hope. Despite all that he now knew, it was a feeling deep down. He knew his father was going to be all right. He knew he would wake.

"That doesn't belong to you," Ben shouted groggily. He was pointing at the thinking cap, still trying to recover from the bull rushing into him.

Vanessa grinned. "Nor does it belong to you. You should have thought of that when you took it from Mr. Millner, but instead, you left him destitute."

"You don't know what you're doing," Ben bellowed. "You must put it back!" His voice carried desperation.

"You've taken everything from me and now you want me to give back? Don't be absurd!" Vanessa replied. She held the thinking cap high into the air. "You don't think that I did this for myself, do you?"

Mr. Millner came running into the room, sweating profusely. It made his hair a ragged, tangled mess. "They're coming, they're coming. He's awake!" he burst out. It sounded like nonsensical gibberish.

"Quick, help me, Mr. Millner! Get the thinking cap," William called out. But Mr. Millner didn't move. Instead, he sheepishly looked away. William's stomach sank as he realized that Mr. Millner wasn't there to help.

"Awake? What do you mean?" Vanessa said. She brushed the comments aside as rubbish born from insanity. She violently grabbed Mr. Millner by the arm. "You are no one. I want him back," she said. "Here you go, Dad." She shoved the cap into his hands.

William's hair stood on end. How can Mr. Millner be her dad? He couldn't believe his ears.

Mr. Millner's hands gleefully twirled as he danced like a madman. "I missed you," he said. He stroked the thinking cap like it was a small pet before putting it on his head. The moment it was seated on his crown, a metamorphosis occurred. His eyes narrowed, his back straightened, his hair untangled, and his demeanor changed. Like a lightbulb being turned on, his memories, his thoughts, his genius came rushing back to him. It was an addiction that he had long been denied. The crazed look in his eye vanished.

"My, that feels good. I never should have taken this off," Mr. Millner said, ripping his eye patch off. He swatted away the flies that surrounded him.

William hardly recognized Mr. Millner. His frail frame didn't seem like a starving, crazed man any longer. His awkwardly crooked green eye twisted in its socket until it aligned with his blue eye. He was tall and neatly slender. It suited his appearance like a tie fits a tuxedo.

"Why are you doing this?" William asked. He struggled to get to his feet.

"Can't you see?" Vanessa replied. "Because your father opened the puzzle organ, this happened. He left me broken with no family. They took everything from me. You of all people should know how much that can hurt." She paused, happier than imaginable. "It's poetic justice in a way, isn't it? I had my father taken because of what your father did, and now your father is gone from your life."

William could hardly agree. Two wrongs never make a right.

"We had to take the thinking cap. We had no choice," Ben shouted in protest. He looked terrified seeing Mr. Millner's transformation. "You have unleashed a power that you don't understand!"

Vanessa shook her head. "Don't you see? I will have my father back. I don't care what the cost is."

Footsteps sounded down the hall. "William," Charley's voice yelled.

"I'm here!" William called back.

Charley came stumbling into the room. He wasn't alone. Hobbling with one arm around Charley came a weak Arthur McFadden.

Despite all that had happened, William felt inexpressible joy. It ran into his legs and sent him racing across the room. Tears pooled in his eyes as he embraced his father.

Arthur held William as best as his frail arms could. "I'm sorry," he stammered.

"Impossible! How did you wake?" Vanessa shouted. She stumbled backwards in surprise, nearly tripping on the broken floorboards. "It doesn't matter. None of that matters now!" She clenched her fists in anger.

"I don't want to take all the credit, but I did rescue him from the coffin," Charley said. He tilted his head to the side, confidently brag-ging at his accomplishment.

"Come, my dear, it's time we were going," Mr. Millner said. He held his nose high in the air.

"You're not going anywhere," Arthur shouted. His was voice weak but powerful.

Mr. Millner sniffed the air in disgust. "Don't say we have to do this again, do we? Last time you tried to take the thinking cap from me, you almost died."

"You've hurt too many people with that thinking cap," Ben said. "Give it back or face us all!"

"Very well," Mr. Millner said. He bent his knees and stretched out his hands with his fingers crooked downward. His thin, pale fingers danced like he was a puppeteer.

Like metal being warped into shape, William felt his mind being twisted. It was a force that reached out from Mr. Millner's fingers. He hunched forward in pain. It wasn't just a physical pain. His mind wasn't working for him anymore. It had become his enemy. He fell to the floor. There was nothing he could do, a prisoner of his own mind. Seconds passed like hours, minutes like months, until it stopped.

Mr. Millner stood upright and released his grip.

William breathed a sigh of relief as his mind was released.

"Now, if you will excuse me, my daughter and I must be leaving," Mr. Millner said.

On the cold hard ground, William knew they were defeated. How can I fight an enemy like that?

Click came a sound from behind Mr. Millner. Mr. Wyatt appeared with one of his guns, his hand pumping the action. Miss Lockit was next to him. "Mate, you're not going anywhere if I have anything to say about it," he announced.

"And you're not going to hurt anyone either," Miss Lockit stated.

Taking aim at Mr. Millner's head, Mr. Wyatt pulled the trigger.

Boom. The gun sounded just as Miss Lockit pushed the barrel into the air. The bullet hurtled across the room and struck the thinking cap as it toppled from Mr. Millner's head.

Like a fish out of water, Mr. Millner shrilled and sunk to the ground. His back hunched and his eyes warped. He was changing.

In the middle of the room, the thinking cap lay on the ground. The bullet hole still had smoking rising. All eyes were on it. In a mad dash, everyone came running.

William dove for the thinking cap and grabbed tightly. His hands pulled back with all their might. Strained to the max, stitches tore from patches. The seams unraveled and, like a zipper coming undone, pulled away. The thinking cap tore in two.

Squeezing tightly, William stumbled backwards and landed on his backside. He looked down to find one part of the thinking cap still in his grip. The other half was in Vanessa's hand.

Mr. Millner shrilled in agony at the sight. "No, no, we need it. Look what you've done!"

There was a sense of awe as they all looked at the cap. Everyone had fought desperately for it. Now it lay in pieces.

"For now, it's over," Ben said. There was a sense of reprieve about him.

Vanessa's dreams were dashed before her eyes. She looked at the company gathered in the room. A sense of panic came about her, knowing that she was far outnumbered. With the thinking cap reduced to rags, and only half of it in her hand, her fight was over. The sense of victory that had so gracefully lifted her pride to the surface now vanished. She looked down at the half of the thinking cap in her hand and then at William, still clutching the remainder. "Give that back, you wretched creature!" Her voice shrilled with anger. She started to stumble toward William.

"I don't think so," Mr. Wyatt said, standing in front of William and pumping the action to his gun.

Vanessa stopped in her tracks. The defeat was unbearable. The stone-cold look, that made Vanessa appear so stern before, was gone. The will to fight faded. The battle was over. She clutched the thinking cap in one hand and lifted Mr. Millner, who was tearfully screaming and pounding his fists on the ground, with the other. "This isn't the end," she scornfully vowed. Like he was a lost puppy, she dragged Mr. Millner into the darkness. No one tried to stop them.

Chapter 29

END OF BEGINNINGS

William swung his feet on the edge of his bed, toes dangling above the floor. Last night, knowing his father was safe, had been a relief. He'd slept through most of it. "What's going to happen to Mr. Millner?" he asked his father sitting next to him.

Arthur put his arm around him. "I wish I could tell you. Without the thinking cap, he's not a threat anymore."

"What about this place?" William asked.

Arthur thought about it for a moment. He looked around the room, seemingly gathering memories from the walls. "I imagine that things will be better. It has always been a place for extraordinary people to learn, and I wouldn't be surprised if it becomes a school again one day. At least, that is what Ben hopes for. He has always done the best he can to take care of it. I don't think he's going to stop anytime soon. Now that this is over, maybe that can happen."

"Ben? But aren't you angry at him?" William asked, raising his tone in surprise. He wasn't sure what to think of Ben. Even with some clarity of the past, it didn't erase things that Ben had done.

Arthur nodded. "Ben and I have our differences, but I can think of no better person for the job." He stood and packed a few more items of clothing into a bag. "I know that may be hard to understand right now, but he has done more for me than you could imagine. His methods may be rough, but his intention is always good. Besides, after what I have done to him, he has the right to beat me up a little." Arthur smiled and looked to the ceiling like he was thinking into the past.

William wasn't sure what to make of that. He clearly didn't understand everything that had happened between his father and Ben. He was a little reluctant to ask. It didn't feel like the right time; however, he was certain he would find out someday. "Will we ever come back?"

Arthur stopped packing. He didn't seem prepared to answer. He didn't even turn his head to respond face to face. "Maybe. Someday." He shook his head back and forth like he was dreading what may happen in the future. "If trouble ever brews again, we will both be back. Let's just hope that isn't anytime soon. There's a lot that I have to teach you."

William had a nagging feeling this was far from over, and he wasn't quite sure what his father would teach him. He had always found a casual amusement in paper boomerangs, picture puzzles and special glue, but now he had real reason to pay attention. He wondered what they would learn if they stayed at the institute. It wasn't home, but it had grown on him. Its twisting halls and endless rooms offered much to explore. It felt untapped, like an adventure waiting to happen.

The door flung open and in marched Mrs. Burbank, with Mr. Wyatt clamoring behind her. She was holding a pen in one hand and a long list of rules in the other.

"Please, madam," Mr. Wyatt said, trying to slow her down.

Commandingly, Mrs. Burbank marched in, ignoring him. "Do you have any idea how many rules have been broken?" she screeched. The moment she saw Arthur, she stopped dead in her tracks. "Arthur. Is it really you?" she clamored.

Mr. Wyatt said, "Sorry, mate, she came through town. She stopped at my shop and nearly ravaged the place putting rules on everything. When I told her what happened to you and your father, she demanded that I bring her here to prove it. Which reminds me, I have to get back. Left Miss Lockit in charge, and she hates registers. Apparently, she has no need for monetary goods and thinks I don't either. She gives everything away for free."

Arthur turned to Mrs. Burbank. "We are ready to head home," he replied with a nod.

"I . . . I . . . I . . . never thought—" Mrs. Burbank stumbled, trying to find her words.

William would have thought she was angry, but instead, she seemed filled with a strange mix of joy and disappointment. He couldn't tell which emotion dominated.

Ben came running into the room with his arms wide open. He was on a collision course with Mrs. Burbank. "Snookums!" he screamed.

Mrs. Burbank turned the brightest shade of red that William had ever seen. Her list fell to the floor and her hands burst forward, ready to embrace Ben.

William's jaw couldn't have dropped open further had a thirty-pound weight been strapped to his lower lip. Bug-eyed, he jolted backwards, watching the two of them embrace as Ben bounced atop her round stomach.

When the smooching slowed, Arthur asked, "Would you mind helping us with some bags?" He raised one in the air.

William was relieved that his father had tried to stop the public display of affection. He could hardly embrace that it was even real. He looked upward to make sure he didn't have the thinking cap atop his head showing him some parallel universe. He couldn't tell if the two of them were married or just a couple. Either way, he was disgusted by the kissing and wasn't sure if he wanted to know more about their relationship. "I guess Ben really is my uncle?" he whispered. He didn't expect an answer, but his father gave him one anyway.

"More or less, I suppose."

Mr. Wyatt, clearly embarrassed by all the hugging and kissing, grabbed a bag and rushed out of the room. "I'll put it by the car," he called over his shoulder.

Charley met William at the front door of the institute. He was admiring his newly repaired van. The duct tape was gone, and there was a fancy new set of speakers that Mr. Wyatt had installed. "Do you like it?" he asked as he grabbed some luggage and threw it in.

William nodded, half committed. It still looked like it was going to fall apart. "Looks like a babe magnet to me."

"Nice!" Charley replied. He nodded his head.

Mrs. Burbank refused to get near the van. She dropped a bag at the door and stormed off.

William jumped in and climbed to the back seat. Through the window, he saw his father talking with Ben. He couldn't hear what was said, but they parted with a handshake. The next thing he knew, his father was in the passenger seat up front. Charley turned the key and the motor roared to life. The stereo let out a familiar blast of rock music. Charley head-banged in tune with the rhythm, and the car rolled down the cobblestone road.

William watched from the back window as the institute faded off into the distance. He recalled a final quote from his father's wall: "Don't worry about the sun setting. Tomorrow, it will rise again."

FROM THE AUTHOR

You may ask yourself what prompted me to write a book. To be honest, I ask myself the same question. I always come up with an answer, but it isn't always the same. Really there is only one way to answer this question: start at the beginning. . .

Let me paint the scene for you. A handful of friends and I sat in a circle. Prior to the event, we had each dutifully created a character with our most prized magical powers. They were the embodiment of wishful thinking even though they were just on paper, and you can rest assured that mine had muscles bulging from every inch of his body. Of course, this had nothing to do with reality. Since I don't love the word "fat", we will just say that I was a little on the portly side. As I leaned forward in anticipation, a role of chub would come over my waist band. To complete the picture, reddish brown curls atop my head finished it off. It wasn't Dungeons and Dragons I was waiting to play, but did that really matter? There was no shortage of dwarves, fair maidens, magical swords and treasure. Each was accompanied by a story that was legendary. Okay, so they weren't legendary, but they were entertaining at the very least, and watching your character's fate be decided by the clicking of dice rolling on the table was mind-bogglingly entertaining. Fast-forward a few dice rolls later and my character is dead with the entire party in chaos. Then it hit me. All these stories were amazingly fun, so I turn to my friend, "We should write a book." He chuckled a bit and looks at me like it was an impossible and ridiculous task, but the idea was never something that I could shake.

Alas, my dungeon searching days were a brief but pleasant memory in my life, but they planted the idea of creating a story. There was nothing concrete about my ideas. The setting and characters changed a thousand times over the years whenever I had the chance to be a story-teller. Truthfully, most of these moments came when I was babysitting. No need to laugh! I was poor and didn't get an allowance. Babysitting was a way for me to put a few dollars in my pocket, and I have vivid memories of lying on the ground and telling stores to kids until they fell asleep. Beyond that, there wasn't much in my life that involved story telling. I probably avoided any chances to talk about my love for fiction to escape being identified as a nerd. This played out once when a friend of mine wanted to go around high school calling each other by our dwarf given names. I heartily declined! However, I still fulfilled the need for a good story by playing a video game or reading a fantasy book, and the real life I lived drastically moved toward becoming a life-guard and going to the gym. In fact, several hours a day were devoted to lifting weights. I never quite achieved the lofty goals of my alter ego that I wrote on paper and so closely followed with dice rolling, but I can confidently say that I had some hefty meat on my bones. The fat melted and I felt pretty good. It turned in to wrestling through high school, which is another story that I will have to save until later.

Life moved on and so did my goals. I lived in Japan for several years, and when I returned, I married my high school sweetheart. Up until that point, I had written nothing, and I definitely wasn't prepared to say, "Honey, I like Dungeons and Dragons and wanna write a book." No sir! Instead, I hit the books in college, and who would have thought that the red-headed kid that spent a ridiculous amount of time in the gym had any brains? Well, I excelled in college. Honestly, I am just of average intelligence, but what I lack for in intellect, I make up for in work ethic. When I was put against other students, I would blow their mind with how much homework I would do to learn material. I was a hardcore study machine! It made me learn something about myself. When I want something, I go get it, and in the end, it paid off by allowing me to study another area of passion in my life, medicine.

For those that don't know, becoming a doctor takes a long time. To give a real-life estimate, in order to get the credentials of MD after my name and become a practicing orthopaedic surgeon took a solid fifteen years after high school. Yes, you read that right. As you can imagine, there was very little time to tell stories, write stories or even have an indulgence from a book or video game. My life became textbooks. However, remember what I told you about being a go-getter? When I put myself to accomplish something, I keep pushing. I literally hate failing. No, I don't always succeed, but I am certainly gonna break a few bones trying before I give up. Thereafter, I pushed through medical school, orthopaedic surgery residency, and fellowship. It was brutal at times to say the least. There are more details that I could give, but I am holding back. This is not the right time or place to tell the tale, but I love my job and the work I do as a physician. Suffice to say that there is no part of my life that training didn't touch. The aftermath was both good and bad in so many ways that I could fill a book talking about it, and one of the worst of these moments came to me right before I started fellowship. I was miles away from my hometown, had three children and a lovely wife, but I was broken. I cannot say it more clearly. The things that led up to that moment in time crushed my soul. To make it worse, I was financially broke. I needed something. It was something I had to have. I couldn't describe it then, nor can I describe it now. Maybe a desire to reach back to my roots; to help me escape the reality that I was facing even if just for a second. So, I sat down at my computer that was resting on the bare carpet of an empty apartment with no furniture. I had no plot, no back story, no characters, but I rolled the dice and wrote.